War of the Wildlands

Tales from Nōl'Deron

Lana Axe

AxeLord Publications
ISBN-10: 0615897134
ISBN-13: 978-0615897134
Cover Art by Michael Gauss

For Eric.

Prologue

"The Young Ones will care for the forest," Elnar said. "In all matters, they will respect the woodlands and tend to its needs. The forest gods will protect them from harm as long as they fulfill this task. They shall grow and flourish here in these woods."

"They have sworn an oath, and we must leave them to it," Tienna replied.

The two elves gazed upon the lush green forest that was to be home to their children. New life was appearing all over the land as the forest gods busied themselves preparing a home for the new arrivals. Birds everywhere lifted their voices in song to herald the birth of the young elves.

As she took Elnar's hand, Tienna's eyes filled with tears. "Leaving our children to care for themselves never gets easier."

"We cannot watch out for them forever," he replied. "They will be safe and happy here in the forests. Our island children have done well, and our woodland children will too."

The pair began walking beneath the massive trees, their feet making no sound against the soft green carpet of the forest floor. A warm spring breeze swept over them, sending tiny seedpods flying through the air.

A small yellow butterfly perched itself on Tienna's shoulder. She stopped to admire the friendly creature as it fanned its wings lazily on the breeze. "I would have you journey with us to our new home," she said. "You represent hope, and our people always have need of you."

The butterfly danced and circled around her, leaving a faint trail of yellow dust as it flew. Tienna smiled, knowing that it would accompany them on their journey. She squeezed Elnar's hand and closed her eyes, allowing the breeze to wash over her.

"Where shall we go now?" she asked.

"We will retreat to the Westerling Vale and give all of this land to the Young Ones."

"The Vale is a land of great beauty," she replied. "I think our people will be happy there."

"We shall," he replied. "The Young Ones will grow, but we shall fade. This is their home now."

The pair continued through the forest and did not look back.

The Young Ones settled in and created villages of their own. In all manners, they respected the forest and took no more from it than they needed. Their numbers multiplied, and their clans prospered under the watchful eyes of the forest gods.

The gods had charged them with a simple task: protect the forest, love it, and respect it. The gods would protect them from all harm, so long as they completed this task. As time went on, however, the Young Ones forgot about their gods and the oath they had made.

Chapter 1

As he did every morning, Yori woke before dawn to begin his work at the smithy. He rose from his small cot and pulled back the curtain that separated his tiny living space from the rest of the shop. He splashed water over his face and around his neck and ran his fingers through his sandy blond hair. Carefully, he positioned a worn red headband at the precise level to cover the pointed tips of his ears. Life was easier in the city of Enald if its citizens could forget for a moment that his father had been an elf.

The shop was open-air with a low wall surrounding it, forcing customers to enter through the area farthest from the furnace. This design helped to avoid accidents from careless citizens, children, and animals. For the last few years, the shop had doubled as Yori's home. His aunt and uncle's cottage was too small to fit everyone comfortably, and the shop was safer having someone present all night. The cool fall weather made for pleasant nights, despite being out of doors. In the winter, he would move his cot closer to the furnace to stay warm.

Grabbing a leather apron from a hook near the anvil, he quickly tied it around himself to cover his tattered gray shirt. He began adding charcoal to the furnace and squeezed the bellows to fan the flames. His Uncle Ren always treated him well, but if the furnace was not hot enough to begin work at dawn, Yori could expect to receive an open-handed smack to the side of his head. To avoid the embarrassment, he always tended the fire first and made its maintenance his top priority throughout the day.

As dawn broke, Yori was still laying out tools for his uncle's use in the day's work. Out of nowhere, he heard a young girl screaming. Startled by the sound, he dropped the pliers in his hand, which fell to the ground with a thud. Realizing the cry had come from his young cousin, he immediately rushed toward the sound. As he stepped out of the shop, he saw arrows whizzing in every direction, and panicked citizens were running away. One lone little girl stood frozen in fear near the well.

Without a thought for his own safety, Yori rushed to the child and grabbed her in his arms. Just as he lifted her to run back to the smithy, his left calf was struck by an arrow. He dropped to his knees, barely setting the girl back on her feet. She wrapped her arms around his neck and buried her tear-stained face in his shoulder. Again he lifted her, ignoring the searing pain in his leg. Turning his back to the oncoming arrows in an effort to protect the girl, he limped as quickly as possible back to the safety of the shop.

Placing the girl behind the anvil, he grabbed the axe near the wood pile and readied himself for a fight. He had never been trained in fighting, but he had learned to defend himself as a child. As an outcast, his world had been full of bullies, and he had realized that fighting back felt much better than just accepting a beating. They may have beaten him worse for his efforts, but at least he had earned his lumps. He did not know exactly what he was facing or why his town was being attacked, but he was ready to defend his young cousin against whoever was approaching.

As quickly as the attack had begun, it ended. Citizens once again came out of their homes and began filling the streets. Yori set down the axe and knelt before the sobbing girl.

"Are you hurt, Meladee?" he asked.

The little girl shook her head. She raised an arm and pointed to the arrow sticking out of Yori's leg.

"It looks worse than it feels," he said, attempting to ease the girl's fear. In truth, his leg was throbbing and still bleeding a considerable amount.

Ren rushed out of his small cottage and ran to the smithy. "Yori!" he called. "Have you seen Meladee?"

"She's here," Yori replied.

The girl remained seated until her mother, who had run out of the cottage in her nightdress, rushed to her side. Meladee threw her arms around her mother and continued to weep.

"Yori's hurt," she managed to say through her sobs.

Ren knelt down to have a closer look at the arrow sticking out of Yori's leg. "This is going to hurt," he said, his dark eyes sympathetic. "You might want to bite down on the corner of your apron."

Yori, confused by the comment, looked down at his uncle just in time to see him grab hold of the arrow. In an instant, he yanked the shaft and pulled the arrow free. Yori screamed in pain and fell to his knees, grabbing at his injured calf.

"I told you to bite down on the leather, didn't I?" Ren said with a smile. "You'll be alright. Let's clean it and get a bandage on it."

As he watched his uncle retrieve an iron rod and place it in the fire, Yori realized what his uncle had meant by "clean it". He was going to cauterize it to stop the bleeding and seal the wound from infection. Yori's head swam as his Aunt Trella brought over a bowl of water and some cloth.

"It will only hurt for a second, and then you will feel much better," she said. Gently, she began wiping the wound with a wet cloth.

Ren approached, a red-hot iron rod in his hand. "Don't scream too much or you'll scare Meladee," he said. "Oh, and don't move around too much or I'll have to sit on you." He offered Yori a small stick of wood to bite down on, which the young man graciously accepted.

As the hot metal touched the wound, Yori moaned and grunted in agony. After a few seconds, the procedure was over. The pain had dulled but persisted. All the bleeding had stopped, and Ren offered Yori a hand getting back to his feet. Placing weight on the leg was agony, but he had very little choice. There was work to be done, and he could not spend the day sitting.

13

"They were Wild Elves," Meladee said quietly, her brown eyes still full of tears.

"You shouldn't be leaving the house alone," her mother chided. "You could have been killed."

"Did you see them, Meladee?" Yori asked, bending to her level.

The little girl nodded.

From the design of the arrow, Yori was forced to accept that the little girl must be correct. The speckled feathers and runed tip of the arrows left no doubt in his mind that Wild Elves had just attacked their city. This could only bring trouble for him and his family. The townspeople already disliked him for being a half-breed, but now they might think he was a traitor.

Yori had never known any Wild Elves except his father, but he was killed when Yori was very young. His mother always spoke fondly of him, even though loving him made her an outcast among human society. According to her, the elves were not happy about it either. They refused to allow a human to live among their clan. Therefore, the couple chose to live independently at the edge of the woods. When she died, her brother took Yori in and put him to work in the smithy. He was not treated as a son but as an apprentice. Still, he was grateful to have someone looking after him in any way.

"This wasn't the Sycamore Clan," Ren said, looking at Yori. "Your father's clan is too far from here. I would wager anything it was the Oak Leaf Clan. They're nothing but trouble."

Members of the Oak Leaf Clan had been banned from trading in Enald's marketplace. On several occasions they had been accused of stealing and causing disturbances. They had gotten the reputation as troublemakers, but none of them were ever given a trial. If a human accused a Wild Elf of wrongdoing, then the elf was presumed guilty. King Domren had no use for elves in his kingdom, and he sanctioned all punishments against them.

"We may as well get to work," Ren suggested. "If we carry on like everything is normal, maybe we'll be left in peace." His voice contained very little hope. Since most people in town were aware of Yori's parentage, trouble was likely to find them.

Meladee squeezed Yori tightly before her mother led her back to their cottage. The poor child was covered in black soot from being held tightly against Yori's dusty apron. She would protest having a bath and would dislike having to wear clean clothes. She much preferred her tattered play clothes, which she only wore while she was in the smithy. She loved her cousin dearly and would rather spend the day in the hot, dirty shop than anywhere else as long as Yori was there.

Yori retrieved the pliers he had dropped earlier and continued to prepare his uncle's workbench for the day ahead. He checked on the furnace and decided it was hot enough for now. "Where should I begin?" he asked.

"Fetch that sword we've been working on. We need to finish up the hilt and get the whole thing together." He scratched at his beard as he spoke.

Yori did as he was told. For several weeks, they had worked together on a sword for one of King Domren's lieutenants at the palace. His father was originally from Enald and had purchased swords made by Ren's father. The quality of those swords was superior to the ones being crafted by the palace's smith, and the man had insisted Ren craft one for him in the tradition of his father. Yori himself had done half the work and was quite pleased with the outcome so far.

The sword's hilt was inlaid with ebony stones which Yori had shaped and polished meticulously. He offered the hilt to his uncle, who inspected it closely.

"This is well crafted," he said. "You're ready to fit it to the blade."

Yori carried the sword to his workbench at the back of the shop. As soon as he turned his back, one of Enald's wealthier citizens appeared in the doorway. He was dressed in a fine burgundy tunic and wore a large feather in his hat.

"What does that one know about the attack this morning?" the man said, pointing at Yori.

Yori turned to face the man, his eyes darting nervously to his uncle.

"He knows he got an arrow in the leg for rescuing my daughter," Ren replied, his tone suggesting he was well prepared for an argument.

"If he's been sneaking around with those savages, I'm going to inform the mayor," the man threatened. "His kind are not welcome here. You should have done away with him when he was a baby."

Ren grabbed a hammer from his workbench and walked toward the man. "I suggest you get out of my shop and leave the boy alone."

"Boy?" the man scoffed. "I know for a fact he's at least seventeen. He's a man and should be fighting his own battles by now. A war is coming, and he will betray this town if he gets the chance."

"My family is here," Yori said. "I don't even know any elves other than the ones who trade goods here. They weren't the ones who attacked us."

"So you know which clan it was?" the man asked. "Apparently you do know a thing or two. Perhaps you should come and speak to the mayor yourself and save him the trouble of sending the guards."

"Get out of here before I bury this hammer in your skull!" Ren's tone meant business, and his face was serious. He tightened his grip on the hammer.

Seeing that he had truly angered the smith, the man decided to back down. He turned and strode briskly from the shop.

"I should have kept my mouth shut," Yori said, his pale green eyes focusing on the floor. "I always say the wrong thing."

"Don't worry about it," Ren replied. "It wouldn't have mattered what you said. That asshole came here looking for a fight, and he nearly got one."

Yori turned back to his workbench and tried to occupy his mind with his work. He was worried that others in the town would also come to accuse him, and he hated the thought of causing trouble for his uncle. For now, he would simply focus on his work and avoid visiting other areas of the city.

"You'll have to sleep at the house tonight," Ren said. "I don't know how safe you'll be out here. We'll just have to make some room."

Yori nodded and tried to hide the relief he felt. The last thing he wanted was to be alone at night with a town full of angry citizens. If the attacks continued, his life could very well be in danger.

Chapter 2

Reylin proudly entered the Overseer's hut, followed by his troop of archers. His twin sister glared at him with her hazel eyes and shook her head as he passed by. He shot a devilish grin at her and continued walking until he stood before the Overseer.

"Explain," the Overseer demanded. His dark eyes stared intently at the young elf.

"We put a few holes in the city of Enald," Reylin said. "That's all." He casually ran his fingers through his red hair as he spoke.

"The entire clan needs to be informed before a raid is carried out. We cannot afford to split up the troops we have. Who would have protected us had we been attacked while you were away?"

"The sword maidens," he replied. "My sister would have protected you personally." Reylin laughed along with several members of his troop. The Overseer had been far too passive in their fight against the humans, and Reylin was not going to miss the opportunity to insult him.

"This won't be tolerated," the Overseer replied. "We must stand together or not at all. You should visit our kin of the Silver Birch Clan and discuss joining our efforts. They have more elves than we do, and we will be more efficient fighters if we join forces."

"I'll consider it," Reylin replied. With those words, he turned and exited the hut, grabbing his sister's arm on the way out. He led her away from the hut and stopped when he had reached the farthest edge of the village.

"You can't keep going off on your own," she said. "You're going to get yourself killed, and then where will we be?"

"Relax, Reylana," he began. "No one even saw us. We shot a few arrows and kept going. We probably didn't even kill any of them."

"Then you're wasting arrows," she said seriously. Her auburn hair caught the sun's rays and flashed red, reflecting her mood. She loved her twin brother, but he could be very difficult to understand at times. "We should plan a proper raid that includes archers and sword maidens alike."

"Yes, ma'am," he replied, his tone mocking.

"I'm serious," she replied hotly, looking down at her brother. "You men aren't the only ones who can fight. You're just the only ones who can fight and hide at the same time. You can send them running and we'll be there to stop them."

Reylin paused for a moment and thought. "That's actually a good idea, Sis," he said. "We can attack one of their farming villages from the tree line and you and your girls can be waiting on the other side. Nothing sends a message to your enemy like slaughtering a village full of fleeing cowards."

"It's no less than they've done to us. Entire clans have been wiped out. Every week new elves are finding their way here to join up with us. There are no clans now within a day's walk of Na'zora."

"If we can manage to win this war there won't be a Na'zora. I'd like to see that king's head mounted above my hut." Reylin's tone was serious. He hated the Na'zorans as well as all other humans. They were responsible for the death of his parents along with countless other elves. His kinsmen were constantly being pushed deeper into the Wildlands and away from their traditional homes. The humans did not care whether they were able to adapt. They would prefer if all elves were wiped out permanently.

"I'll gather some of the women so we can start planning," Reylana said before hurrying away. She glanced back at her brother, who had gone over to speak with his troops. He was a hothead for sure, but she knew his actions were carried out with the best intent. He had only gone to Enald to frighten its citizens and let them know that the elves of the woods would fight back to protect their homes. They were sick of being bullied by Na'zora's king, and they would do whatever was necessary to defend their right to exist.

Seated on a log bench at the center of town was Essa, the leader of the Oak Leaf Clan's sword maidens. "Essa," Reylana called as she spotted the dark-haired elf. "I need to talk with you."

Essa had been busy polishing the blade of her broadsword when Reylana approached. She put the blade away and eyed her cautiously. "What are you up to?" she asked suspiciously.

Reylana laughed and said, "You know me. When have I ever been up to anything bad? Come with me. We're going to discuss plans to attack one of the human farming villages."

Essa joined her friend as they walked back to Reylin's small hut. Several men were already inside, noisily sharing their ideas.

"Ok, everybody shut up," Reylin said loudly as his sister entered. "Let's see what the ladies have to say."

"Nothing much, really," Reylana began. "Essa leads the sword maidens for our clan, so I'll let her do the talking."

"First of all," Essa said, "I want to know what village and when. Secondly, I want to know why you went out today without consulting me? We'd have been happy to come along and chop a few heads."

"It was just a small scare tactic, Essa," Reylin said, rolling his hazel eyes. "Don't act so left out. You're as bad as my sister. Sometimes you should just let the men handle it."

"You can handle it all you want," Essa remarked. "But when it comes to fighting, you should let the women take charge. We know attack plans better than those who hide in the trees. We're at the front of the line. You men are just our backup."

Men began shouting and arguing at her words. They were offended by her comment, and they wanted to let her know it. Wild Elf men generally stand a head shorter than the women, allowing them greater stealth when moving through the trees.

Neither sex, however, is any less fierce than the other.

"Quiet!" Reylin shouted. "She's just trying to get under our skin. She's ticked that we didn't let Her Majesty come with us. We're big boys, Essa. We do what we want. Next time, we'll work together, ok?"

Essa nodded and took a seat at the small dining table at the back of the room. Reylin and Reylana both sat as well. A small hand-drawn map of the area was laid out on the table. From this map, they would determine which village had the best layout for them to attack with stealth. The women would need to be concealed until the men could force the villagers in their direction. Then, when there was no chance of escape, the women would attack. No one would be left alive. Domren's men had been ruthless in their attacks on the elves. No elf had been spared for any reason, and the elves were most willing to retaliate in the same fashion. The time for small skirmishes was coming to an end. A war was about to begin.

Chapter 3

King Domren shifted anxiously on his horse as he peered deep into the woods. "Do you think Aelryk's men are in position?" he asked.

"Until Mi'tal makes his way here, we have no way of knowing," General Luca replied. His gray eyes were stern, his passion for battle ever-present on his face.

"He should have been here by now. I don't like waiting." The king let out a heavy sigh and clenched his teeth. His dark eyes focused into the trees, hoping to catch any sign of movement. Wild Elves are masters of stealth within the forests, and he wondered if he was already being watched.

From behind, he heard a horse approaching. He turned his head to see Mi'tal coming up from the rear of his company. The young, black-haired man hurried past the soldiers and went straight to the king.

"Majesty," he said, "Aelryk and his men are in position and are awaiting your lead."

"Finally," the king said. He raised an arm and motioned his troops to follow. Drawing their weapons, they charged into the thick forest. The Silver Birch Clan was about to experience the king's wrath.

As they entered the village, they showed no signs of slowing. The surprised elves were sent fleeing in all directions. Many were trampled by the horses and several others were cut down as they ran. Women and children were not spared, nor were elderly clansmen who could not possibly offer a fight. The warriors rushed to their huts to retrieve their weapons. They had been given no sign their village would be attacked, and they had not been prepared for battle.

Mages at the rear of the company began firing off spells. Most of them cast fireballs at the huts, while others fired energy blasts to knock the fleeing elves off balance. Those who managed to get to a weapon were quickly dispatched by the energy blasts, dropping their weapons as they fell. The elves who did not find their feet quickly were trampled by the horses as they charged. Within minutes, the first village lay in ruins.

Domren's troops rode on toward the second village. It was larger, but with Aelryk's company charging from the opposite end, there was little chance of encountering any significant resistance. The elves had been alerted by the cries coming from the neighboring village, but that had also signaled Aelryk to begin the attack. He was young and had little experience in battle, but he was obedient and very capable of following the orders his father had given him.

Arrows whizzed from the highest branches, shot by the few elves who had managed to make it to the trees. Their swordswomen dodged the horses as they charged past at full speed. Foot soldiers were no match for mounted cavalry. Many of them began to run into the woods as well. Domren smiled to himself to see the bravest among the elves fleeing. He hoped to continue the attacks until every Wild Elf was driven to the far side of the Blue River or killed. He did not care whether they had to be annihilated or left willingly. His mission was to expand his kingdom, and the elves were in his way.

The mages began setting fire to the huts in this village as well. They tossed their fireballs casually and sipped at their potions as if they hadn't a care in the world. Human mages do not regenerate their power naturally. Instead, they rely on a steady supply of potions to continue being useful in combat. The mages enjoyed testing their prowess in battle, as they normally sat around discussing magical theory and practicing little tricks to amuse the nobles. Today, they were proving their worth to their king, and they were making it look like child's play.

Once the second village lay in ruins, Aelryk came riding up to his father. The two men were similar in appearance, both with dark hair and eyes. Aelryk, however, stood half a foot taller and had a far more pleasing countenance than his father.

"Good morning, Father," he said. "It seems everything has gone to plan."

"It has," Domren replied. "You have done well for your first true battle. Gather your men and we'll head back to the palace."

Aelryk did as he was commanded, and the company set off eastward, leaving the smoking villages behind them. Mi'tal rode next to Aelryk at the front of the company. Before his death, Mi'tal's father had been charged with the personal safety of

King Domren. Mi'tal had taken it upon himself to act as a protector for the young prince. He could be impulsive at times, and Mi'tal had always been there to pull the prince back in his anger. Usually it was just a petty argument over some minor insult. Today, however, marked a new chapter in the prince's future. He would be riding into battle regularly, and Mi'tal planned to be there to protect him, even if it cost him his life.

"Well done today, my lord," Mi'tal said, his brown eyes sincere.

Aelryk nodded. "Father had everything set up very well. I would have been an idiot to mess it up. Nonetheless, I thank you for the compliment." Aelryk grinned at his friend, and the two of them laughed.

"Soon you will be planning your own strategies," Mi'tal commented. "You will make a fine war leader. Your men love you, and they will fight for you no matter the cost."

Aelryk considered the notion for a moment. He was young, but he wanted to be fair with his troops and gain their respect. His father ruled using fear, and everyone jumped at his command. He wasn't sure if that was the kind of commander he wanted to be.

31

Normally, his father would bark commands at him without expressing any gratitude once his wish had been fulfilled. Aelryk believed in discipline, of course, but his father's manner was a little rougher than his own. It was not in his nature to be cruel. He preferred to treat others with the respect they had earned, and if someone needed to be punished, it should be done with fairness. Justice was not in his father's vocabulary. Trials were held for show when a noble was accused. Anyone else could only hope for a swift, painless execution. Most were not that lucky.

When it came to the elves, King Domren was unwavering. He wanted them either exterminated or moved as far away as possible. Aelryk had not yet mentioned his thoughts on diplomacy to his father, but he hoped to have the opportunity soon. Today's show of strength should convince the elves to accept the king's terms. If he could convince his father to let him speak with the elven leaders, perhaps more battles could be avoided. The elves would certainly wish to retaliate, and Aelryk did not like the idea of his citizens being slaughtered. He was determined to bring the idea to his father as soon as he found the opportunity-and the courage as well.

Chapter 4

Yori sat down to dinner with his family. His leg still throbbed, but the wound had not reopened. His aunt placed a steaming bowl of stew in front of him along with a slice of freshly baked bread. Yori was convinced there was no better cook alive than his aunt. His mother had been a terrible cook. Her bread was always hard and flat, and she never made a dish she didn't burn. Despite the cooking, he had loved her dearly. She was warm and loving and always made him feel special.

"Is that sword in one piece yet?" Ren asked.

"Yes," Yori replied with a mouthful of food. Swallowing, he added, "It's ready for your inspection."

"Good," Ren replied. "I told the lieutenant I'd deliver it in the next couple of weeks. I wouldn't want to break my promise."

They finished their meal in silence, and Yori helped stack the dishes to be washed.

"That's fine, dear," Trella said. "You go and rest. I'll see to the dishes."

Yori nodded and walked to the pile of blankets that had been laid out on the floor for his bed. It wasn't as comfortable as his cot, but he felt safer sleeping indoors tonight. As soon as he sat down, Meladee popped up out of her bed and ran to him. She plopped herself next to him and leaned against his side.

"Tell me a story, please?" Her soft brown eyes pleaded with him, and he could not refuse.

"Ok, but just one," he replied. "Let's see." He paused for a moment and then continued. "There once lived a gnome named Jack. He was the most clever gnome that ever lived. One day a giant threatened to stomp Jack's little village into dust."

Meladee gasped as she pictured the tiny gnomes being crushed beneath a gigantic foot.

"Don't you worry," he continued. "Little Jack knew just what to do. 'Hey you giant!' he shouted. 'You've got those big feet but no shoes! You can squash us better with the fine pair of boots I saw.' The giant wasn't very smart, of course, so he followed Jack to see this fine pair of boots. Jack led him to a crevice between two huge boulders that was just wide enough to fit the giant's foot inside it. 'Right here!' the little gnome cried. The giant scratched his head and said, 'Don't see nothin' but no rocks.' And his big face was all contorted and confused like this," Yori said, miming the action to the delight of the little girl.

"Well, clever little Jack had an idea. 'Stick your foot just there, and the magical rock boots will go right on your feet.' Giants aren't very smart, so he did as the little gnome said. Wouldn't you know it, the giant's foot stuck fast in the rock, and he pulled with all his might but couldn't break free. Little Jack laughed and returned to his village. The other gnomes cheered and thanked Jack for saving their lives. They threw a big party and named him the new mayor."

Meladee applauded at the end of the story. "Another!" she cried.

"Your mother is going to be very angry if I keep you up too late. Off to bed now," he said, patting the child on her head.

"Ok," she said, disappointed. Slowly, she got up and went back to her bed. Pulling the covers up to her chin, she grinned at her cousin. He smiled and waved goodnight before lying down himself.

The next morning he rose before the rest of the family and slowly made his way to the smithy. Outside the entrance, someone had dumped a pile of horse manure. *A gift from my wealthy friend, no doubt,* Yori thought, remembering the man who had accused him of conspiring with the elves.

He proceeded through the door to light the furnace. Nothing inside the shop appeared to have been disturbed, so he went about his work as usual. He used the coal shovel to clean up the mess out front and carried it over to the woods to dump it. He thought he heard voices coming from the treetops, and he hurried back to the shop. If there were elves in those trees, he didn't want to be seen anywhere near them. He hoped they were only there to have a look at the town and nothing more. He feared how the citizens might treat him if a second attack took place.

When Ren finally arrived at the shop, Yori placed the finished sword in front of him. It was the finest work he had ever done, and he was quite proud of it. It was rare for him to work on any sword, let alone

one crafted for a nobleman. It was more a showpiece than a weapon for the man who would be receiving it. Staining such a beautiful item with blood would be a shame.

"This is very good, Yori," Ren said as he turned the sword over in his hands. "I'm sure our customer will be pleased." After a moment, he added, "You can take it to him at the palace."

"Me?" Yori said, stunned.

"Yes, you. It couldn't hurt to have you away from town for a few days."

"I've never been there before. I don't even know where it is." Yori did not like the idea of travel, especially alone. He had never been anywhere but Enald, and he had no desire to leave.

"I'll give you directions. If the weather is good, it will only take you a couple of days to walk there." Ren looked at Yori, who was obviously still unsettled by the idea. "Look," he began. "It won't be that bad. The palace district is very large and full of lots of different people. Just hide your ears like you always do, and no one will notice the difference. If no one there knows about your parentage, you won't be treated any differently. You're tall enough that no one will suspect a thing."

37

Ren made a valid point. Except for Yori's ears, no part of him appeared elfish. Perhaps in the palace district he would be treated like an average human. The thought gave him a small amount of courage, and he nodded his acceptance. Though he was still unsure about traveling, he would try to make the best of it.

"When will I leave?" he asked.

"You can head out tomorrow," Ren replied. "Maybe I'll get a bonus for finishing early."

Yori nodded and carried on performing his chores for the day. He would need to have the sword polished and glowing before he wrapped it up for travel. The thought of carrying back coin did not sit well with him. He hoped the roads were safe for travelers and tried to remember any recent rumors of crime or bandits. Nothing recent came to mind, and he was grateful for it. With a great amount of effort, he pushed the following day's task from his mind and focused on the work before him. He couldn't bear to think about the look in Meladee's eyes when he would tell her he was leaving. The poor little girl would probably be devastated. For now, he would focus on his work and forget about the day ahead.

Chapter 5

The elf woman staggered blindly through the forest. She hoped she had chosen the right direction, but the severe throbbing in her head and blood running into her eyes had muddled her mind. Her strength was failing, and she did not know if she would reach her kinsmen before collapsing. As if by some miracle, an elven village came into view.

"Help me, please!" she cried with all her strength. Despite her best efforts, her voice sounded no louder than a whisper. Finally someone spotted her, called to the others who were close at hand, and ran in her direction. The red-haired elf caught her just before she hit the ground.

"I've got her," Reylin said to his companions. "I'll carry her back to town. Go and fetch Doni."

Reylana caught sight of her brother as he carried the wounded elf to the center of the village. Doni, the healer, rushed out of his hut to meet them. Reylin placed the woman on a low wooden bench and looked in Doni's eyes. They did not look hopeful, and Reylin feared she would not survive.

"What happened to her?" Reylana asked as she approached.

"Isn't it obvious?" Reylin shot back, his hazel eyes fierce. "Humans attacked her. They probably killed everyone in her village."

"Where is she from?" Reylana asked, kneeling at the woman's side and taking her hand. She had lost consciousness, but perhaps the small comfort of a friendly touch could soothe her.

"I'd say she's Silver Birch by the look of her. She's wearing one of those shell bracelets their women like so much." Reylin pointed to the bracelet, which had only a few shells left and was caked in blood.

"I don't think I can help her," Doni said. "This head wound is beyond repair. I've given her some herbs to ease her pain, but I have no medicine to heal this type of damage. I'd say she was struck with a hammer from a moving horse. Obviously, the blow was offset and not enough to kill her instantly. That probably would have been easier for the poor girl."

"I'll carry her inside your hut," Reylin said. He scooped the woman up once more and proceeded to the healer's hut. At least there she would be more comfortable, even if her wounds proved fatal.

Reylana waited outside the hut, her face wet from tears. "I don't know how much more of this I can take," she said as Reylin emerged.

"That's why we have to keep fighting," he replied. His anger was growing, and she knew he was ready to fight this very moment.

"We have to stick to the plan, Reylin," she said, laying a hand on his arm. "We attack tomorrow as it is. Let's get something to eat and try not to think about it for now."

They joined their friends at the center of the village. Most of them were enjoying the ale and discussing the following day's raid.

"How's the girl?" Essa asked.

"Not good," Reylana replied. "Doni doubts that she will live. Do you think we should send someone to their village to see if anyone else is alive?"

"I doubt it's safe," Essa replied. "The humans have probably left troops behind."

"There won't be many, and they won't be expecting us," Reylin said.

"That's true," Essa said. "I guess a few of us could go and have a look."

"You stay here," Reylin said. "I'll take some archers with me. Who wants to come?" he asked, turning to the men. Several of them raised their hands. "Let's get going then," he said. They set out in the direction of the Silver Birch village.

Reylana fixed herself a plate of elk meat with raspberry sauce and sat down next to Essa. "I worry about Reylin," she began. "He never stops for a moment. All he does is obsess about revenge against the humans. I want that too, of course, but I think his judgment is clouded by his anger."

"The death of your parents was difficult for him," Essa replied. "It's natural for him to want revenge."

"Yes, but we have to go about it the right way," she began. "He doesn't think things through, and the men follow him without question. He's going to get himself killed, I fear."

"We're all likely to get killed," Essa pointed out. "This war will most likely continue until we're all dead. The humans won't stop coming unless we kill their king. Then we have to hope the new king isn't as bad, which he probably will be. It's hopeless, but we have to fight back. I won't sit by and watch our homes be taken without a fight."

Reylana nodded and remained silent. She finished her meal and waited impatiently for her brother to return.

After a few hours, Doni emerged from his hut with the sad news that the woman had passed away. "She is a part of the forest now," he said. "I'll be in my hut should the scouts return with more injured."

It was nearly sunset before Reylin and his troops returned. They brought no survivors with them, but they did carry some equipment they had taken off of the slain soldiers. The Na'zorans had left behind a small group of fifteen guards to finish off any wounded elves and search for information on upcoming raids. They were fools to leave behind so few. Reylin's men had killed them all and taken their weapons and armor.

"Before I killed one of them, I asked why they were digging through piles of rubble. He said they were searching the burned-out huts for information on raids." Reylin broke out laughing. "Why would we be stupid enough to write such things down? That must be what humans do. Whatever is written can be stolen and read by others."

"I wish we still had a rune carver," Reylana remarked as she sorted through the weapons. "I wonder if the Sycamore Clan still has one. They're the nearest now that the Silver Birch are scattered or dead."

"There weren't enough bodies around for them to be wiped out," Reylin replied. "They've gone into hiding somewhere. They'll either show up here or start again elsewhere. I doubt they'll rebuild for now, but we'll probably encounter them somewhere in the forests."

"That's a bit of good news, at least," Reylana said. "There's no time to get these new weapons ready for tomorrow's raid, but maybe some of these things will serve us in the future. You better get some sleep before we head out in the morning." She gave her brother a kiss on the cheek and said, "Sleep well." She retreated to her own hut to rest and try to put the day's events behind her. The morning would bring vengeance and blood.

Chapter 6

As dawn broke over the forest, Reylana and the other sword maidens were already in position. They had chosen the perfect spot just outside the farming village. A small series of rolling hills provided perfect cover where the women could not be spotted from the town itself. A light fog had settled that morning, thanks to the autumn weather, and its presence only aided the elves in their attempt at stealth. The men were stationed in the forest on the opposite end of the town, and soon they would begin the attack.

The crowing of a single rooster brought many villagers from their homes to begin the day's work. As soon as a handful of them were in sight, Reylin signaled the attack. Arrows began to fly from the trees, none of them missing their targets. The Wild

Elves were excellent archers, and they did not intend to waste many arrows today.

Villagers began fleeing back to their homes, but Reylin's men were prepared. They had carried with them a handful of red-runed arrows which they now prepared to fire. As the arrows struck the villagers' homes, they immediately burst into flame. The fires spread rapidly, consuming the houses within seconds. Terrified villagers rushed from their homes, heading straight for the waiting sword maidens.

Essa struck the first blow against a pudgy woman who could run surprisingly fast for her size. At Essa's side, Reylana swung her sword as a frightened man nearly crashed into her in his flight. The archers had descended from the trees and were still taking aim at the villagers, shooting many of them in the back. Seeing that they were about to be left out of the fight, Essa signaled the women to charge into the village. Together they ran toward the remaining humans and easily cut them down. Not a single one of them had taken up arms.

Essa stayed her sword as a frightened boy ran toward her in a panic. He was screaming "mother" as he recognized the lifeless form at Essa's feet. Without a hint of fear, he dropped to his knees at his slain mother's side. Essa lowered her sword and stared at the boy. Suddenly, an arrow pierced the side of the child's neck, and he slumped to the ground. Looking up, Essa could see that only Reylin still had his bow at the ready. The other archers had already begun salvaging arrows from the corpses in hopes of using them once again.

Essa strode with purpose toward Reylin, the anger obvious in her steps. "We do not kill children!" she shouted. When she reached him, she shoved him roughly, forcing him to take a single step back. Essa's large, muscular frame gave her a more intimidating presence than most elven women. "Kill the men, fine. Kill the women, fine too. They should have armed themselves instead of running like cowards. The children have done nothing and cannot fight back. That is where we draw the line. We are not murderers."

Reylin was unfazed by her reaction. "We have to send a message," he replied casually. "This is no more than they've done to our children, and we have to be as brutal as they are. If we are soft, they will never fear us. If we're not a threat, they'll never leave us alone."

"Reylin, he was only a child," Reylana said softly, kneeling near the boy's body.

"That child would have grown up and joined the human army. In a few years, he'd be slaughtering our kind too. You should thank me for getting rid of him." Reylin stormed off, followed by his troop of archers. They proceeded back into the woods in the direction of their village.

"I won't fight alongside your brother again," Essa said to Reylana.

"We have to stick together, Essa, or we have no hope of defeating the Na'zorans."

"I'd rather be killed than fight the way he does. I couldn't live with myself after that." She motioned to the boy on the ground, the grass beneath him soaked in blood.

Reylana didn't know what else to say. She loved her brother, but she did not agree with his actions. The murder of their parents had changed him from a carefree young elf into a heartless warrior. He thought of nothing but revenge.

They returned to the village to find the men celebrating at the center of town. They all had mugs of ale and were complimenting each other on their prowess in battle. Reylin appeared to be the only one who remained sober.

"Reylana," he called, motioning for his sister to come closer.

She approached him and stood silently, waiting to see what he had to say.

"You're not going to scold me like Essa did, are you?"

"No, I'm not. I don't agree with what you did, but I understand your reasons." She swallowed, looked away, and added, "I wish it didn't have to be this way."

"It is this way, Sis," he said. "Our only chance is to join forces with all of the remaining clans on this side of the river. We're all in danger, and we should work together."

"Agreed," she replied.

"Well?" he asked.

"Well what?" she said, puzzled.

"You have a big mouth. You could go and talk to the other clans." He took a sip of ale and grinned at her.

"Why don't you go? If they say no, you can beat them into submission."

"If only it were that easy," he replied with a mock sigh. "Seriously, I'm needed here. These guys need a leader who isn't afraid to make hard decisions. You're prettier and more persuasive than me. You should go."

"I wouldn't know where to begin," she said.

"Just tell them we should all join up and see what they say. Obviously it's a good idea. If they say no, they're traitors to our entire race." His voice became more and more angry as he spoke.

Reylana stared at him for a second. "I guess I could try. Essa's pretty pissed, so I probably won't be going into any battles for a while anyway."

"No battles under her command," Reylin pointed out. "She isn't your boss, and this is a war. We do what we have to, which includes putting new leaders in place. You can lead the sword maidens when you return."

"Thanks, but no," she replied, shaking her head. The last thing she wanted was a command. It was too much pressure, and she didn't like screaming orders at people who were only half listening. Wild Elves are free spirits and do not follow orders in the same fashion as humans. Human soldiers are highly disciplined and do not think for themselves. A Wild Elf fighting in the forest has to use his own wits, even if it means disobeying his commander.

"You don't have to go at once," Reylin said. "We barely have enough people to defend the village as it is. After today, we can expect Domren and his goons to come after us."

Chapter 7

Mi'tal waited patiently at the inn for the prince to arrive. Frequently, the prince would meet him here for lunch rather than eating at the palace with his father. His father only talked about military strategy, but Aelryk preferred the relaxed nature of the inn. Mi'tal admired the prince's desire to be near regular people, even though his father preferred to stay as far as possible from the common man.

Mi'tal himself could fit in anywhere. He was a nobleman, but he lacked the arrogance that often came along with a title. He was taller than most other men and had a hefty warrior's build which gave him the appearance of a soldier rather than a noble. The inn suited him just fine.

As Aelryk entered the inn, few people took notice. He was tall and handsome with dark hair and eyes, and the ladies rarely ignored him. Today, however, only Mi'tal seemed to be interested in his arrival. He raised his mug and nodded as the prince took a seat across from him.

"An ale, please," Aelryk said to the young serving girl who was passing by. She abruptly stopped in her tracks and turned to obey the prince's command.

"There was an attack on a farming village in the south," Aelryk began. "Father wants swift, immediate retaliation." His ale arrived, and he handed the girl a silver coin. She stared at him a little longer than would be considered polite, and her face began to blush. He gave her a broad smile before she went back to her work.

"Do you know which clan was responsible?" Mi'tal asked.

"Does it matter?" Aelryk replied. "He wants them all killed, and he doesn't care who we attack in response to the massacre. None of those citizens were armed."

"Personally, I'd prefer to find the ones responsible," Mi'tal commented. "I don't like senseless killing. Surely we can live beside some of those clans in peace."

"I agree," the prince said, sipping at his ale. "I spoke with one of the lieutenants who was at the scene shortly after the attack. They had runed arrows that set fire to the homes there. That would suggest the Sycamore Clan, but we can't be sure. They could have crafted the arrows for any other clan."

"Which clan lives closest to the site of the attack?" Mi'tal asked.

"The Silver Birch were the closest, but they're scattered now. I doubt they'd have been able to regroup so fast. The Oak Leaf Clan would be the second closest. They are suspected of attacking Enald earlier this week."

"I guess we'll be heading for them next, then," Mi'tal said. "I don't like fighting women. Even women as ruthless and bloodthirsty as those elves are still women. It doesn't feel right to fight them, and the men are impossible to catch when they're hiding in the damn trees." Mi'tal sat his mug down hard, shaking his head as he spoke.

"It is somewhat unsettling to fight women until you realize that they will kill you given the chance. They're fierce warriors and as capable in battle as any man. Don't let your guard down with them for a second. They won't hesitate to kill you."

Aelryk's words were true. Most Wild Elf women are trained in fighting from birth. Some choose other paths, of course, but the vast majority become sword maidens. They spend long hours practicing their craft, while the men hunt game to provide food for their families. The men are not any easier to deal with in battle. Their skill with a bow is unmatched in all of Nōl'Deron, and they are deadly accurate. Typically, they employ stealth by hiding in the treetops before taking aim at their victims. Crossing into their territory without permission usually leads to certain death. Unless a man wanted to know what it felt like to be a pin cushion, he stayed clear of their woods.

At the back of the inn, a group of merchants were having a heated discussion about King Domren's taxes and the hardship they were causing. To fund his war against the elves, the king had raised taxes on every citizen, especially the merchants. They were required to give an outrageous twenty percent of their profits to the king. The men sent to collect the taxes would demand more coin every time. They refused to believe that anyone kept honest records of their sales, and as a result, they took it upon themselves to threaten the merchants into paying more.

Aelryk strained to hear the merchant's speak.

"We should go directly to the king and appeal," one man said. "He may not know that his tax collectors are corrupt."

"He knows," a second man insisted. "He prefers it that way. He's a ruthless tyrant who cares only for his wars. The common man be damned."

Aelryk looked in their direction, contemplating the man's words. An abrupt silence followed. Realizing they had been overheard by the prince himself, the men were quick to gather their things and leave the inn.

"Do you think my father's taxes are unfair?" he asked Mi'tal.

"Taxes are always heavy when we're at war," Mi'tal said.

"The collectors, do you know them?"

"Not one," he replied. "All I know is that any position giving a man power over another man's money is a dangerous one. It leads to corruption, and few men are immune to it. Most men who are given the opportunity to steal a little gold here and there will take it, especially if there is no chance of being caught."

"Who audits the auditors?" Aelryk quipped.

"Exactly my point," Mi'tal agreed.

Aelryk made a mental note to mention the subject to his father. Once again, he felt the familiar dread in the pit of his stomach. He knew it was inevitable, but he did not look forward to speaking with his father about such matters. Domren was not a man who took advice well. He disliked being questioned, and his advisors had learned to simply agree with him. They were more concerned about their own lands and titles than the well-being of the kingdom. Aelryk knew change was needed, and he hoped that one day he would prove a worthy leader for his people.

Chapter 8

Yori packed a few meager possessions into a heavily patched knapsack. Among them was a second shirt that was in much better condition than his usual one. His uncle had insisted he wear something that wouldn't offend his wealthy customer. He also packed a few provisions that his aunt had prepared for his trip. Lacking the funds to stay at an inn, he would have to carry a bedroll and find someplace along the way for sleeping.

Meladee watched with sad eyes as he slung the bag over his shoulder. He knelt down and took the little girl's hand. "I won't be away very long," he said.

"Promise?" she replied, the tears spilling over from her eyes.

"I promise," he replied. He hugged the girl and retrieved the sword from his workbench. Ren had placed it inside a leather scabbard and wrapped it in cloth to protect it during the journey. It scarcely resembled a sword, and Yori was grateful for it. He did not want to appear armed should someone recognize him as a half-elf.

The morning's weather was pleasant for traveling. A soft breeze was blowing through the air, shuffling the dried leaves that littered the road. The trees were giving off their last brilliant display of red and gold before succumbing to the long sleep of winter. Luckily, the air was not cold, and Yori did not regret his lack of a coat.

He encountered very few travelers along the road. A traveling merchant on a horse trotted lazily past, pulling a small covered cart behind. At midday, he stopped for a short break at the roadside. Sitting beneath the shade of a tall oak tree, he crunched one of the fresh, crisp apples his aunt had packed for him. Tossing the core into the woods, he started off down the road once more. At sunset, he neared a farmhouse and wondered if the family inside would mind if he slept in their barn. The clouds had been gathering throughout the afternoon, and he feared it might rain in the night.

Adjusting his headband to be sure his ears were still covered, he approached the small farm. A blonde-haired lady was leading a silver horse into the barn for the night. She caught sight of him and paused.

"Hello there," he said. "I'm on my way to the palace district and wondered if you would mind if I slept in your barn." His timing was perfect, as a gentle rain was just beginning to fall.

The lady looked him up and down and obviously didn't see him as any type of threat. "If you'll rake out the stalls before you turn in, you're welcome to stay," she replied, wiping her brow with her sleeve. "My son has gone to join the army, and there are more chores here than my husband and I can handle."

"I'd be happy to help," Yori replied. "Thank you."

She handed him the horse's lead rope and went back inside her house. Yori led the horse inside the barn and tied him just outside the stall. He picked up the pitchfork and began sifting through the straw. Once he was satisfied with its cleanliness, he disposed of the soiled straw and droppings in the large pile behind the barn. He added a fresh bale of straw to the stall and walked the horse inside it. As he closed the gate, the horse gave a friendly neigh. He petted its nose and spread his bedroll on the floor just across from the horse. The work was a small price to pay for a dry place to sleep.

When he awoke the next morning, he was surprised to find a plate of sliced bread smeared with blackberry jelly. He devoured the food greedily and licked the sticky sweetness off his fingers. He repacked his bedroll and placed it over his shoulder along with his knapsack.

Unlatching the gate, he led the horse out to the pasture to graze. The woman was already tending to her chickens and gathering eggs in a basket. He carried the plate from his breakfast to her and said, "Thank you for the food, ma'am."

Taking the plate, she replied, "You're welcome. Are you looking for work?"

"No, I'm just running an errand for my uncle," he replied.

"Oh," she said, sounding disappointed. "If you run into any other young men needing work, send them my way. There are lots of repairs needed around here, and I don't know if my son will ever return. Safe travels to you."

"I will. Thank you," Yori replied, feeling sorry for the overworked woman. He returned once again to the road to complete his journey to the palace.

By nightfall, he was within sight of the palace. Just outside of the town, a group of merchants and other travelers had set up camp and were laughing and talking around a campfire. Yori thought it would be safer to join them rather than sleeping alone at the edge of the woods. He approached the men, who greeted him cheerfully.

"Join us, young man," a robust man said, lifting his mug. Yori nodded and took a seat near the fire. "You headed to the palace?" the man asked, offering him a mug of dark brown ale.

"Yes," he replied, taking the mug and tasting its contents. It was bitter and very strong.

"Lots of lovely young girls in this town," the man replied, raising his eyebrows up and down and grinning.

Yori smiled back, realizing the man was drunk. Tasting the ale again, he decided it wouldn't take much to accomplish the task. He had never tasted any ale so strong before. He wondered if it was the variety preferred in the palace district.

Another man produced a lute and began to play. The music was cheerful, and the assembled party began to clap in time to the beat. Those who knew the tune began to sing along. Never before had Yori been a part of any celebration, and this one seemed to be happening for no reason. Life in Enald did not offer many opportunities for him, and he enjoyed the moment.

Along with the free-flowing ale, the men shared their bread and salted pork. It was the best Yori had eaten since he left his home, and he was grateful. It was a nice feeling to be accepted without question. No one here was suspicious of him, and no one knew his secret. Here, he was simply a young man traveling along the road.

A bright blue sky greeted him the next morning. He changed into his clean shirt, thanked his new friends for their hospitality, and continued into the city. He wanted to deliver the sword first thing and perhaps explore the town a bit when he was finished.

The palace's market district stretched on for what seemed like forever. There were scores of stalls selling a wide variety of goods, and he was sure it was at least four times larger than Enald's market. It was still early, but citizens were buzzing everywhere. There were more people here than he could possibly count. He wondered how easily he could blend in here, and how long he would have gone unnoticed had he grown up in a town this size.

Making his way to the palace was slow. The large crowds of people were in no hurry to move, and most of them walked back and forth between merchant stalls, browsing the goods and comparing prices. At last, he approached the huge iron gates of the palace where two guards stood at attention.

"State your business," the one on the right said, sounding bored.

"I'm here to deliver a sword to Lieutenant Perrin," Yori replied.

"Go ahead," the guard said, waving his hand. "The page inside will give you directions to his chambers."

Nodding, Yori entered the palace. Immediately, he was struck by the vastness of the interior. The stone floors were polished, and the walls were bright. Fancy brass sconces lined the walls, illuminating the room with a soft white glow. A large staircase with intricately detailed banisters filled the entire back wall and led upwards to rooms of unimaginable comfort. His uncle's small home could fit in the entryway at least five times over.

A dark-haired page greeted him at the door. "What can I do for you, sir?" the boy asked.

"I, uhm..." Yori stumbled on his words for a moment. Never before had he been referred to as "sir". "I'm sorry," he started again. "I'm here to see

Lieutenant Perrin. I've brought the sword he commissioned from the blacksmith at Enald."

"Follow me," the boy said. He led Yori up the vast staircase and down a long corridor. The walls were lined with paintings featuring all manner of noble lords and ladies. All of them wore fancy clothes, and some of the men carried fine swords. A few were painted with children or small dogs at their feet. They were so life-like that Yori had to restrain himself from the childish urge to touch them.

The boy led him into a sitting room that contained the most lavish furnishings he had ever seen. There were various chairs placed all around the room, each complete with its own velvet cushion. Yori couldn't imagine having such a comfortable place to sit.

After a few minutes, Lieutenant Perrin entered the room. He was average height with a thick build. His eyes were bright, and his dark hair hung loosely at his shoulders.

Remembering his manners, Yori waited to speak until he was spoken to.

"You've brought the sword, then?" the man asked.

"Yes, my lord," he replied, presenting the bundle to the lieutenant.

He laid the sword on a large writing desk and unwrapped it slowly. "Oh, this is nice," he remarked. "This is very nice." He lifted the sword in his right hand, checking the balance. Giving it a few swings, he tested the quality of the work. "Your master has certainly lived up to his father's reputation."

"Thank you, my lord," Yori replied.

"Are you his apprentice?"

"I am, sir," he said.

"Did you help forge this at all?"

"Yes, my lord," Yori replied, forgetting his modesty. "I inlaid the hilt as well."

"Most apprentices aren't so bold. They only admit to lighting the fires," Perrin said, laughing.

Yori looked at the ground, unsure how to respond.

Perrin turned the sword over in his hand and looked closely at the ebony inlays. "If I did work this good," he began, "I'd want the credit for it as well. Apprentices can be much under appreciated. I was once one myself." He winked at Yori. "I purchased this as a gift for Prince Aelryk. Would you accompany me to give it to him?"

Yori looked at the man with a stunned expression. He had never imagined meeting any member of the royal household, and he had no idea how to behave in front of a prince. There was no reason this man should want him present, but it would be impolite to refuse. Ren would be beyond angry if the customer wasn't fully satisfied, so he nodded in agreement.

He followed the lieutenant back down the corridor and up a second flight of stairs. At the top of the stairs, they entered the first door on the right which led into another sitting room. The page darted into the adjoining room to announce their arrival to the prince. Yori's heart was pounding, and he hoped he didn't make a fool of himself. He felt underdressed and completely out of place in these surroundings. Now he was going to be viewed by a prince, who would probably be insulted by his mere presence.

The prince entered wearing a black satin tunic. "Good day, Perrin," he said, his voice cheerful. He ignored Yori, obviously seeing him as an insignificant servant.

"Your Majesty, I've had a court sword crafted for you as a gift. It's early for your birthday, but I have never been good at waiting." Perrin presented the sword to the prince.

"This is very fine work," he said as he inspected the hilt. He gave the sword a few swings as Perrin had done and ran his hand along the flat of the blade. "Truly this is a thing of beauty. Is this ebony?"

"Yes, Your Majesty," Yori replied without thinking. Perrin turned to look at him and smiled.

"This is the sword's maker, my lord," Perrin said. "Well, one of them. A blacksmith named Ren from Enald has crafted it, but this young man is responsible for the inlay."

"Indeed," Aelryk replied. "You have an excellent eye for detail. I imagine you could etch runes as well, had you been born with the ability."

Perrin laughed loudly. "I'm afraid you'd need an elf for that, my lord." The prince laughed as well.

Yori had a sudden urge to jump out of the window. He stood frozen in place, hoping he was not asked to speak again. He feared his voice may abandon him.

"What is your name?" the prince asked.

"It's Yori, my lord," he managed to say.

"Yori, you have my compliments. You must pass them along to your master as well. Perrin, I thank you for this lovely gift. I shall wear it at all of the court celebrations."

Perrin bowed, and Yori followed suit. Together they walked back to the palace entrance where Perrin handed him a purse full of coins. "It's been a pleasure, Yori," he said. "Please give my best to Ren."

With that, Yori exited the palace. As he returned to the market district, his head still swam from the morning's events. Just seeing the inside of the palace would have been enough, but meeting the prince himself had been surreal. Though he would never consider spending any of his uncle's money, he decided to have a look at the local wares before once again departing for home. The road before him was long, and traveling solo was lonely business.

Chapter 9

A thick fog hung over the forest as Reylin began his watch. Scouts had reported soldiers in the area, and he had ordered his clansmen to take to the trees. Only a few archers and the sword maidens remained on the ground. They had no intention of running, and they would defend their village to the death. The elves who were unable to fight hid themselves high in the trees. They were the young, the elderly, and those who had no skill in battle. Their healer Doni was among them. He had taken a good amount of supplies into the trees with him in case the warriors were wounded in battle.

Reylin listened closely to the sounds of the forest. The birds chirped happily overhead, and the wind gently rustled the golden leaves, escorting them delicately to the ground. In the distance, he heard the crack of a small branch and knew that the Na'zorans were on the move. He readied his bow, signaling the others to prepare themselves as well.

Suddenly, horses burst through the tree line and into the village. Immediately, he loosed an arrow, knocking one soldier from his horse. His clansmen loosed arrows as well, and several men fell to the ground, clutching the arrows sticking out of their flesh. As their formation began to break, the sword maidens charged into battle. They quickly dispatched the men who had fallen from their mounts and began slicing at the legs of the men who had yet to be struck by arrows.

As his dark eyes drank in the scene, Mi'tal tightened his grip on the slender wooden handle of his war hammer and swung it at the charging women. The first to charge his direction was a tall, dark-haired elf with a savage look in her eyes. She screamed as she swung her blade to meet his hammer. Before she could draw her sword back a second time, he struck, hitting her directly in the head. She crumpled to the ground and did not move again. A second woman charged him, barely giving him enough time to block her blade. He struck the auburn-haired elf in the back and continued charging through the ranks.

Prince Aelryk's stallion was spooked when a horse in front of him suddenly changed direction and charged straight at him. The horse reared, throwing the prince violently to the ground. Mi'tal, who had witnessed the event, dashed to the prince's side. As he dismounted his horse to help Aelryk to his feet, an arrow grazed his left shoulder leaving a deep gash. Ignoring the pain, he grabbed the prince's arm and pulled him up. Grabbing the horse's reins, he used the animal for cover while he and Aelryk moved away from the center of the fighting.

"Are you alright, my lord?" Mi'tal asked, breathing heavily.

"I think I just had the wind knocked out of me," the prince replied. "We need to get back on our horses and reform the charge. Somehow these elves knew we were coming."

As Mi'tal looked around the battlefield, he realized that the elves had every advantage. Though his troops were certain they had the element of surprise, it was clear that the elves had known of their presence. It was a stupid mistake on their own part. Of course the elves would have scouts scouring every edge of the forest. A large group of mounted soldiers would be impossible to miss. Most likely, the elves had been expecting an attack ever since the massacre at the farming village. They must have been lying in wait, hoping for the opportunity to turn this war to their advantage. Today they had succeeded.

Arrows continued to fly from the trees as men and horses fell to the ground. The vast majority of the wounds were lethal, piercing the men through the eyes, neck, and heart. The mages at the rear of the assault stayed away from the fighting. From a distance, they began tossing fireballs at the huts, setting the village alight. The elves ignored the fire, and no one came running from the burning homes. With their clansmen safely evacuated to the trees, the elves would not be distracted by fleeing, unarmed citizens.

Moving through the treetops, the elves inched closer to the mages. In one coordinated attack, four arrows were loosed and simultaneously struck the four mages. Three of them were hit in the neck, while the third was hit in the ear. He had lowered his head slightly just as the arrow came whizzing his direction. The elves considered the mages to be the greatest threat of all the human soldiers, making them a prime target. The chaos had left them completely unprotected, and now they were dead.

"We need to get out of here," Mi'tal called to Aelryk.

Grabbing at the reins of a fleeing horse, the prince pulled himself onto the saddle. Mi'tal mounted a horse as well, and they began motioning and yelling for their troops to retreat. More than half already lay dead, and many others had been wounded. Once a dozen or so had managed to gather, they retreated back into the forest. More of the remaining soldiers followed, leaving the dead behind.

The elves did not pursue the fleeing soldiers. They had accomplished their goal and proven themselves worthy adversaries. No longer would the Na'zorans attack frightened, unprepared elves. From now on, they would deal with a mighty elven force that was not afraid to fight back.

"Reylana!" Reylin called as he looked around the battlefield. His sister's auburn hair normally made her stand out among a crowd, but he had not seen her since the battle began.

Hearing her name, she cried, "I'm here!" She walked slowly toward her brother. After the men had retreated, she began to feel pain in the back of her left shoulder where she had been struck with a war hammer. The pain was becoming severe, and a large purple lump was forming. As she approached Reylin, she looked at the ground and realized most of the fallen were Na'zorans. Unfortunately, a few of her elven sisters lay dead as well.

"Are you hurt?" Reylin asked as she grew closer.

"The back of my shoulder is bruised and maybe broken, but I'm not bleeding. Where's Doni?"

"Dead," he replied. "The flames from one of the mage's fireballs leapt at the tree where he was standing. I saw him fall directly into the fire. There's nothing there now but ash."

Reylana looked over at the tree where Doni had been. "I'm sorry to lose him. He was a fine healer. Did any of his supplies survive? We're going to need those."

"Some of the archers are looking for them," he replied. "We'll just have to help each other instead of relying on a healer."

He inspected the lump on his sister's back. It was rapidly becoming darker, and she winced when he touched it. "I think something is broken in there, Sis. We need to get your arm stabilized so it can heal."

"I can't use a two-handed sword very well with one arm wrapped up," she protested.

"You'll never use it at all if your arm heals crooked." He looked her straight in the eyes, his tone serious.

"Ok," she said reluctantly. He removed his vest and began ripping the fabric to create a makeshift sling. Wrapping it around her arm with a delicacy that she found surprising, he said, "That should do for now. Maybe another clan still has a living healer that can look at it."

"You still want me to visit the other clans?"

"Of course I do. We'll be much stronger if we stand together. We have no homes now, so we're all going to be living in the trees. They can't keep burning our villages if we have none. With nothing holding us in place, we can form an army to match the strength of our enemy. We're going to win this."

Reylana looked at her brother's hopeful expression and sighed. She knew a village could be rebuilt in time, but this had been her home since she was born. Everything was changing and not for the better. "You should have some of your men start scouting the area to locate the other homeless clans. We need to know the locations of each clan and which still have villages that could be vulnerable. Those will probably be hit next and will need protection."

"Now you're starting to sound like a war leader," Reylin commented with a smile.

Chapter 10

A bright, cloudless sky settled over the palace district as Yori moved through the marketplace. The aroma of freshly baked bread filled his nostrils, reminding his stomach that he had not yet eaten that day. He hoped that one of the merchants might have a menial task for him to perform which would earn him a few coins for a good meal. Eventually, he would be starting out on his long walk home, and he did not intend to go with an empty belly.

As he continued through the marketplace, he noticed a young woman was following him. From a distance, she repeatedly glanced at him and looked away quickly when he saw her. She carried a basket of wildflowers, and her light brown hair cascaded in soft ringlets over her shoulders. Bright yellow ribbons accentuated her tresses and brought out the brightness in her eyes. Looking at Yori once more, she gave a shy smile. He smiled back and stared at her curiously.

Slowly, she made her way from behind a merchant's stall and began walking casually toward him. She browsed at each stall along the way, pretending she wasn't interested in him at all. Finding an ounce of hidden courage, he began to move in her direction until he was standing next to her in front of a stall filled with fancy cloth and lace. As she admired a roll of embroidered satin, she glanced at him and flashed a smile.

"Hello," he said.

"Hello," she echoed, turning to face him.

Yori had very little experience speaking to women, especially pretty ones. This girl was breathtaking, and he found himself at a complete loss for words.

"It's a fine day," the girl said. "Are you a traveler?"

"Yes," Yori replied, thankful that she had continued the conversation. "I'm from Enald."

"I've never been there," she said, shaking her head slightly and causing her ringlets to bounce. Yori's eyes locked on the moving tresses as they danced upon her breast. Seeming to notice where his gaze had ventured, she slipped her arm in his and compelled him to walk alongside here.

"My name's Arla," she said as she walked.

"I'm Yori," he replied, wondering where they were going. This was his first time walking arm in arm with a girl, and he was concentrating on his stride in an attempt to not trip over his own feet. Looking like a fool was one thing, but the thought of looking foolish in front of such a pretty girl was mortifying.

"It's a pleasure to meet you, Yori," she said. "I baked a fresh apple pie this morning. Would you like to have some?"

"Umm, sure," Yori said, surprised by the question.

She continued to lead the way out of the marketplace and down the narrow street to a residential area. The neighborhood was filled with small houses built only a few feet apart from each other. The street seemed fairly clean, and few people were around.

Arriving at her home, she opened the door and motioned him inside. "My father is out for the day," she said. "He's gone on business and won't be back until dark."

She sat on the edge of a bed near the side wall of the house. Yori stood awkwardly, staring at the girl.

"Come and sit," she said, patting the bed next to her.

Yori obeyed and sat next to the girl. She gave him a flirty smile and kissed him quickly on the lips. Yori was too surprised by her actions to respond. No one had ever kissed him before, and he was unsure how to proceed. She looked away shyly and glanced back up at him.

"Aren't you going to kiss me?" she asked in a mischievous tone.

Yori said nothing. After a moment of silence, he placed a hand on her cheek and kissed her soft, warm lips. Though he'd never kissed anyone, he had watched closely as young lovers in Enald had passed by him in the marketplace. He was fairly certain he was imitating their actions well.

Arla seemed pleased with the kiss and giggled happily as he released her. She began unlacing her bodice, allowing her bosom to show through her thin chemise. Slipping the dress down off of her shoulders, she revealed her nakedness to Yori, who sat in awed silence, hungrily devouring the sight before him.

Instinctively, he moved closer to her, placing a hand on one breast. He caressed it gently and began kissing her neck passionately. Wrapping her arms around him, she began kissing him along his neck and nibbling at his earlobe. Forgetting himself in the moment, he allowed her to continue working up his ear until she slid her fingers through his sandy hair, removing the headband that hid his secret.

Seeing the pointed tips to his ears, Arla recoiled with a scream of fright and clutched her chemise to her chest. She backed away quickly and stumbled to the door. Yori sat stunned, not knowing what to say. He knew why she was upset, but he had no idea how to calm her.

The girl began to scream as she flung open the door and proceeded, undressed, into the streets. "Help me!" she cried, her throat raspy with terror. "Someone, please! He's tried to rape me! An elf! A *Wild* Elf!"

Yori's eyes went wide with fear. He stood frozen in the doorway, holding his breath and staring at the young woman. Another woman came running over to her and helped her wrap the chemise around her body to cover her nakedness.

Pointing at Yori, Arla cried, "He's an elf! He tried to force himself on me! An elf!"

A small crowd began to gather as they heard the commotion. Two guards approached and grabbed Yori's arms. One of them punched him in the stomach, forcing the air from his lungs. He offered no resistance, for fear they might kill him on the spot. His messy hair barely covered his ear tips, and he could not possibly deny the crime of being an elf.

The guards dragged him to the palace dungeons as half the citizens in the marketplace watched. Tossing him roughly inside a stone cell, the guard slammed the iron door shut and turned the key. Yori sat on the damp stone floor and buried his head in his hands. He was certain they would execute him. An elf could not expect a fair trial in Na'zora.

His mind swam with the possibility of being tortured before he was killed. Tears began to flow as he wished with all his heart that he had departed the palace district immediately, rather than wasting time around town. If only he could change that one moment, he would be free to return home to his family. He thought of little Meladee and how sad she would be when he did not return. The best he could hope for was a swift execution, but he knew that was unlikely. In the cramped stone cell he would find no comfort, only despair.

Chapter 11

For two days Yori languished in the cramped cell.

He was given a few bread crusts and just enough water to make him feel constantly thirsty. No one had spoken a word to him since he arrived. The only sounds in the dungeon were the footsteps of the guards, the dripping of water, and the occasional cries of a fellow prisoner.

A pale torchlight illuminated the darkness in the hallway. Someone was approaching his cell, but his eyes were blinded by the sudden light. The footsteps indicated that two men were coming his direction. Fearing they would take him to his execution, Yori began to breathe heavily and closed his eyes.

"You're tall for an elf," a voice commented. "For a male, anyway."

Yori looked up at the man standing outside his cell. He wore fine boots and a brocade tunic. Behind him was a younger man, who glanced nervously from side to side.

"I never would have guessed you were an elf. You hid it well, my friend," the first man said, moving closer to the bars and lowering the torch slightly.

The face revealed by the light stunned Yori. His heart missed a beat as he recognized the face of none other than Prince Aelryk.

"I believe it's customary to stand when your prince approaches," he said.

Yori scrambled to his feet, still in a state of shock. "Forgive me, Your Highness," he said, stammering. His balance was poor from sitting so long in one position, and he leaned a hand against the bars to steady himself.

"You have been accused of attempted rape," the prince began. "Are you guilty?"

"No, my lord," Yori replied.

"Then the girl is a liar?"

"I think she was frightened when she discovered I am half elf, my lord." The last thing Yori wanted to do was accuse a Na'zoran citizen of lying.

"I believe you," Aelryk said. "I am young, but I am a very good judge of character."

The prince took out the fine sword that Yori had helped craft. Yori held his breath, expecting the sword to pierce his heart. Perhaps this was the swift execution he had hoped for.

Instead of running him through, the prince spoke again. "This is a very fine sword. If you are an elf, you can learn to etch runes."

"I am only half, my lord," Yori began. "My father was an elf, but my mother was human."

"It doesn't matter," Aelryk replied casually. "I'm told a drop of elven blood is all that's required. You have a talent for crafting metals, and it shows. I will offer you an opportunity for freedom. Seek out your elven kin and learn the art of rune carving. Once you are proficient, you will return to Na'zora and work for me."

"Surely the elves would kill me as I approached," Yori replied, shaking his head.

"A quick death at their hands is far better than what my father has in store for a raping half-breed," the prince said matter-of-factly.

Yori considered his words for only a second. He had no doubt the prince spoke the truth, and he did not wish to find out what King Domren's punishment would be. "I will go," he said. "If I live, I will return when I've mastered the runes."

"Guards!" Aelryk shouted. One of them came running at the sound of the prince's voice. "Release this man. He is going on a mission for me that will most likely result in his death. I pardon him of all charges."

The guard bowed slightly to his prince and sorted through the keys that were tied to his belt. Finding the correct one, he unlocked the gate to Yori's cell and opened the door. Bowing again to Aelryk, he disappeared once again into the darkness of the dungeon.

Aelryk turned to the young page whose face still showed his uneasiness. Being in a dungeon, even as a free man, was not a pleasant experience. "Get this man some clean clothing. He's about your size, so bring him something of your own. Nothing too fancy, just a simple shirt and pants. He'll also need a decent pair of boots."

The young man bowed and ran out of the dungeon quickly. Any task was better than standing in the oppressive dungeon. The prince motioned for Yori to follow him, and together they ascended the stairs leading out of the dark, cold prison.

"You'll want to keep your hair covering those ears as best you can until you're safely out of the palace district. Your kind trade at some of the market villages along our border, but few people here will tolerate an elf."

Yori nodded, squinting his eyes as they adjusted to the light.

The page returned carrying a green shirt and a brown pair of pants which he offered to Yori. Slung over the boy's shoulder was a pair of leather boots that had hardly been worn.

"Well done," the prince said, clapping the boy on the back.

Yori changed into the new clothes, wishing he had the opportunity to bathe first. He had no desire to hang around, however, and decided it would be best to wait until he was safely back on the road that would lead him home.

Once he had finished dressing, the prince handed him a small purse. "This will help you if you encounter any more trouble. Most guards are easily bribed. They may expect double when they find out you're an elf."

"Thank you, my lord," he said, tucking it safely away in his pocket.

"You are on your honor," Aelryk said. "I expect you to keep your word and return here someday. If you do not, I will assume you have died."

"I am grateful for your kindness, my lord," Yori said. "I will return one day."

The prince nodded and looked him in the eye. Yori felt it strange that a nobleman, especially a prince, would have such trust in him. Most Na'zorans did not see elves as honorable or trustworthy.

The prince, however, was different. He judged a man by his character and actions. His instincts told him that Yori was a good man that had been falsely accused. In sparing this elf's life, he might earn two things. First, he might earn the respect of whichever clan the young man encountered. Surely he would relay his story, and the other elves would judge the prince's actions as commendable. Secondly, if the young elf succeeded in mastering the runes and returned, Aelryk would have earned himself a rune carver.

Only elves have the ability to etch magical runes, and no human, whether rich or poor, had ever managed to employ an elf for the task. They would staunchly refuse, even to the death. This young man, however, was a child of both worlds. He had grown up in the human world, and Aelryk hoped that he would return to it.

Chapter 12

Aelryk continued ascending the steps until he reached the main floor of the palace. Making his way to his father's council chambers, he paused momentarily outside the door and took a single deep breath. His father had finally set aside a precious few minutes of his time to speak with him as he had requested.

"You're late," the king remarked as Aelryk opened the door.

"Forgive me, Father," he replied, knowing full well he was actually early.

"What is it you want?" The king sat at the end of a long, rectangular table in an ornately carved high-back chair. His expression was one of boredom.

Apparently he did not care much for whatever his son was about to say.

"I'd like to discuss the situation with the elves," Aelryk began. "They are attacking our citizens in the outlying villages and leaving none alive. Those people are unarmed and have no chance to-"

"We cannot station troops at every village," Domren broke in. "We barely have enough men as it is. If we start splitting our forces to protect every single village, the elves will easily destroy our army."

"That wasn't my idea, Father," the prince said, trying to hide his frustration.

"Then what?" the king asked impatiently.

"We have already destroyed the majority of elven villages on this side of the river. There are no reports of any rebuilding, so they are certainly in a weakened position. Perhaps they will be willing to negotiate and rebuild their villages farther from our borders."

Domren gave his son an annoyed look. "Those savages will live among the trees. They don't need those measly huts we've destroyed. Why would I want to negotiate with them when I can simply wipe them out? If we negotiate, they'll want something in return. I'm not giving them anything."

"But Father-" the prince began.

"I've heard enough from you," the king interrupted, waving his hand dismissively. "I have a bit of news that concerns you. I have agreed to an engagement between you and the eldest daughter of King Olin of Ra'jhou. The prophet Orzi has foretold that she will be an excellent match. You will soon be wed."

"Father, this is hardly the time to be planning weddings. There is a war happening, and I have other matters which are more urgent."

"Exactly," the king said. "In exchange for taking a daughter off of his hands, King Olin will be adding some of his troops to our own. With our forces combined, we will destroy the elves entirely."

Aelryk stood in silence. He had no idea what words might convince his father to negotiate rather than continue the fighting. Both sides were suffering heavy losses, and it weighed heavily on the prince's conscience. There was little choice for him other than to follow his father's command. After all, he was only a prince and not yet a king. Soon he would be ordered to continue the raids, and there was nothing he could do about it.

Defeated, Aelryk bowed before the king. "Your Majesty," he said.

Outside the council chamber, Mi'tal patiently awaited the prince. As the door opened, he smiled at him curiously, examining the expression on his face. It did not appear that the conversation had gone well.

"Did you speak with him about the taxes?" Mi'tal asked, breaking the silence.

"I didn't have a chance," the prince began. "I started out asking about negotiations with the elves."

"That was bold," Mi'tal commented. "How did he take it?"

Aelryk stared at his friend and remained silent.

"That bad, huh?" Mi'tal said, shaking his head. "Well, at least you tried."

"He also informed me that I'm to be married to a princess from Ra'jhou."

"Congratulations, my lord," Mi'tal replied. "I'm sure she's quite lovely."

The two began to walk down the long corridor to the palace entryway. Exiting out into the town, Aelryk said, "This just isn't the time for weddings or celebrations. If only the king would listen to someone other than himself."

"If I may be so bold, Your Highness," Mi'tal began, "you could send emissaries to speak with the elves without your father's knowledge."

Aelryk stopped walking and asked, "How do you mean?"

"You don't need to send an army," he said. "Your father won't take any notice of two or three missing people."

"Secret talks," the prince remarked. "Do you think the elves would allow the emissaries to live long enough to talk? They have no reason to trust us."

"All you can do is send someone under a banner of truce and hope for the best."

"Are you willing to go yourself?" the prince asked.

"If you command it of me, my lord," Mi'tal replied firmly.

"You are indeed brave, my friend."

The pair continued walking down the dirt path until they reached the armory. "Is there any chance of knowing which clan might be most likely to talk?" Mi'tal asked.

"So far the Sycamore Clan is the only one that still has a village. Either they will hate us slightly less than the others, or they will have taken in all the displaced elves, which means they will truly despise us." The prince thought for a second. "There are probably hundreds of elves that have taken to the trees. Na'zorans journeying through the Wildlands are not likely to be spared." He shook his head and added, "I don't know what to do."

"We could release the elves that are being held," Mi'tal suggested. "That would be a sign of good faith. Perhaps one of them would convey the message."

"My father has been using them for slave labor at the docks. He's going to notice if they disappear."

"Tell him you've enlisted their help in the army. They could polish armor and sharpen swords, as far as he need know."

"My father would be happier if they were being used as practice dummies," the prince commented.

Mi'tal raised an eyebrow, approving of the idea. "He'll think you're following in his footsteps. Just imagine his pride." Both men began to laugh. "No one at the docks will question you for taking the elves away. It may be some time before your father is made aware of it."

"You're right, my friend," the prince said, laying a hand on Mi'tal's shoulder. His mind was made up. Without informing his father, he would attempt to make peace with the elves on his own. Perhaps the idea was folly, but he had to try. Otherwise, the fighting would continue until the elves were wiped out, and there would be no one left to protect the forests from his father's desire to expand the kingdom. Villages and farms would dominate the land, and the ancient forests would be no more.

Chapter 13

Frost filled the forest air as autumn began to give way to winter. Most of the trees were stripped bare, their slender branches naked and exposed before the world. Birds became scarce, most of them preferring the warmer climates to the south. The brave few who stayed blasted their calls to the sky, defying the winter itself.

Reylin and his archers gathered near a campfire to discuss their next attack. Reylana had joined them, as she was still unable to fight alongside the other women. Her shoulder had grown stiff, but the pain was duller than before. Still unable to wield a sword, she was preparing to leave and visit other clans in the area.

"Reylana will be heading to the Sycamore Clan soon," Reylin began. "They are the only clan we are aware of that still has a living rune carver. A pretty girl should do a good job of convincing him to help. Hopefully his clansmen will be willing to join the fight as well. They haven't been attacked yet, but their day is coming."

"What of the Mountain Clan and the Mulberry Clan?" a young, dark-haired elf asked. "Has there been any word of them?"

"None of us have traveled that far north," Reylin replied. "Someone will need to visit each of them and try to convince them to fight as well. I don't know whether they've been attacked or if any of them are still alive."

"Do you think the clans across the river would join us?" a second archer asked. He was older and had traveled farther than any elf of the Oak Leaf Clan. "The Na'zorans haven't made it that far, but once they wipe us out on this side, I'm sure they won't let a river stop them."

"You could certainly cross the river and find out," Reylin said. "You've been to some of their villages before. Maybe they haven't moved."

"Send my father," the elf replied. "I can still fight. He is too old, but he remembers where the clans are located."

Reylin nodded in agreement.

"So now you're sending more of us away," Reylana commented. "Who will be left to defend our people?"

"I will," Reylin said. "The majority of our archers will still be here along with all of the sword maidens. We can create a distraction while you and the others gather our army."

Reylana nodded. She hated the idea of her clan going into battle without her. Her arm, however, was not going to allow her to fight efficiently. The best she could do for her people was secure the aid of the Sycamore Clan and its rune carver. With runed weapons, they would possess superior arms to those of the Na'zorans.

"I feel very strongly that our clan should move away from this area," Reylin began. "The humans will be expecting us to stay around our ruined village, and that will only make us easier targets. I suggest that the elderly, the children, and the nursemaids move across the river with the clans who have yet to be attacked. They will welcome them, I'm sure, and they will be safe there. Those of us who can still fight should move north and stay near Na'zora's border. We can attack the villages there, and I don't think they will see it coming. I have no doubt that they will increase their presence to the settlements near here, which gives us another reason to move north."

"I agree," Essa said, approaching the campfire. She was still unhappy with Reylin, but the good of her clan was her first priority. He was ruthless, but he had a talent for planning battles. "We need to get going soon. The rains are coming."

A gentle thunder rolled high in the clouds as if summoned by Essa's words. The late fall rains would make life without huts difficult. The trees had already dropped the majority of their leaves and would not provide the best cover from the rain.

"Nearly all of our animal skins were destroyed in the fires. We have nothing to stretch over the limbs for roofing," Essa said.

"We can't exactly tan hides while we're traveling and fighting," Reylin replied. "The clansmen we're sending away will be fine. Those of us who are fighting won't be staying in one place long enough to care. We'll just have to make do."

For some time the clansmen talked quietly among themselves. Finally, they decided who would be traveling to the Mountain and Mulberry Clans. Two older clansmen had been chosen and would have to be informed.

Reylana was regretting her injury more and more. She disliked that her brother was moving the clan farther away, and that she could not join in the fighting. Their clan Overseer had been killed when their village was destroyed, and Reylin had stepped up quickly to take over command. He had no desire to take the title, and he was too young for anyone to consider giving it to him. However, they did need a leader during the war, and there were few who could lead a battle better than him. Reylana sighed to herself, wishing she was fit enough to travel alongside him.

She gathered up the nuts and dried fruit she had prepared for her journey and placed them inside a small pouch that hung from her belt. Placing her sword on her back was difficult without the use of her left arm. The sling still prohibited her movement, and she knew she wouldn't be able to swing the sword if she needed it. With only one hand, she couldn't hope to do more than clumsily bash someone with it. Still, it was better than no defense at all. It was unlikely she would encounter a problem in the forests, but she wouldn't leave her sword behind.

Eventually her arm would heal, and she would be able to rejoin the fighting.

Once she was ready to set out, she went looking for Reylin. He was perched on a limb, busily crafting arrows for the fighting ahead.

"I'm all set to leave," she called up to him. Her tree-climbing skills were quite awkward without the use of both arms, so she chose to remain on the ground.

Reylin hopped down from the branch and wrapped his arms around his sister. "Be well, Sis," he said. "Remember how much we need the Sycamore Clan's help. You have a very important task ahead of you."

"I doubt they'll say no," she said with certainty.

"I can't imagine they would," he replied. "But if they've been attacked, they may not be so easy to find. I have no idea how many of them may be left. If their rune carver is dead, it's up to you to find someone else."

"I'll do whatever I can," she said. "I hope to see you again soon."

Glancing back over her shoulder at what had once been her village, Reylana's eyes filled with tears. This had always been her home, and she wondered if it ever would be again. Her life was changing too quickly, and she yearned for the carefree days of her childhood. She missed her parents and their wisdom. Things had always seemed simpler when they were around.

A gentle mist began to fall over the forest, and streaks of pale lightning illuminated the sky. The thunder drummed lazily through the clouds as if it had no desire to be noticed. Reylin climbed back into the trees and watched as his sister moved deeper into the dense forest, disappearing within its protective cover. In her hands rested the hope of their clan and all their kinsmen. Their only chance to survive this war depended on the weapons she would secure for them.

Chapter 14

A chill lingered on the air as Yori arrived within sight of Enald. He stood at the edge of the village and sighed quietly to himself. He was not looking forward to telling Meladee that he would be leaving for good. Those soulful eyes of hers would no doubt leave him feeling entirely guilty. She would not understand that he had no choice in the matter. All she would know was that her dearest friend was abandoning her for good.

Mustering his courage, he continued into the village and through the streets until he came at last to Ren's smithy. Stepping inside, he heard his uncle say, "Welcome back. You were gone a bit longer than I expected."

Meladee rushed at him, throwing her arms around his waist. "Where were you?" she asked accusingly.

Yori knelt to her level and took her little hands in his. "I'm sorry I didn't come back right away," he said.

"You must have met a girl," Ren said, grinning.

"Sort of," Yori replied, his gaze falling to the floor.

Ren noticed the change in Yori's expression and asked, "Did something happen?"

Yori was silent for a moment but finally answered, "Yes, something did." He drew in a deep breath and let it out slowly before continuing. "I did meet a girl, but when she found out I was an elf, she had me thrown in the dungeons. The prince himself released me on the condition I find my father's clan and learn to etch runes. He wants me to work for him."

Ren stood in stunned silence. This news was a bit much to swallow all at once. Not only would he be losing his apprentice, but the young man was setting out on a quest to fulfill the wishes of a prince. It sounded far-fetched and highly improbable. Why would the prince take an interest in a half-breed peasant?

"The prince, you say," Ren began. "He is personally sending you on a mission?"

"Yes," Yori replied. "The sword you sent me to deliver was for him. It was a gift. Lieutenant Perrin introduced me to the prince, and when I got into trouble, the prince himself let me out of the dungeons."

Ren stared at him in disbelief. He wondered briefly if the young man had suffered a head injury. Yori knew nothing of his father's clan or of runes. He did not even know that his father had in fact been a very skilled rune carver.

"What do you know of your father and his clan?" Ren asked.

"Very little," Yori replied. "I know he was from the Sycamore Clan, and he traded goods here in Enald where he met my mother. That's about it."

"He was a rune carver," Ren stated flatly. "King Domren had insisted he come to work for him, but your father refused. He would not craft weapons that would be used against his people. His refusal is what got him killed."

Yori silently absorbed the information his uncle had given him. He was not aware that the king had any knowledge of his father, or that he had demanded his father's services as a weapon maker. Until now, he had not even known his father was a smith.

Ren spoke again despite Yori's silence. "How could the prince have known this when you didn't?"

Shaking his head, Yori replied, "I don't think he knew it at all. He complimented my work on the hilt of his sword and said I would make a good rune carver. Until he found me in the dungeons, he had no idea I had elven blood."

"You did excellent work on the sword, Yori. You will make an exceptional rune carver one day. I only hope you are able to find your father's people in the Wildlands. It isn't safe to travel there, and I can't give you any information as to their whereabouts."

Yori handed his uncle the purse full of coins the lieutenant had paid him for the sword. Ren accepted the purse and handed a few of the coins back to Yori. "The elves don't deal in coin, but you've earned a share of the profits."

Yori accepted the coins gratefully. "Thank you, Uncle."

Meladee, who had been observing their conversation in silence, suddenly began to sob. "You can't go away," she said through her tears. "Don't leave, Yori."

Yori knelt once more to comfort the girl. "I have to," he began. "When the prince tells you to do something, you have to do it. That's just how it

108

works, Meladee." His green eyes looked at her apologetically. She did not understand. All she knew was that her best friend was leaving her, probably forever.

Trella returned to the smithy, a basket filled with cloth in her hands. Her eyes went immediately to the sobbing young girl. Giving Ren an accusing glance, she reached down and picked her up. "What's wrong, my darling girl?" she asked. "Mama will make it better."

"Yori's leaving again," Meladee squeaked, burying her face into her mother's shoulder.

"You've only just returned," Trella said, looking at Yori.

"I know," he replied, "but I can't stay. I have business to attend to on behalf of the prince."

Trella's mouth dropped open slightly as she heard his words. "Will you at least be staying for dinner?" she asked. "This business can wait until the morning, surely."

"Of course," Yori replied, sounding relieved. He was glad Trella didn't ask for more of an explanation. In many ways she reminded him of his mother, and he did not want to tell her he had just been thrown in prison. Even if he had not truly committed a crime, he still felt too ashamed to express those words to his aunt.

"It looks like the prince has provided you with some fine garments," Trella commented. She reached out to touch the sleeve of Yori's shirt. "This is very fine indeed. Look at this, Meladee. This is a rich man's clothing." The little girl lifted her face from her mother's shoulder and stared at Yori. "You see, sweet girl, he has a very important friend, and he has to leave us in order to serve him. It is a great honor, and we must be brave and let him go." She kissed the girl on her cheek.

Meladee nodded and her tears began to slow. Her mother always knew just what to say to make her feel better.

"I'll get dinner started," Trella said. "Don't stay too late," she added, looking at Ren. She retrieved her basket and carried Meladee back to their home.

"I'm going to miss having your help around here," Ren said. "You do fine work."

Yori smiled nervously and nodded. Ren rarely gave compliments, but his words were always sincere. He wondered if his uncle ever thought of him as a son rather than just an apprentice. Having never known his real father, Ren was the closest thing he had to one.

Tonight would be his last night among his human family. If he managed to find his father's clan, he hoped they would accept him. There were many questions they could answer for him regarding his father. Yori knew next to nothing about him and wondered what kind of person he had been. Perhaps they even had a few things in common. With luck, he might survive the Wildlands long enough to find out.

Chapter 15

Lisalla stood on her balcony gazing at the Wrathful Mountains. This spectacular view had greeted her every day since she was born, and now she was preparing to leave it behind. The mountains stood tall and proud in the distance as she peered at the mist that hid the white caps from view and wondered what life on a mountaintop must be like. A sense of freedom came over her as she pictured herself high in the mountains, looking down upon the clouds. Closing her eyes, she tried to embed the image to her memory in case she was never able to return.

Soon, Lisalla would be leaving to meet her husband. Prince Aelryk of Na'zora was described as strikingly handsome as well as good-natured. Her excitement over her upcoming marriage was marred only by the fact that she had to leave her home. In her dreams, a prince had always traveled to Ra'jhou to marry her and take over her father's throne. In reality, she would have to travel to a land she had never even visited and someday become their queen.

"My lady," Danna said as she walked out onto the balcony. "You still haven't decided on a wedding gown. Most of your things are packed, and we really should bring wedding clothes with us. Your father says the ceremony will take place immediately."

Lisalla smiled at her maid and asked, "Are your things prepared as well?"

"Yes, ma'am," the young woman replied. "It's you I'm concerned about."

"I'll choose something," Lisalla said with a sigh. "I just don't understand why we have to be married so quickly. I want some time to know my husband before we wed."

"I'm afraid that isn't how things work for royalty," Danna said sympathetically.

"Maybe we can have more fun finding you a husband," Lisalla said, playfully tugging at Danna's long dark hair.

Danna blushed and pushed her hair back over her shoulders. "I think that's going to have to wait a while," she said.

"Come and sit with me," Lisalla said, pulling on Danna's arm. The two sat together at the intricate metal table near the balcony's railing. Lisalla closed her eyes and turned her face to the wind, her blonde ringlets dancing lazily on the breeze. Taking in a deep breath, the crisp mountain air filled her lungs. The days were growing shorter and the air cooler, but winter would not dampen her spirits. Her life was changing, and she was determined that it be for the better.

"Tell me about Na'zora, Danna. Have you ever been there?"

"No, my lady," Danna said. "I hear it is a very nice kingdom, and the palace overlooks the sea. The weather is a bit warmer there, and it doesn't snow as frequently as it does here. The summers can be very hot and humid, though." Danna thought for a few seconds and added, "I hear the food is very good."

Lisalla laughed. "Who can think of eating when wedding nerves set in?" she asked. "My main concern is whether this prince will like me."

"He will love you from the moment he sees you," Danna replied. "He is said to be very handsome, and you will have beautiful children together."

"Let's go and look at those gowns shall we?" Lisalla stood, followed by Danna. They passed through Lisalla's spacious bedroom and out into the palace corridor. Their footsteps echoed along the brightly polished marble floors. Descending the stairs, Lisalla took her maid's arm and leaned in close. Whispering, she said, "What color do you think the prince would like?"

"I'm afraid I don't know, my lady," Danna replied.

They continued walking arm in arm until they reached the dressmaker's quarters. Lisalla's mother was extremely passionate about her wardrobe and insisted a royal dressmaker be kept on staff at all times. She was given elaborate quarters next to the queen's own chambers and was on call at all hours. Four sewing assistants were also housed in servant quarters adjoining the royal dressmaker's rooms. When the queen demanded a gown, she did not like to wait long for its completion.

Stepping inside the brightly lit room, the girls finally let go of each other.

The royal dressmaker greeted them warmly. "Welcome, Your Highness," she said. "Please, have a seat. I will bring out the gowns I have prepared."

Clapping her hands together, the dressmaker summoned her assistants. Seeing that the princess had come, they darted off to retrieve the gowns. Within seconds, several elegant gowns of varying colors were presented before her. "Do you have a specific color in mind?" the woman asked.

Lisalla glanced at Danna and smiled. "Not yet," she said.

The servants laid the gowns on a large wooden table that had been covered with a blue velvet cloth. The room had several windows, allowing a good amount of light to fall on the garments. Lisalla began inspecting each gown and running her fingers over the fabric. Danna followed suit with a dreamy look in her dark eyes.

Lisalla moved rather quickly through the dresses until she came to a simple lavender gown. "This one," she said, stroking the fine lace that adorned the dress. "I like this one."

"My lady that one is too plain for a wedding," the dressmaker said. "The girls shouldn't have brought that one." She gave a severe look to her servants, who bowed their heads apologetically.

"No, it's perfect," the princess insisted. "I can see it isn't quite finished, but this is my dress." She lifted it from the table and held it in front of her. Her bright blue eyes and pale skin were accentuated by the lavender hue of the fabric, and her blonde ringlets cascaded on top of the lace, emphasizing the two distinct colors.

Danna gasped as she looked upon her friend. "It's so beautiful on you," she said as tears filled her eyes. "You look like a bride."

Lisalla smiled warmly and asked, "How soon can you have this finished?"

"An hour, my lady," the dressmaker replied. "Do you have any special requests for it?"

"Can you weave some silver threads through the lace to give it a bit of sparkle? Also add some small pearls, since I'll be living near the ocean."

"Of course, Your Highness," the woman said, bowing.

Lisalla handed the gown over to one of the servant girls and again grabbed Danna's arm. "We need shoes now, don't we? Let's go and visit the shoemaker in the marketplace."

"My lady, we don't have time to go all the way to the market. You have to be ready to leave by morning."

"Your Highness," the dressmaker said. "I can have satin shoes with lace trim ready for you as well. They will match the dress perfectly."

Lisalla tried to hide her disappointment. "That will do nicely. Thank you." She regretted that she wouldn't have one last chance to visit the marketplace. Shopping was one of her favorite activities. She loved to see all the new items from across the seas. It brought to her mind images of far-off lands where the items had been crafted. She doubted she would ever travel to those places, but having small pieces of those lands brought to her was enough to satisfy her thirst for adventure.

The girls returned to Lisalla's room where Danna began hurriedly packing more of the princess's belongings. Lisalla sat on a cushioned chair facing a large window.

"I hope my prince likes lavender," she said.

"When he sees you in that dress, it will become his favorite color," Danna replied.

Lisalla couldn't help but laugh. She was growing more and more excited and also a bit nervous. *Tomorrow I will leave my home, and in a week I will meet my future husband.* "I hope you are right about everything, Danna."

Chapter 16

Recent storms in the area had created choppy waters near the docks in the Kingdom of Na'zora. The elven slaves wore thick chains, and their backs bore the scars of the fierce beatings they received when they refused to work for the humans. Only ten of them remained out of the twenty-three who had been taken captive. Thirteen had been beaten to death because they refused to work or could not perform the duties required of them. The slaves spent their days carrying heavy loads to and from the merchant ships docked at Na'zora's coast. They were given one small meal at the end of their long work day and lived in a tiny warehouse that was infested with rats.

Today the slaves worked without complaining. After weeks of servitude, they had learned the best way to stay alive was to keep their mouths shut and do as they were told. Constantly looking for a method of escape, their hearts were always hopeful. They had yet to give up and resign themselves to the situation. For now they would bide their time and work, hoping that one day they would escape and take revenge on their captors.

Aelryk and Mi'tal approached the docks casually, trying not to give anyone cause for suspicion. Aelryk's plan was to free the elves from their bondage and send a message with them back to their clans. He did not intend for his father to find out exactly what he was up to. His command would not be questioned by the dockmaster, but he did not intend to reveal his true reason for freeing the slaves. Should his father find out the truth, the prince feared his reaction. King Domren was not above punishing his own son, especially if he felt betrayed.

"Good day, dockmaster," the prince said as the man came into view. He was short and deeply tanned from many years of labor under the sun.

Bowing slightly before his prince, the man replied, "Good day, Your Highness. How may I be of service to you?"

"I have need of your elven slaves for a project of my own. I trust it won't cause you too much inconvenience."

"Of course not, my lord," the dockmaster replied, not hiding the displeased look in his eyes.

"For your trouble," the prince said, handing the man a purse full of coins.

Opening the purse, the man's eyes widened. Inside were dozens of gold coins, more than three times the worth of ten elven slaves. "You are a generous and kind lord, Your Highness," the man said, bowing again.

"I would appreciate it if you would keep this matter silent. If anyone inquires where the slaves have gone, simply tell them they were sold to a wealthy noble who does not wish his name to be revealed."

"As you request, my lord," the man replied. Right away he began chaining the elves together. One elf, a tall blonde woman, tried to resist by spitting in his face. He immediately swung the chain, striking her on her cheek. A large red gash appeared on the surface of her skin.

Aelryk took a step forward, but Mi'tal placed a hand on his chest to hold him back. "Not now, my lord," he said quietly. "We don't want him to grow suspicious."

Aelryk stared at the dockmaster, his eyes filled with hatred. Witnessing such cruel treatment without being able to intervene was almost too much to bear. He vowed to himself to find a suitable punishment for the dockmaster at a later time.

After the elves were chained, the dockmaster led them to their new master. Handing off the lead chain to Mi'tal, he said, "They'll probably resist for a while, but a good beating will soon set them right."

Mi'tal nodded and accepted the chain. Aelryk bit his tongue to prevent himself from screaming. It was appalling to meet someone with so little regard for another living being. They were at war with these people, but prisoners deserve to be treated with some respect. If one of Aelryk's men were taken captive, he hoped the elves would treat him well. Even in war, honor can be found.

"Gather around, all of you," Aelryk said, as Mi'tal ushered them together. "I am Prince Aelryk, heir to this kingdom. I'm going to free you, but first we must get you safely to our borders. You will have to remain chained for the next two days to avoid suspicion. If I unchain you, most of you will probably run and be captured. I won't be able to offer much help in that situation. You will be at the mercy of whoever has managed to catch you."

The elf men and women looked suspiciously at the prince and glanced at each other in silent communication. No one spoke a word, and Mi'tal wondered if they were planning something despite the chains. "I will be escorting you," he said. "You have my sincere vow that none of you will be harmed. We are going against the king's wishes by doing this. The prince wishes to negotiate a peace agreement with your clans and would like you to convey that message to your kinsmen."

The elves stared at him, still refusing to speak. They had no idea if this was a trick. Their previous treatment at the hands of the Na'zorans would suggest this man was dishonest. However, being chained together did not leave them much choice. Whether they wished to or not, they would be forced to follow this man to their fate.

"I apologize for the way you have been treated during your stay in my kingdom," the prince said. "I have had no part in it, but I can assure you that any other prisoners taken during this war will be treated better. You have my word on it. Please inform your clan leaders of my desire to make peace. The attacks will continue and many lives will be lost on both sides until we have reached an agreement. Convincing my father will be difficult but not impossible. I am willing to do whatever is necessary to secure peace."

Turning to face Mi'tal, he said, "The carriages should be waiting for you at the stables. Make sure the drivers remember to stay silent about all of this."

"Yes, Your Highness," he replied, bowing. "Follow me, please," he said to the elves. To his relief, the elves followed willingly while he held the chain loosely in his hand. As they approached the stable, Mi'tal spotted the two plain wooden carriages that would carry the elves to their freedom. Once they were placed inside, no one would know who was being transported. The windows would remain covered, and the elves would remain chained to avoid any chance of escaping.

Both carriage drivers appeared nervous, but they helped Mi'tal split the elves into two groups of five. Each group was loaded into a carriage, and Mi'tal took a seat next to the lead driver. With a nod, Mi'tal ordered the drivers to head for the western border.

The wooden carriages rolled noisily over the stone streets of the palace district. Few citizens took any notice as they passed, and Mi'tal felt free to relax in his seat. For now the elves were remaining quiet, and no one was aware that he and the prince had just committed treason. If the king happened to find out about this, they could both expect to be thrown in the dungeons. Aelryk would be forgiven in time, but Mi'tal's only hope would be for a single stroke of the headsman's axe. His loyalty to the prince, however, was much stronger than his loyalty to the king. Though Aelryk was still young, Mi'tal could plainly see that he was a much more respectable ruler than his father.

* * * * *

As evening darkened into night, the carriages stopped to make camp at the edge of a small farming community. Mi'tal opened the doors himself to allow the elves to sleep outside in the fresh air. Blankets had been stored in a trunk on the back of the second carriage, and the drivers distributed them among the elves.

"Are we going to have to sleep while chained?" a young elf asked. This was the first time any of them had spoken since the journey began.

"I'm afraid so," Mi'tal replied. "If you were to escape now, you might still be in danger. You have no reason to trust me, I know. If I unchain you, I can't be certain you won't run."

"What you mean is, you can't be certain I won't cut your throat while you sleep," the elf said, glaring at his captor.

"There's that as well," Mi'tal stated calmly. "Neither of us is much capable of trust it seems. We are at war after all."

"Are you really going to free us when we reach the Wildlands?" an older elf with graying hair asked. "You don't plan to use us for slave labor anymore?"

"I have no intention of doing so," Mi'tal answered. "As soon as we reach the border I will release the chains, and you can go where you will. I hope you will consider carrying the prince's message to your clansmen."

"I might consider it," the older elf said. "If you keep your word, perhaps your prince will keep his as well. It's a shame that the king has no interest in peace. He's the one we are fighting against."

"That is true, but Prince Aelryk hopes to negotiate a treaty and bring it before his father. He is certain that once everything is agreed between our two peoples his father will acquiesce."

"Domren is a tyrant and a murderer," an elf woman said.

Taking a closer look at her, Mi'tal realized it was the same woman who had been struck by the dockmaster earlier in the day. "I regret the poor treatment you have received at the hands of my people," he began. "You must believe that the prince will do everything in his power to negotiate this peace. Not all Na'zorans are like the dockmaster who mistreated you."

"You're all sheep," she said. "You follow a tyrant king no matter how cruelly he treats his subjects. He's beaten you all into submission, and now he has come for us. He will destroy the forest and claim the land for himself. If this prince truly wants peace, he should cut his father's heart out and claim the throne himself. If he does that, I will carry his message to my people."

The woman's harsh words landed heavily on Mi'tal's ears. She was correct that Domren was a tyrant. He judged his own people mercilessly, and a fair trial was no longer a common occurrence. The king did not like to be questioned, and any advisor that did so risked being put to death. Luckily, Aelryk was able to see the error of his father's ways. He had grown up to be the opposite of his father, and Mi'tal was certain he would make a far better king.

"A man who murders his own father would be a poor king," he replied. "Even with all his shortcomings, King Domren is still our sovereign. We must obey him."

"You're not exactly obeying him now," the older elf commented. "What would he do if he knew you were freeing us?"

"Most likely he would have us all killed," he replied. "Let's hope he remains ignorant of our situation."

As darkness overtook the land, the elves began to settle in near the base of a large oak tree. Mi'tal and the drivers stayed close to the carriages and took turns sleeping while one stood watch. The nights were growing colder, and the sun would not be up before they would have to depart again. The farmers would awake before dawn, and the carriages would need to be loaded to prevent the elves from being seen.

When the stars began to fade, Mi'tal gently shook one elf from each group. He requested that they remain silent and board the carriages for the last leg of their journey. Bread and honey were waiting for them in the carriages. The older elf was surprised to see that he was being fed, and he thanked Mi'tal for his hospitality.

Near mid-afternoon the Wildlands came into sight. Na'zora's borders had extended up to a section of dense forest, which Mi'tal hoped was not guarded by any Wild Elves. "Stop here," he told the driver as they neared the tree line. "We don't want to be in range of their archers if they are hiding in those trees." The driver obeyed without hesitation.

Mi'tal hopped down off of his seat and opened the doors of the first carriage. As promised, he removed the chains from the elves and handed the key to the driver of the second carriage. The man accepted the key nervously and proceeded to release the second group of elves from their chains.

"You are free now," he said. "Please take our message to your people. If it leads to an end to this war, you will have done a great service to your own people and mine as well."

"I will take this message for you," the gray haired elf said. "My name is Tod, and I am a member of the Mulberry Clan. I hope this prince of yours is telling the truth. If so, my clan's Overseer will listen."

"Thank you, Tod," Mi'tal replied respectfully.

"What is your name?" he asked.

"It is Mi'tal, First Guard of His Royal Highness Prince Aelryk of Na'zora."

"You are a rare thing, Mi'tal," the elf said. "You are a human who keeps his word. If you say this prince is honest, I will trust you. You have treated us well and freed us as you promised. I will not forget it."

Mi'tal nodded and watched as the elves disappeared into the thick forest. He hoped his message had reached more than just the one elf, but he had no way to be sure. At least he had put forth the effort and extended the olive branch. It was up to the elves to accept or reject it.

Chapter 17

A chilly dawn descended over Enald as Yori prepared to leave his family behind and begin his journey into the Wildlands. The mood was somber, and silence lingered heavily throughout the small house.

Trella had prepared a large quantity of nuts and dried fruit for his journey. She had baked two extra loaves of bread which she wrapped carefully and placed in his worn knapsack. Having never spent any time in the forests, Yori had no idea which plants might be edible. He vaguely remembered picking berries with his mother when he was very young, but he had no idea which kind they were. With his luck, he would find something poisonous and make himself sick. The provisions his aunt had provided for him would seem like a feast in the dense forest.

Though he would be late opening his shop, Ren had decided to see Yori off that morning. "I have some traveling advice for you," he said as Yori finished packing his knapsack. "There is a good possibility you'll run into this war between the king and the elves. The best way to avoid it is to travel south near the borders of Al'marr. They are not at war, and there are no rumors suggesting they have the intention of joining one. Your mother once told me the Sycamores live near the bank of the Blue River just north of Al'marr. If they're still there, that will be your safest road."

Yori nodded, digesting the information. His uncle's advice seemed sound. If he traveled near Al'marr's border, he would spend less time lost in the woods. He had no idea how to navigate through a dense forest and feared he would end up walking in circles. The road to Al'marr is clearly marked as one heads south. From there, he could only hope that the route to the river was marked as well. Even if it wasn't, he still felt safer being near civilization.

"I would also advise you to hide your ears near human settlements and uncover them when you're in the woods. Hopefully that will save you some trouble along the way." Ren shook his head, his expression troubled. "Do you know anything about surviving in the woods?"

"Not really," Yori admitted.

Ren swallowed and looked at the floor. "Maybe your elven instincts will kick in," he said.

Trella approached them and spoke quietly. "Meladee is refusing to see him off on his trip. She's lying in bed crying, and she won't listen to me."

"I'll talk to her," Ren said, laying a hand on his wife's shoulder. He hurried to the little girl's bed to see if he could calm her.

"We're all going to miss you," Trella said. "Meladee is upset, but she'll be alright. Ren is going to be lost without you. He thinks of you as his own son, you know."

Yori was surprised to hear those words. He had never felt any special bond between himself and his uncle. Ren had never been one to show affection, and Yori had considered himself the man's apprentice and nothing more. "He does?" Yori asked.

"Of course," she replied, smiling warmly. "I know he's not the warmest person, and he does like to yell at you when you mess up at the forge. That's just how he is. Even if I bore him a dozen sons, he would still think of you as his eldest. He loves you, Yori. I do as well."

Since his mother had passed away, Yori could not recall anyone telling him that he was loved. Until this moment, he had not missed hearing the words. His eyes began to fill with tears, and he reached an arm around his aunt, squeezing her tightly. She laughed softly and hugged him as well.

Releasing from their embrace, Yori looked up to see Ren holding Meladee. She buried her face in her father's chest and refused to look at Yori.

He stroked the back of her dark hair and said, "I'm leaving, Meladee. Won't you at least say goodbye?"

The girl squirmed a little, pressing her face harder against her father. She did not utter a sound.

Trella placed a hand softly on Yori's shoulder. "She's just too little to understand. She loves you, and I know she will miss you dearly." She reached into the pocket of her apron and pulled out a dark blue knit cap. "I managed to finish this for you last night. It will help keep you warm as the weather gets colder, and it will also help hide your ears when you need to."

Taking the cap, he said, "Thank you, Trella." He brushed through his sandy hair with his fingers and placed the cap on his head. Since losing his headband, he had felt exposed. Everywhere he looked, he worried that people were staring at him and judging him because of his ears. Covering them once again, he felt a little more at ease. At his height, no one would guess he wasn't fully human.

As he opened the front door, the sunlight rushed inside to greet him. The cool air brushed against his face and filled his lungs. Winter would be here too soon, and he would be homeless. Luckily, he had thought to pack an extra blanket. It was old and torn, but it was still capable of providing warmth. Reaching the door, he turned back to look at his family. "I hope I see you all again someday."

"You will," Trella said reassuringly.

Handing Meladee to her mother, Ren grabbed Yori and hugged him tightly. Yori was surprised by the gesture but accepted it wholeheartedly. "Safe journeys, Son," Ren said. "You take care of yourself out there and come back to us."

Yori nodded and smiled nervously. He patted Meladee on her back and said, "Goodbye, Meladee. I'll miss you." Again, she did not reply. Her sobbing was barely audible as she continued to press her face into her mother's shoulder.

Not wanting to prolong the goodbye, Yori turned and walked quickly to the edge of town. He intended to travel along the road and follow the merchants that were leaving to peddle their wares in Al'marr. Perhaps one of them had work he could do in exchange for a little companionship on the road. Though he had so far only traveled once, Yori knew just how lonely the road could be.

As he reached the road, he sighed with relief. Several merchant wagons were heading south this morning. One elderly merchant had paused on the road to tighten the ropes holding his load in place. Two reddish-brown mules brayed impatiently as their master fiddled with the ropes. Yori gave the man a friendly wave as he approached. The bald old man glanced up and nodded.

"Could you use some help?" Yori asked.

"Sure could," the man replied. "These old fingers just don't work the way they used to. Damn ropes won't cooperate either."

Yori chuckled and pulled at the ropes. Giving one sharp tug, he secured the blanket over the load and tied off the ropes.

"You've got some strong arms there, young man. You heading down south?"

"I am," he replied.

"I'd be glad to have you along to the markets." The old man extended a hand for Yori to shake. "Name's Atti," he said. "You've got a real strong grip there," he commented, pulling his hand away from Yori.

"I'm Yori," he replied.

"What's got you heading south?" Atti asked.

"I was apprenticed to the blacksmith here, but he can't afford to keep me. I thought I'd look for work someplace else." Yori felt bad lying to the kind old man, but he certainly had no intention of telling him the true story.

"Looking for a little adventure as well, I'd guess," Atti said, his dark eyes twinkling. "When you're young there's nothing better than going far from home and seeing the world. I've been all over Nōl'Deron myself. Nowadays I just travel from Na'zora to Al'marr and back. I just can't move like I used to."

The mules brayed again, wondering what was keeping the men so long. The two of them climbed onto the wagon seat and started down the road.

"So what kind of goods are you carrying?" Yori asked.

"Bits and pieces," Atti replied. "There's some pottery and cloth and other household goods. Time was I'd carry jewels and high value items. I just can't defend them like I used to, though."

"I'd want an armed escort for that," Yori said, laughing.

"Back then you could borrow a few guards to travel with you. Now they're all off fighting in a war."

"What do you think of the war?" he asked curiously.

"It's a damn shame. The elves make good trade. They give you a good deal, and they make high quality stuff. Now I have to pick that stuff up in Al'marr. They don't allow the elves to trade in Na'zora anymore."

"Do you know any elves in Al'marr?"

"I do, as a matter of fact," Atti replied. "The Sycamore Clan is just outside the border near the Blue River, and they trade freely in Al'marr's market cities. I've traded with them for more years than I can remember. Good people, those elves."

Yori was astonished by this stroke of luck. Not only could this man tell him how to find the Sycamore Clan, he was taking him straight to a town where he might find some of the clan's members. That sounded far better than wandering through the forest while trying to avoid being shot. He smiled to himself and relaxed in his seat.

Chapter 18

Reylin led the way as his clansmen journeyed north. The elderly and children along with their nursemaids had already been sent across the river, and now the clan's warriors were on the move. Stealthily, they traveled near the Na'zoran border. Two scouts scanned the area ahead to be sure the path was safe. The rest of the group hung back among the dense foliage, their weapons constantly at the ready.

"Reylin," a voice called. A young elf appeared suddenly, dropping from a branch high above. Lon was one of the clan's bravest warriors, even at his young age of seventeen. "Not far to the east I saw a small village. There were no guards nearby, and the humans there did not seem like they were prepared for any kind of battle. It looks to be a town full of sheep and cloth weavers."

"I could go for a little mutton," Reylin said with a smirk. He signaled his troops to gather near him. Essa strode forward to stand at his side. "There's a village nearby, and I say we raid it," he said. "We can even earn ourselves a good amount of meat."

"No killing children," Essa declared, her voice adamant.

"I don't give a damn what you do with the kids, Essa. Leave them to starve in the wilderness for all I care. They're just going to grow up and kill us like their fathers do."

"My sword maidens won't fight if you don't agree." Essa looked around at the women, many of whom nodded in agreement.

Reylin looked around at the men and said, "We'll spare them too if it will shut you up."

Essa looked displeased but said nothing. The group set out following Lon eastward to the village.

Reylin observed the setting and decided that surrounding the village was going to be impossible. Much of the land sprawled eastward for miles. These were large, spacious farms, and there was no active center to the town. "Looks like we'll just have to charge in," he said. "The trees are too far back to offer cover while we shoot, and those people are never going to run within reach of our swords."

Essa nodded in agreement. "Ready the charge, ladies," she commanded.

The village was alive with movement. People were walking here and there tending to their farm chores while children played in the fields. The archers crept silently to the north and south sides of town, hoping to pick off any citizen who tried to flee. The farmers would most likely stand and fight as the sword maidens rushed the village.

Silently, the charge began. Essa had ordered the women not to cry out and to run as quickly as possible. If the alarm went up too soon, the citizens would flee before the maidens could reach them.

Just as they reached the edge of town, the shouting began. Women were grabbing their children and leading them away from the charging elves. Just as they had hoped, the men grabbed whatever weapon was at hand: hay forks, woodcutting axes, and shepherd's crooks. These tools did not stand a chance against the maidens' broadswords, but the men were prepared to fight in any case.

Essa charged wildly at a blond-haired farmer wielding an axe. He swung down hard as Essa came within reach, but her two-handed sword blocked the

143

blow. She swung at him with her blade while the farmer made a weak attempt to block it with the axe handle. The force of her swing splintered the handle into pieces, and the man staggered back, surprised by her strength. With one swift move she slashed open his chest. Silently, he crumpled to the earth.

Reylin and the archers picked off the women as they tried to flee. As they had promised, the children were spared. They ran eastward toward the Na'zoran city of Duana. Reylin knew that could only spell trouble for his people, but he did not dare break his word. Any more trouble out of Essa and their clan may be divided. He could not risk infighting. Every Wild Elf who could fight was desperately needed if there was any hope to win this war.

Once the fleeing citizens were dealt with, the archers moved to assist the sword maidens. Anyone who had yet to fall to their swords was quickly taken down by their arrows. Their victory secured, the men began retrieving any useable arrows they could find. The fate of the elven smiths was uncertain, and they would not risk wasting precious arrow tips. These were forged of steel, not simple bone or rock. Such arrows were useful in hunting, but in times of war, steel or iron was preferred. A few of the recovered arrows bore etched runes which greatly increased their chances of surviving to a second or third use. As he inspected the arrow tips, Reylin hoped silently to himself that his sister would find a living rune carver among the Sycamore Clan.

As she wiped the blood from her blade, Essa looked up at Reylin and nodded her head. "Good fight. This was more honorable than before."

"It was," he agreed, "and now those children can sound the alarm. Within hours, we could be tracked to wherever we choose to spend the night."

"Na'zorans don't have the skill to track us in the Wildlands. They are blind and ignorant in these forests."

"Let's hope they stay that way," he replied.

The sword maidens slaughtered two sheep and prepared the meat for travel. It wouldn't be safe to hang around much longer with the children raising the alarm, so the majority of the group returned to the dense forest to feast and celebrate. A few men stayed behind to search the village for any goods that might be useful and set fire to the homes once they had finished.

Lon was the last to rejoin the group. With him, he carried several pairs of iron scissors in a linen bag. "I'm guessing they use these to trim the sheep," he told Reylin. "They look like iron. When we find a smith, he can melt these to make new arrow tips."

"Well done," Reylin said, handing him a mutton rib. "The rest of us were too busy thinking about our stomachs."

"Who can blame you? We haven't had meat in weeks." Lon tore at the rib with his teeth.

"What's next for us, Reylin?" Essa asked.

Swallowing a bite of mutton, he replied, "We keep heading north and raiding wherever we come to. Some of our clansmen should be reaching their destinations by now, so hopefully we'll be joined by other warriors soon. We just have to keep moving to avoid the Na'zoran patrols."

"Their king will be furious when he hears of these attacks," Lon said, still chewing on his food. "I hate those mages, and I'll bet he brings more of them into the fight."

"Let him bring them by the dozens," Reylin replied. "Our arrows kill them just as well as any other man." He flung a bone away into the cooking fire.

"He's right," Essa said. "Mages are tricky. We don't know what to expect from them. They might even think they can attack us in the deeper sections of the Wildlands."

"I doubt that," Reylin said. "They might have new tricks to perform, but they're still cowards at heart. We'll be safe if we hide deep in the forest, and we don't have to raid every day. We just have to make sure our presence is known."

Essa nodded her head in agreement. The warriors finished their meals and took to the trees to spend the evening in silence. Reylin climbed to a high branch and began the first watch of the night. Any Na'zoran who came looking for his clan this night would fall the instant he came into sight. None would be spared while Reylin stood watch.

Chapter 19

The sun was setting fast in the late afternoon sky as Reylana neared the area where the Sycamore Clan was last known to dwell. She could sense that a pair of eyes had spotted her, and she scanned the treetops looking for her kinsman. Movement stirred among the dried leaves, and an elf dropped quickly to the ground.

"Welcome, friend," he said as he approached. His head was shaved bald except for a thin strip down the center that grew long enough to tie back into a ponytail.

"Sycamore Clan, I'm hoping," Reylana said, her weariness apparent in her voice. She had traveled for days without stopping, and her shoulder still ached from the blow she received in her last battle.

"That's right," he replied, a broad smile spreading over his face. "I'm Nat. What brings one so lovely as you our direction? You're Oak Leaf, right?"

"I am," she began. "My name is Reylana. My village was recently destroyed by the Na'zoran army, and I've come seeking aid."

"I've heard rumors about the war, but so far it hasn't reached our village. We're better protected being farther away from their borders. I'll take you to our Overseer. I'm sure everyone will want to hear what you have to say."

"I hope so," she said, following the elf to his village. As she approached, she could hear the sounds of laughter and children playing. Nat had spoken true. This village had yet to be touched by the war. Reylana's heart fluttered at the sight of their perfect little village. Dozens of huts stood proudly among the trees, and a large festival area still bore the signs of a recent celebration. This was the home she had longed for since her own village had been reduced to ashes.

Nat led the way to the Overseer's hut. Stepping inside, he introduced her to the muscular elf who provided leadership for the Sycamore Clan. Though his hair was beginning to gray, his body was still in good shape. "Overseer, this is Reylana of the Oak

Leaf Clan," Nat said. "She's come to discuss the war with us."

"Welcome, Reylana," he said. "I hope you have come alone by choice. Does the Oak Leaf Clan still survive?"

"They do," she replied. "We are scattered, though. Those who cannot fight are crossing the river to safety. The warriors have journeyed north to continue the raids."

"So the rumors are true then," he commented, looking down at the ground. "I feared as much, but so far our clan has avoided any attacks. Tell me, is there any news of the other clans?"

"As far as I know the Silver Birch Clan is worse off than we are. They were driven from their homes and scattered throughout the Wildlands. My brother is hoping to locate them and bring them into our own group. I have no news of the other clans. A few elves from my clan were heading out in hopes of finding them."

"I hope they are successful," he replied.

"Me too. I've come to you hoping that you still have a rune carver among your ranks."

"We do, but he is getting on in years. His apprentice is learning, but he isn't progressing as quickly as his master would like."

"We are in desperate need of runed weapons," she said, the urgency apparent in her voice. "They are our only hope of defeating the Na'zorans or of standing a chance against their mages."

"Though we haven't encountered their armies yet, I have no doubts as to the value of such weapons. So far, we have only used them for hunting."

"They are badly needed in war. I don't know if any other rune carvers still live."

He paused to think for a moment. "We will call a meeting of the clan tomorrow to discuss the matter. Nat can show you where to find dinner and a bed."

"Thank you, Overseer," she said with a nod of respect.

Nat and Reylana exited the Overseer's hut. At the center of the village, a large cooking fire was just being lit.

"That's where you'll find dinner," Nat said. "The hunters brought back elk today. There's plenty for everyone."

Reylana nodded, her stomach beginning to rumble. She hadn't tasted meat in quite a while, and freshly roasted elk sounded wonderful.

"My hut is the one between those two trees," Nat said, pointing. "My mate and I stay there. There's room for one more, and we have blankets to spare."

"Thank you," she replied, still thinking about the food.

"I better get back to my watch," Nat said. "I'll see you later." He turned and walked back into the forest.

Reylana joined the elves who were gathering around to cook the elk. Even with one bad arm, she was still able to help with some light cooking. She was greeted warmly by the others and helped herself to a mug of ale. As one woman cut chunks of meat and skewered them, Reylana placed them over the fire and turned them as necessary.

As the scent of the roasting meat filled her nostrils, she said, "This smells fantastic." Her mouth was beginning to water.

The older woman nodded, handing her more meat to place on the fire. She was a quiet sort of person, but she was highly skilled at seasoning meat. Reylana had never been a very good cook, but she envied those who had the skill.

Once the meat had finished cooking, many of the elves gathered around the fire to enjoy a meal. The cooler weather meant fewer fresh greens to be found, but the clan had done well preserving jams which contained the finest fruits the summer had to offer. Their sweetness mingled in perfect harmony with the smoked meat, and Reylana could not remember the last time she had eaten so well.

The clansmen were friendly and welcomed her with open arms. For now, she enjoyed the company of a carefree clan and chose not to burden herself with talk of war. Convincing this clan to join the war could wait until tomorrow. Tonight, she would sleep with hope returned to her heart.

* * * * *

The next morning was dark and cloudy with a sorrowful chill to the air. Winter had finally swallowed the land, providing shortened days and bitterly cold nights. With no huts and no opportunity to rebuild them, her clan could only look forward to a rough few months.

It was midmorning before the sun began to peek out from behind its cloudy mask. Its rays, however, provided little in the way of warmth. Reylana made her way to the center of town, where the Overseer was already gathering the clansmen together.

An elderly elf stood to the left of the Overseer. He had bright green eyes and thin gray hair. Despite his age, the elf appeared to be quite strong, and the muscles of his right arm appeared larger than his left.

That must be the rune carver, she thought. *All my hopes rest on his shoulders.*

Catching sight of Reylana, the Overseer waved her to the front of the crowd. "Please be seated, everyone," he said. "Our guest has arrived. Go ahead, Sister."

She turned to face the assembled elves. "My brothers and sisters, I have come seeking help in the war that is spreading across the Wildlands. The Silver Birch Clan is nearly destroyed, and my own village has been reduced to dust. Our warriors continue to fight the Na'zorans, but without help from all of the clans we will surely fail. We need more warriors, and we need runed weapons if we are to prevail."

Several voices spoke at once. The Overseer spread his hands, imploring the crowd to quiet down. "Darin," he said, addressing the elderly smith. "Let us hear what you have to say."

"I can't speak for the warriors," he replied, "but I can speak for myself. I will etch runes for any elf needing a better weapon. Unfortunately, I don't have the resources or the strength to forge new weapons for an entire army. You'll have to settle for your regular weapons with the addition of runes."

"There is little more I could ask of you," Reylana replied. "I thank you with all my heart."

155

Darin nodded, wishing he could do more. He was too old to march into battle, but he would support his kinsmen in any way possible. "My apprentice does most of the smithing, so anyone needing a new weapon will have to speak with him. He hasn't mastered the runes yet, so I'll have to do those myself."

"What say the warriors?" the Overseer asked.

Again many voices spoke at once. A dark-haired archer stood to address the crowd. "If villages are being raided and ruined, we are needed here to defend our own. I won't go riding off and allow the humans to take my home."

Many voices sounded in agreement. "You could seek them out and stop them before they made it here," Reylana said, losing her patience. "They will come for you in time, and you may not be able to stop them. My clan was prepared, but we still lost everything."

A tall sword maiden stood and began to speak. "I would go and fight this war, but I also fear leaving our home unprotected. I may fight one group in the north while a second attacks my village. The elderly and children would be here to die at their hands. I cannot leave my home. Not yet." She sat back down, her head bowed.

"You could help us stop this war before it gets worse," Reylana said, pleading with the elves. "If you don't help us, we will fail. Your clan will not be spared. You may be the last one on their list, but you will face the same fate as the rest of us."

The voices in the crowd made it clear that the majority of elves had no intention of entering the war. They were too far removed from the Na'zoran border to be bothered with the scuffles between elves and humans. Reylana could find no words to convince them.

"It seems we will not be joining you after all," the Overseer said with regret. "Personally, I agree with your remarks. I fear Na'zora will strike at us in time, and I wish there was some way to avoid that fate. However, leaving our village unattended is not an option."

Reylana stared at him dumbfounded. "Did you become Overseer through cowardice?"

"Careful, Sister," he said. "Your list of friends here is short. You may stay as long as you need, and our healer will be happy to tend to your injury. Darin has already agreed to assist you, and I hope you will consider that enough for the time being."

As quickly as it had begun, the meeting came to an end. The elves dispersed and went about their business. Nat approached Reylana once the crowd was gone.

"I'm sorry," he said. "There are some of us who would gladly join you in battle. I will speak to them and see if the Overseer would object to a small group of us coming with you. We have enough warriors to protect the village if only half of us join the war."

"Thank you, Nat," she said, tears spilling from her eyes. She had come all this way and failed. Her brother had trusted her with one important task, and she had been unable to complete it. The runed weapons would certainly help, but who would be left to wield them? Too many of her kinsmen had already died, and she wanted no more of the war. She wished she could be complacent like the members of the Sycamore Clan. If only she could pretend that the war was not her problem, then she could live on in peace and ignorance.

Unfortunately, she could not dismiss the facts and pretend there was no war. Once she was healed, she would return to her clan and continue to fight. To do anything less would be unimaginable. She was still a warrior, and she would continue the fight, even if it meant her death and the deaths of those she loved.

Chapter 20

"We'll be at Al'marr by midday," Atti said as he and Yori continued along the road. "One time I took a ship out of Al'marr and went all the way to the Sunswept Isles. Beautiful place, that is. Those elves aren't friendly though. They hate everybody who isn't them, and I bet they hate each other too."

"What did you do there?" Yori asked curiously. He had heard very little of the Sunswept Isles, and he had never met anyone who had been there.

"Well, they have this big college there where they teach magic. They need all kinds of supplies, and I thought I'd make a fortune by selling gems over there. They use them in their magic, and supposedly they're highly prized."

"Let me guess," Yori said. "You didn't make a fortune." He grinned at the old man.

Atti laughed and said, "No, I didn't. Those elves act like nothing a human merchant brings is ever good enough. They nitpick and try to cheat you on the prices. I didn't bother trying to sell them any other goods since they buy most everything else from Ral'nassa. That place is full of more uppity elves, but I guess they like them better than us humans."

"Do you know what they do with the gems?"

"Not really. I've heard they have lots of different uses in magic. I've seen swords that have special gems set in them that supposedly contain magical powers. I've never met a smith in Na'zora or Al'marr that could do such a thing. I suppose you have to go to the Sunswept Isles or Ral'nassa for that. Assuming you can stand those uppity bastards long enough to learn anything. I got out of there after only two days, and I don't plan to ever visit Ral'nassa. I can't imagine those elves being any more welcoming."

Yori wondered how the Enlightened Elves of the islands could be so different from the Wild Elves. If the old legends were correct, they all came from the same place originally. The First Ones, or Westerling Elves as they were now referred to, had given rise to both the Woodland Elves and the Island Elves. The two groups had followed different paths: one worshiping nature, and the other lusting for magical power.

The two continued along the road as the early winter sun tried its best to warm the sky. The chill in the air showed no signs of bending to the sun's will and continued to steal the heat from every warm body it encountered. The wind joined in the game, multiplying the chill as it danced across the road.

Finally, a border town came into sight. Yori could hear voices shouting in the distance, and the smell of freshly roasted meat wafted on the breeze.

"That's the biggest market town on the northern border of Al'marr," Atti said. "They call it Marrel. Don't confuse that with the port city in the south called Marron. I wonder whose silly idea it was to name them so close to the same thing."

"Is Marron where you took the ship to the islands?"

"Yes it was," he replied. "You thinking about going there?"

"Maybe someday," Yori said, shrugging.

"I hope they treat you better than they did me, but that was at least thirty years ago. Maybe things have changed."

They arrived in Marrel, and Atti drove his wagon to a large warehouse. Yori gladly helped the old man unload his wares, most of which were already sold to the local merchants. Atti had done business in Marrel for so many years that he had standing orders to fill. He spent very little time having to find new business or convince others to buy from him. His reputation as honest and fair had provided him with a loyal customer base.

Once they had finished unloading, Atti said, "You sure you want to keep traveling? I could use a strong young man to help move these goods back and forth. I can pay a decent wage."

Yori considered the idea briefly. "Thank you, Atti, but I'll have to pass for now. I appreciate the offer."

"Alright," Atti said. "You take care out there, and if you pass by my way again, feel free to say hello."

"I will," Yori replied. He shook the old man's hand before leaving to explore the town. It was easily three times the size of Enald, with merchant stalls spread as far as he could see. It was so similar to the palace district's market that he couldn't help but remember the events that had occurred there to change his life forever. He scanned the nearby stalls for any signs of elves or elven goods. Seeing nothing, he decided to grab something to eat and perhaps inquire of some of the local merchants.

He found a tavern that was nearly bursting at the seams with customers. Squeezing his way through the crowd, he managed to find the bar and a serving girl. She was young and buxom with dark eyes and a broad smile.

"What can I get for you, handsome?" she asked.

Yori felt himself blush, and his mouth went dry. "An ale, please," he managed to say. "And can I get some meat and bread as well?"

"Sure thing," she said. "Five coppers, please." She held out a hand for the money.

Reaching into the small purse given to him by the prince, he pulled out a silver coin and handed it to the girl.

"This is Na'zoran money," she said with a smile. "It's a pleasure to have you in Al'marr."

Yori had expected some change in return, but the girl simply put the coin into her apron pocket and batted her eyelashes at him. Too stunned to speak, he did not say a word. She was certainly pretty enough to earn a large tip, and Yori had never been very good with money. His experience with it was only slightly more than his experience with women.

The girl trotted off into the kitchen to retrieve Yori's food. When she returned, she brought the items he had requested as well as a large slice of berry pie. After she placed the items on the bar, she leaned over and kissed his cheek. Yori stared at her, dumbstruck, until he was startled back to his senses by the sound of coins jingling onto the bar. She had given him change for his silver after all. Flashing him a final smile, the girl headed off into the crowd to see to her other customers.

Once he finished eating, he slipped back through the crowd and walked along a row of merchant stalls. Just ahead, he caught sight of wooden longbows hanging on pegs inside of a shop. Surely a fletcher would know where to find Wild Elves. He made his way to the stall and stepped inside. To his surprise, an elf sat within affixing feathers to an arrow shaft.

The elf looked up and said, "Good day, sir. How may I serve you?"

"Actually," Yori began, "I'm looking for an elf."

"Which one?" the elf asked.

"Someone from the Sycamore Clan," Yori said.

The elf smiled and stood. "I'm from the Sycamore Clan," he said. He approached Yori and reached out a hand. "My name's Hydon."

"I'm Yori," he replied, shaking the elf's hand. Yori suddenly found himself feeling a bit nervous. He wasn't sure exactly what to say, so he remained silent. Removing his cap, he brushed back his sandy hair to reveal his pointed ears. Startled, the elf jerked his head back as if he had just been swatted on the nose.

"How did you get so tall?" the elf asked, stunned.

"My mother was a human," Yori replied. "My father was called Yon. He was rune carver for the Sycamore Clan before he was killed."

Hydon continued to stare at Yori for a moment. "I'm sorry, he said. I never met a half-elf before."

"I'm trying to locate my father's family," Yori said. "Did you know him?"

"I think I did," he replied. "I was just a kid then, though. His father Darin is still the rune carver for our clan."

"Can you take me to him?" Yori asked eagerly.

"I suppose I could," he replied. "Does he know he has a grandson?"

"I don't know," Yori said, looking down at his feet. "I suppose he knows that my father and mother were together, but I can't remember ever meeting him."

"It couldn't hurt to talk to him, I guess," Hydon said. "We don't usually bring strangers back to our

165

village, though. Maybe I could ask him to come here tomorrow." Hydon was inclined to believe Yori's story, but no human had ever come into their village, with the possible exception of Yori's mother. He could not remember her, and he did not feel safe bringing a half-human among his people.

"That'll have to do," Yori replied. "Do you think he'll come?"

"I can't say," he said with a shrug. "If he knows you exist, I imagine he'll want to meet you."

Yori replaced his cap, once again hiding his pointed ears. "I guess I'll look for you in the morning, then."

As he turned to leave the shop, Hydon had a change of heart. He felt sorry for the young man who had come seeking his family. "Wait," he said. "Come to the village with me this afternoon. Darin is too old to travel to the markets. The worst he can do is send you away."

"Thank you so much," Yori said, sounding relieved.

"I have some work to finish, but once it's done one of the others can watch the shop while I take you to the village."

"Could you use any help?" Yori asked.

"Only if you know how to construct an arrow."

"I know how to forge the tips," he replied, hoping that would help.

"You're a smith?"

"I've been an apprentice to one for several years," he replied proudly.

"Then you can definitely help. I'll handle the feathers, and you can secure the tips."

Yori gladly took a seat next to the elf and busied himself with the arrows. After what seemed an eternity, they finally finished and departed for the village. The pair entered the dense forest, the brown leaves crunching under their feet. A warmth permeated the forest air despite the chill of winter. The trees blocked the cold breeze and insulated the small amount of heat left on the ground. As the sun moved lower in the sky, Yori feared the warmth would not last, and the world would again succumb to winter.

After an hour in the forest, they arrived at the edge of the elven village. Yori took a deep breath at the sight of the huts and the scent of the campfires. He felt as if he were home, even though he had never before set foot in a Wild Elf village. These were his people too, and he felt a sense of belonging that he had never experienced before. In his heart, he hoped that they would accept him.

Hydon led the way to Darin's hut. Yori followed, trying to quell his excitement. He did not want to appear as an over-excited puppy begging for a treat. Once he caught sight of the forge, he knew he had reached his grandfather's home. A young, fair-haired elf was hunched over a workbench and did not hear them approach.

"Hello, Lem," Hydon said. "Is Darin around?"

"He's inside," he replied without looking up from his work. Darin had just emerged from his hut and was heading back to the forge. He nodded at Hydon and stopped short when he saw Yori.

"Forest bless me," he said as he stared at Yori. "You must be Yon's boy."

Hydon gave Yori a pat on the back and departed.

"I am," Yori replied. "How did you know?"

"You look exactly like him," Darin replied. "Well, except you're a head taller. What brings you here?"

"I came hoping you could teach me to etch runes like my father did."

"Is that so," he asked suspiciously. "Do you plan to use this knowledge for humans or for elves?"

"I don't know, honestly," Yori replied. "I lived in Enald my whole life, and no one ever really accepted me. Na'zora's prince offered to help me out of trouble if I would learn the runes and return to work for him someday."

"Did he help you?"

"Yes," Yori replied.

"Then it sounds like you owe him."

"I suppose I do," he said, knowing that it would be a very easy promise to break. There was nothing binding Yori to the commitment other than his word.

"I don't like the idea of humans using runed weapons," Darin said. "It is all too likely they will use them against our kinsmen."

"Will you not teach me, then?"

"You are my grandson," the old elf said. "I will teach you what I know, and I will trust you to make the right decision in the end." Darin grabbed him and clutched him tightly, tears welling in his eyes. Looking at this young man reminded him of the son he had lost, and he was overcome with emotion.

Chapter 21

Slowly, the horses made their way through the dense forest. King Domren led the way, followed closely by General Luca. The scouts had reported that they were only minutes away from the Mulberry Clan's village. With luck, they would catch the elves unprepared.

High in the treetops, the king saw movement. An elven scout, perhaps, but it was too late. The elves had little chance of readying themselves for battle in such a short amount of time. If they were truly ready for battle, archers would have filled these trees and began firing as soon as the king's men were in sight. Domren smiled to himself, knowing that the battle was already won.

Drawing his sword, General Luca commanded his troops to do the same. The mages were positioned near the rear of the company, surrounded by highly skilled soldiers. The king would be furious to lose so many mages in battle again.

As they entered the village, they spurred their horses for the charge. Elves were already running frantically, desperately trying to arm themselves or flee. Many of their archers were running for cover in the trees, but Domren was prepared. He led his troops straight toward the archers as they ran. If he could prevent them from reaching the trees, they would be useless in battle. Thundering in their direction, his men trampled several of the elves as they scrambled to get out of their path. Some survived to climb the trees, but the mages had already locked onto their positions.

Two mages provided a magical shield for the other six. Focusing all of their concentration on defense left the other mages free to fire energy blasts at the elves. Coordinating their attacks perfectly, the shielding mages would drop the barrier only long enough for the others to fire and immediately replace the shield afterwards. Arrows flew toward the mages but glanced off as they hit the shining magical wall.

Three archers had taken to a very large tree at the farthest end of the village. Finding it impossible to take down the mages, they concentrated on the king's men instead. Their arrows flew faster and faster, each one mortally wounding a Na'zoran soldier. King Domren stayed well out of their range, chasing down the elves who tried to flee.

In one coordinated attack, the six mages fired a concentrated energy blast which uprooted the large tree where the three archers stood. Two of them jumped for their lives, while the third was crushed beneath the massive tree. The force of the blast knocked four of the mages from their mounts and left the remaining four dazed in their saddles.

Seeing that the mages had spent all of their resources on one attack, General Luca ordered them to retreat. Mages had their uses, but none of them were properly trained in battle. He made a mental note to discuss the matter with the king. If he was going to waste men protecting the mages, they needed to be worth protecting.

The soldiers began lighting fire to the huts to flush out any remaining elves. A nursemaid with an infant in her arms emerged from a damaged hut. She ran desperately with all the speed she could muster, all the while clutching the child to her breast. King

Domren spotted the woman and gave chase. She looked back with terror filling her eyes as the king's horse advanced. With a single swing of his sword, he severed her head from her body. She fell lifelessly to the ground, suffocating the baby beneath her.

Spinning his horse around, the king surveyed the village. His losses had been heavier than he expected. Several of his own troops lay dead with arrows sticking out of their heads and necks. The casualties among the elves had been much greater, but there were not enough bodies around to account for the entire village. No sword maidens had been encountered. The village had been filled with older clansmen and small children. Domren began to fear that the warriors would return and find his army unprepared. They were no longer in formation, and many of his men were pillaging the ruined huts.

From the tree line came a second group of soldiers led by Prince Aelryk. Domren's anger began to build at the sight of his son who trotted casually in his direction.

"Forgive me, Father," Aelryk said. "We lost our way in the dense forest. It would seem you did not need our help after all." He looked around at the desecrated village.

"Their warriors were not here," Domren said angrily. "We could have all been slaughtered, thanks to you." He signaled to General Luca to gather the men. "You can take your men and find the warriors," he told Aelryk. "Let us know how it turns out."

The king led his men back out of the forest while Aelryk and Mi'tal dismounted to inspect the village. All of the elven bodies belonged to those who were either too young or too old to fight effectively. Only a few archers appeared to be in good health and still in fighting condition. Aelryk hung his head.

"This was a massacre," he said. "These people never stood a chance."

Mi'tal inspected the fallen tree and marveled at the force necessary to bring it down. He was no fan of mages, but this feat was impressive. Beneath its massive trunk, he spied the arm of an elf. He moved in closer to see the face of Tod, the elf who had promised to deliver Aelryk's message of peace. His heart dropped to the ground as he realized what must have happened. This elf had convinced his clan that Na'zora was ready to discuss peace, and they had felt safe leaving their village unprotected. Though he had not known of the king's plan, he was overcome by guilt. Every death here was caused by his failed attempt at negotiating peace.

Returning to Aelryk's side, he said, "These people wanted peace. They were willing to negotiate."

"My father did this in retaliation for the orphaned children who came running into Duana a few days ago. The elves killed everyone in their town but spared the children."

"That's more than you can say for us," Mi'tal commented, looking down at the crushed body of a trampled elf child. "Are we going to seek out their warriors, my lord?"

"My father is a coward for not seeking them out himself," he replied. "I will not do it. Let them join forces with the other displaced elven warriors. That is their only chance of becoming a force worth fighting. My father will never yield if he thinks they are too weak to defend themselves."

"How will we manage peace now?" Mi'tal asked.

Aelryk shook his head. "I fear this will escalate the war. I'm sure these elves will think we tricked them into complacency. They won't make the same mistake again."

"This was your father's doing, not yours," Mi'tal said. "I believe they are smart enough to realize that in time. Once their wrath has had some time to cool, they will think more clearly. All hope of peace may not be lost."

"I hope you're right, my friend." Climbing back onto his horse, the prince led his men away from the ruined village. Instead of searching deeper into the Wildlands as his father had commanded, Aelryk decided to patrol along the border. He had no desire to fight the elves today, but he would not allow his own people to be massacred in retaliation. If only his father would allow him to negotiate peace, many innocent lives could be saved on both sides. Though he had tried to avoid admitting it to himself, the prince could no longer deny his true feelings. He despised his father and believed him unfit to rule. Na'zora was in more danger from its king than it ever was from any Wild Elves.

Chapter 22

A bright but cold morning arrived over the Sycamore Clan's village. The entire clan was already stirring as the sun came up, and Yori felt more refreshed than he had in years. Sleeping in a hut under the forest canopy was good for his soul, and he enjoyed it in spite of the cold. His grandfather had already made his way to the forge, and Yori hurried to dress and join him.

"Good morning," Darin said as Yori came into view.

"Good morning," he replied, heading straight for the furnace. He checked the fire to be sure it was hot enough to begin working.

"Your cousin Lem tends to that," Darin said with a smirk. "Looks like you already know more about smithing than he does." The old elf chuckled while his apprentice stared blankly at him. "Come over here, Yori."

Yori obeyed. On the workbench in front of him were several scrolls. Taking one and spreading it across the bench, Darin said, "You're going to have to learn Ancient Elvish if you want to etch runes." He pointed to the symbols on the scroll.

"You expect me to learn to read that?" Yori asked.

"Of course I do. It will be as easy as the first time you learned to read."

"I never learned," he replied.

"What do human mothers teach their children?" Darin asked, bewildered.

Yori gave it some thought and said, "I suppose she couldn't teach me what she didn't know herself. It's not a necessary skill for common people in Na'zora."

"Well, you're going to learn Ancient Elvish. No one here speaks or reads it except me. They use it a lot in the Sunswept Isles, but they're just a bunch of uppity bastards."

Yori smiled, remembering how Atti had described the Enlightened Elves in a very similar fashion. "How long will it take me to learn?"

"Not long, I hope," Darin replied. "Please tell me you're smarter than this one." He gestured his thumb at Lem, who was fighting with a pair of pliers. "While you're at it, you can learn to read the common language too."

Yori focused all of his attention on his reading lessons. There were thirty-two Ancient Elvish symbols to learn, each one representing a different sound in the ancient dialect. By noon, he could recite them in order, but his head felt like it was about to burst.

Taking pity on his grandson, Darin decided to take a break from the lessons. "I've got lots of weapons that need etching, so we'll concentrate on that after we have a bite to eat. You can learn something a little more useful than just letters."

"Sounds great," Yori said, grateful for the chance to get away from the scrolls. "Will I have to speak this old language?"

"Not really," Darin replied. "You just have to know enough to put the right runes in the right order. It's not like you want to converse with a bunch of smart assed, magic-loving, sugar-sucking, full of shit elves anyway."

"Have you had many dealings with Enlightened Elves?" Yori asked.

"A long time ago," he replied. "They're worse than you've heard. They'll ask you to do something, but no matter what you do it's never good enough for them. Never trust them. They'll cheat you if they can."

Lem fetched three bowls of stew from the gathering area of the village. Yori had hoped they could join the rest of the clan as they ate, but Darin had too much work to do and wouldn't leave the forge. Getting to know his kinsmen would have to wait for another day.

Once they had finished eating, Darin placed a pile of iron arrow tips on the workbench. "You know how to forge these, I presume," he said.

Yori nodded. Na'zorans did not typically use arrows, but Yori had crafted them many times for visitors to Enald's marketplace.

"Good. We can skip that part." He fetched a bundle of tools rolled up in a wide leather strip. Inside were thirteen different chisels, each resting in its own leather pocket. Darin took out a chisel and handed it to Yori. "What do you think?" he asked.

Yori examined the chisel, turning it over in his hand. "The iron work is good," he said. "The tip is very fine and quite sharp. Back in Enald I would have used this to etch my uncle's mark onto the blade of a sword or dagger."

"We're going to do something much better with it," he replied. "But it's good to know you've done a bit of delicate work and not just a bunch of hammering. Lem is great with a hammer but terrible with a chisel."

Yori observed as his grandfather began to etch runes into an arrow tip. It appeared to him nothing more than etching any other mark or design into the metal. There were no magic words, no chanting, and no beams of magical light. The entire process seemed a little unimpressive.

"This arrow tip will now explode when it hits its target. Whatever is struck will burst into flame." Darin handed Yori the arrow tip.

As he looked at the runes, he saw a faint red glow within the etching. Stunned, he asked, "How did you do that?"

"Do what?" he asked, giggling.

"The runes are glowing," Yori said. "How do you give them their power?"

"It's the blood in my veins, Yori, and it's in yours as well." He patted Yori on the shoulder and grabbed a second arrow tip. Yori bent down to watch more closely as his grandfather again chiseled a series of four runes into the arrow tip. To his amazement, Darin's eyes flashed green as he chiseled into the metal. Yori realized that the process wasn't the important part. The person doing the etching was what mattered.

"Can anyone learn this?" Yori asked.

"Any elf probably could, but I can't say they'd all be as good at it." He handed the second arrow tip to Yori. "Your father was really something special. He could finish these twice as fast as I ever could. You have his eyes, you know."

"How do these runes work, exactly?" Yori asked. "I don't understand the process."

"Like all elven magic, it comes from within. You'll need to learn a bit of earth magic, but that will come naturally to you. Then it's just a matter of putting the runes in the proper order. As long as you have talent with the metal, you can etch runes. Poor Lem just can't seem to master the fine details. I suppose it takes an artistic talent as well."

Yori had never considered himself particularly artistic. He did enjoy creating the fine details of a sword rather than the everyday tools he used to make back in Ren's shop. He remembered the pride he had felt when he finished the inlay for Aelryk's court sword. The process had taken many long hours, but the joy he felt upon seeing the finished product had been its own reward. It was truly a thing of beauty to behold, and Yori had impressed even himself with the quality of his work.

"Let's see how well you can copy a line of runes," Darin said. "Grab some scrap metal and give it a try. Don't worry about it blowing up on you. The runes you etch won't have any magical properties to them just yet."

Slowly, Yori began to etch the same runes onto the scrap metal that his grandfather had etched onto the arrow tips. Still unfamiliar with the symbols, he would pause halfway through each line to double check the shape of the rune. He did not intend for a single rune to look different from his grandfather's. If he could not yet imbue them with magic, he would certainly learn to etch the correct shape in the meantime. Once he had finally finished, he pushed the scrap metal toward his grandfather for inspection.

Bending down close to the runes, Darin said, "This is very good for a first try. This would actually be good for tenth try." He smiled at Yori and nodded approvingly. "You're going to be good at this," he said. "I can already tell."

Relieved, Yori finally remembered to exhale. He smiled back at his grandfather, who was beaming with pride. Yori had proven himself a fast learner. Now all he had to do was memorize the runes, learn what to etch for a desired effect, and unlock the magical secrets that would give the runes their power. The thought made him nervous but excited too. Before him was the opportunity to do something very few elves could do. As a half-breed he had always been treated as an undesirable. Now he had the chance to become something special.

Chapter 23

Moving quietly through the forest, Reylin scouted ahead of his warriors. He stopped suddenly, hearing footsteps nearby. Just ahead, a small caravan was heading south just outside of Na'zora's border. Reylin wondered who would be stupid enough to travel away from the road in a war zone. He sprinted back to his kinsmen to deliver the news.

"Essa," he said as he reached the group. "There's a small caravan ahead. It looked like merchants, and I saw no guards escorting them."

"Let's get them, then," she said with a smile.

Drawing their weapons, the warriors advanced through the forest to meet the caravan. The wagons stopped short as the elves emerged from the woods. Arrows began to fly through the air, catching the wagon drivers before they knew what hit them. The maidens rushed to open the doors of the rear carriage and ordered the men inside to step out.

A finely dressed man in a feathered hat emerged slowly from the carriage, followed by a balding man with a round, protruding belly. "Don't kill us! Please!" the fat man begged, falling to his knees.

Essa could not abide a cowardly man, and she ran him through without a second thought. The finely dressed man held up his arms in surrender and remained silent.

Reylin approached the man and asked, "What kind of dumbass leads a caravan through a war zone?"

"Apparently a dead one," the man replied.

Reylin laughed. "What was your purpose here?"

"I collect taxes for King Domren," the man responded. "We had confiscated some goods from merchants who refused to pay their fair share. I was taking them back to the palace district."

"You were going the wrong way," Reylin said. "It seems to me you were taking them someplace other than to your pig king."

"The king does not need all of these items. I was bringing them to the market myself and would have given him the profits."

Again Reylin laughed. "I'm sure you would have. You're an important man I take it?"

"I am," he replied. "I am also very wealthy and will fetch a good ransom should you return me safely to my family."

"I don't bargain with Na'zorans," Reylin replied, his eyes cold and full of hate. "You bring gold to a king who uses it to murder my people. You don't deserve to live."

"Reylin," Essa said. "Maybe he's right, and we could trade him for more weapons."

"You want to trust this one? What's wrong with you?"

"I want to do whatever will be best for our kind," she said, shaking her head. "If he's important, the humans might retaliate."

"They're going to retaliate anyway. Have you forgotten what happened to our village?"

The archers were growing impatient with the conversation, and one of them yelled, "Burn him!" Several voices spoke up in agreement.

"No," Reylin said. "Let's peel the skin from his bones and send him home."

The elves cheered at the suggestion and rushed in to perform the grizzly deed. The man screamed and flailed as the elves descended upon him, stabbing him repeatedly with their knives. When they had finished, nothing remained of a man except a red mass of flesh. They loaded the remains into the wagon, and Reylin turned the horses to face east. With a slap of his hand, he sent the horses racing towards Duana. He only wished he could hear their screams when they opened the wagon to discover the grim spectacle within.

After the attack, the elves were in high spirits. They moved back into the forest and away from Na'zora's border. Suddenly, Reylin heard the call of a bird that no longer existed in the Wildlands. That could only mean another clan was nearby. Responding with a similar whistle, Reylin slowly walked in the direction of the sound. The bird continued to call until Reylin was upon it. A scout descended from a branch high overhead and landed in front of him.

"Greetings, Brother," the elf said. "I am Niko of the Mulberry Clan."

"Reylin of the Oak Leaf Clan," he replied. "Is your village nearby?"

"It's a few hours north of here," Niko said. "Our warriors have come to find you. We want to join the fighting."

"That is good to hear."

Niko whistled for the rest of the Mulberry Clan's warriors to join him. Reylin was pleased to see they still had over three hundred warriors in their ranks. They would certainly be stronger now that they had joined forces.

"Do you have any idea where they will strike next?" Reylin asked.

"No, our Overseer has refused all negotiation with the Na'zorans. One member of our clan had been captured but returned home bearing a message from the prince. He claimed he wanted peace, but it was most likely a trick. One of your clan visited us and told us where we might find you. He was old and not feeling well, so he stayed behind in the village."

"Who is protecting your village?" Reylin asked.

"We left behind a few archers. I doubt the humans could have slipped past without our knowledge. They move too loudly through the woods."

A gnawing feeling came over Reylin. Without a decent number of warriors, the Mulberry Clan's village would not stand a chance against an attack. "We should head for your village. Your people aren't safe there, and we need to evacuate them across the river."

Niko nodded his agreement, and the two companies joined ranks before heading north. Night began to fall as they reached the devastation that had once been home to the Mulberry Clan. Piles of rubble that had formerly been huts still smoldered, and the smell of death filled the air. Warriors cried out in agony as they saw their loved ones lying dead upon the earth. Solemnly, they began the grim task of placing the corpses among the trees to honor them in death.

"We should travel to the other villages and evacuate them before it's too late," Essa suggested. "This cannot be allowed to continue."

"The Mountain Clan is the nearest to ours," Niko said. "We should head that way first."

"I've never been that far north," Reylin said. "You will have to lead the way. We should stay close to Na'zora's border, though. If they send out more soldiers, we might be able to stop them before they reach the village."

"Agreed," Niko said. "We can head out in the morning. It appears our Overseer was among the dead." He shook his head. "He was my father."

"I'm sorry," Essa replied softly. "You must lead your people now. I can see strength in your eyes."

He nodded and let out a long, slow breath. "I'll do what I can. Just yesterday we were not at war. We had everything we needed, and our homes were safe. Now we must fight to keep what is ours." He strode off into the darkness, contemplating the road ahead.

Chapter 24

Soft snow began to fall over the Sycamore village.

A thin white blanket was rapidly accumulating on the forest floor. The weather, however, would not hinder Yori's lessons.

"Take off your shoes," Darin said to Yori.

Yori looked up, puzzled. "It's a little cold to go barefoot, don't you think?"

"Take them off anyway," he replied. "You need to connect with the earth beneath your feet."

Hesitating, Yori stared at his grandfather. Realizing that the old elf was indeed serious, he reluctantly bent down to remove his shoes. The feel of the frozen ground beneath his feet was unpleasant, and he soon felt the cold traveling up through his body.

"Now," Darin began, "take that chisel and etch me some fire runes."

Yori grabbed for a piece of scrap metal and began chiseling the runes he had learned for the arrow tips. After finishing the work, he showed the runes to his grandfather.

Sounding disappointed, he said, "This isn't right. You have to concentrate more."

Yori stared at him, not knowing how to respond. Finally, he said, "I'm freezing. What do you want me to concentrate on doing? The runes are correct, aren't they?"

"Of course they are!" Darin shouted, losing his patience. "You mastered those the first day. Now you have to infuse them with magic. Otherwise, they're just useless symbols."

"I don't know how," Yori admitted.

"I'm trying to teach you, but you're not listening. You have to connect with the earth. Concentrate."

Yori took the chisel and scrap metal once again. Wiggling his toes into the cold snow, he tried his best to feel the earth. In truth, all he felt was the cold. He began to etch the fire runes into the metal and passed it back to Darin.

Sighing, he said, "I must not be explaining this very well. Your father came so naturally by his magic that I never really had to explain it at all." He crossed his arms and stared off into the forest for a moment. Just as Yori began to worry that his grandfather was too ashamed of him to continue the lesson, Darin spoke again. "Close your eyes and listen."

Yori obeyed. He heard Lem's hammer as he pounded a piece of metal on the anvil, a baby crying somewhere in the village, and the hissing of a campfire as the flames competed with the snow for dominance.

"What do you hear?" Darin asked.

"A hammer, a baby, and a fire," Yori answered honestly.

"Don't listen to that crap!" his grandfather shouted, slapping his hand against the workbench. Yori opened his eyes and glanced over at Lem, who had stopped hammering to eavesdrop. "Listen to the forest. Tune out everything else, and listen to nature."

Again Yori closed his eyes. He tried his best to ignore the sounds of the village and find any sound from the forest itself. To his disappointment, he heard nothing but the snow falling all around him. Looking at his grandfather, he replied, "I only hear the snow."

"That's a start."

197

Yori was surprised to hear those words. He had expected to disappoint Darin once again.

"Try closing your eyes and focusing on the snow for a moment before you etch the runes."

With a nod, Yori closed his eyes and focused his ears to the sound of the snow. It was coming down harder now, and his feet were quickly being covered by the cold white blanket it left on the ground. Opening his eyes, he gave the runes another try.

Darin inspected the metal closely. "That's better. They aren't glowing red, but they look a little shiny. I don't think they're going to do anything, but you're getting there. Why don't you grab a blanket from the hut and go and sit a while at the edge of the forest. Just try to clear your mind and relax." Yori started to leave when Darin added, "I'll let you put your shoes back on now." He chuckled to himself as Yori grabbed his wet shoes from beneath the snow.

Grabbing a thick fur blanket, Yori made his way to the edge of the village where the forest became denser. He sat upon a low tree stump and stared into the forest. His mind, however, had no intention of relaxing. For the last few days he had studied the runes relentlessly. Nearly every waking moment was spent staring at scrolls and memorizing which runes created which effects. As he had never attended any school, he never considered himself to be very intelligent. He was determined not to disappoint his grandfather, and he wanted nothing more than to learn quickly and efficiently.

As he closed his eyes and attempted to focus on the sound of the snow, his mind swam with all of the different symbols he had learned. They flashed unceasingly in his head until he once again opened his eyes. Before him he saw a world of white amid a dense, unending forest. Taking in a deep breath, he closed his eyes again. Focusing with all his strength, he still could not hear the sound of the snow. The runes had returned into his mind and were taking over his every thought.

Feeling completely defeated, he placed his head in his hands and stared at the ground. In the distance, he thought he heard the sound of running water. Though he had found his father's clan days ago, he had not had the chance to explore the area. All of his time so far had been spent in the smithy. Remembering his uncle's words, he wondered if he was hearing the Blue River nearby. His curiosity overcame him, and he decided to venture into the woods to find out.

The snowfall relented as he pressed on through the woods. He lost track of time and focused solely on finding the river. After an eternity in the woods, he emerged into a clearing and caught his first glimpse of the riverbank. Crossing the white field, he was drawn to its banks as if hypnotized. The swift current bubbled and splashed as it climbed over the unseen obstacles in its path. Closing his eyes, he allowed the sound of the water to enter his soul. The runes no longer flashed over and over in his mind. In their place was the image of flowing, clear water.

As he inhaled deeply, the fresh, cool air filled his lungs. He opened his eyes once more to behold the mighty river before him. The water was fresh and clear with a slight blue hue to at its depths. Yori could not guess how deep the water might be, but it felt like it delved down into eternity. Never before had he beheld a sight so lovely. He felt as if the river itself had reached up and enveloped him in its waters.

Feeling more connected to the earth than ever before, he knelt at the bank and drank a handful of water from the river. It was crisp and clean and the most refreshing drink he had ever tasted. Slowly, he rose again, taking one last look at his muse. Turning, he made his way through the forest and back to the Sycamore village.

As he entered the woods, he felt like a different person. Suddenly, the trees seemed to have a voice as they creaked and swayed beneath the weight of the snow. The withered brown leaves crunched beneath his feet, and a small, unseen creature scampered somewhere beneath the leaves. A jay belted out a call high overhead, piercing through the silent forest with great force. The sound of the river followed behind him, refusing to leave his ears just yet.

He returned to his grandfather, a triumphant smile spreading across his face. "I think I understand now," he said.

With a nod, Darin handed him the chisel and scrap metal, and Yori etched the fire runes into the metal once more. This time, however, his eyes flashed green as he meticulously etched at the steel. Darin inspected the finished runes and smiled proudly at his grandson. "Well done, young man. This looks perfect." He patted Yori on the back, and his eyes narrowed mischievously. "Should we try it out?"

Yori remained silent, staring open-mouthed at his grandfather. Quick as a flash, Darin tossed the scrap metal away from the village into a soft pile of snow. As it buried itself deep into the fluffy white heap, it exploded, sending snow and dirt in every direction. Villagers came running from their huts to see what had happened.

"False alarm!" Darin called out to them, cupping his hand to his mouth. With a wave, he dismissed them all to go about their own business. Yori laughed in disbelief and was joined by both Darin and Lem.

"You learn fast," Lem said. "I've been trying to do that for years." He nodded, approving of his cousin's skill and returned to his hammering.

"Now practice, practice, practice," Darin commanded. "And whatever inspiration you found, make sure you keep it close to your heart. You're going to need it with you for the rest of your life."

Chapter 25

Three elaborate white coaches with scrolling gold carvings passed slowly along the roadways of Ra'jhou. Lisalla and Danna sat in the middle coach, staring out of the windows at the world passing by.

"How much longer until we reach Na'zora?" Lisalla asked.

"They say we'll reach the border in a day or so. After that, it's two or three days to the palace." Danna could not count how many times she had answered that question since setting out from home.

"Why must it take so long?" Lisalla asked. She stretched her neck from side to side, attempting to alleviate the stiffness.

"It would be faster if you didn't insist on stopping at every market along the way, my lady."

"I've never been anywhere before, and I may never get the chance to travel after I'm married. I just want to see as much as I can while I have the opportunity." She gazed out of her window to see a sprawling meadow a short distance away. "Signal the driver to stop."

Danna tugged on a rope which rang a small bell next to the carriage driver. In less than a minute, the carriage came to a halt. Lisalla did not wait for the door to be opened. Instead, she opened it herself and stepped out into the sunlight.

"I'd like to take a walk in that meadow," she said as her guards came to her side.

Danna followed as Lisalla approached the meadow. Swaying golden stalks reached past their knees, forcing them to hold their skirts as they walked. The ground was soggy from recently melted snow, but Lisalla paid it no heed. Dirty shoes were a small price to pay for an adventure, and the frosty winter air would not dampen her spirit.

"My lady," Danna called, falling behind. "Can we return to the carriage yet?"

"We've only just left the carriage," the princess replied. Ahead of her, a herd of spotted deer ran by. They were the most majestic creatures she could remember seeing. She turned to look at her maid, who was desperately trying to keep her balance upon the soggy earth. Sighing, she walked slowly back to Danna and took her by the arm. To Danna's relief, they returned to the carriage and climbed back inside.

"I hope I never spend so much time in a carriage again," Lisalla said.

"You might have to visit far-off places once you're queen." Danna smiled cheerfully, imagining her friend as Queen of Na'zora.

"As long as I don't have to travel by carriage. Maybe I could travel by ship."

"An adventure by sea," Danna said, a dreamy look in her eyes. "Let's imagine we're sailing off into the unknown. That will help pass the time."

"Am I taking my prince with me?" Lisalla asked, laughing.

"I suppose that's up to you, my lady."

"Alright," she replied. "I have just boarded a ship and am sailing to a distant land. The boat hits a reef, and we're all dashed overboard. I make my way to an island filled with primitive natives."

"Oh my," Danna said. "Please tell me I wasn't on the ship."

"You can stay home if you like, but I'm going to see this island. The natives are tiny little people who have never seen a woman as tall as me. They think I'm a goddess."

"That doesn't sound bad at all," Danna commented. "Maybe I'll come along after all."

"The weather is always warm, and the natives are all very friendly. They only eat the finest fresh fruits, and they never require me to sit in a carriage."

Danna giggled. "Do they force you to marry their king?"

"They don't have a king," Lisalla replied. "They govern themselves, and everyone is treated fairly."

"That's very different from what I hear of Na'zora, my lady." The carefree tone had left Danna's voice. She was truly concerned about the kingdom where they would spend the rest of their lives.

"That's only because Domren is their king. If I have any say in the matter, Aelryk will make a good king. I won't stand by silently if he treats his subjects as poorly as his father treats them."

"They are at war with the elves, you know." Danna almost whispered the words, as if some unseen elf might overhear them.

"I've heard as much," Lisalla replied. "I don't understand it. Their king wants to expand his borders, so why not do it where there are no elves? Why do men have to go around killing each other?"

"I don't know, my lady," Danna said. "Perhaps it's just in their nature."

"It shouldn't be, and I refuse to believe it's in every man's nature. A man should protect his family. That doesn't include raiding other villages and killing innocent people."

"You think the elves are innocent?"

"I don't know," she said with a sigh. "What I do know is that Domren is a tyrant, and he has no mercy for anyone. He expects your full cooperation, or he orders your execution. I will not allow my husband to rule in such a manner."

"A princess is expected to please her husband and produce an heir. He may not want your advice on politics."

"He will have it just the same." Lisalla tired of the conversation and went back to staring out of her window. She did not know Prince Aelryk, but she knew in her heart he would be different from his father. Her childish dreams set aside, she tried to picture what her future husband might look like. She envisioned a handsome man with dark hair and kind eyes. If she found him to be unkind in real life, she was determined not to go through with the marriage.

She would run far away, even if it meant giving up everything she owned. She would not marry a man like King Domren.

Chapter 26

Prince Aelryk slowly made his way to his father's council chambers. All of the king's lieutenants were meeting to discuss the details of their next attack on the Wild Elves. Aelryk's stomach felt like he had just swallowed a large stone. He had no desire to join any more battles, and he knew that was exactly what his father would have in mind.

As he entered the room, the conversation came to an abrupt halt. "How nice of you to finally join us," the king said.

"Your Majesty," the prince replied, bowing. He took a seat at the far end of the table, as far from his father as possible.

"As soon as we have finished conversing, you will be heading south near Al'marr. There is a large elven clan there which has avoided any contact with our troops. I want them eradicated."

"If they haven't attacked us, why are we attacking them?"

"We will attack them to prevent them from joining forces with the other elves. We can't allow them to gather an army of considerable size."

"How do we know these elves are even considering such a thing?" Aelryk could see the blood rising into his father's face. Questioning him like this in front of his councilors was unwise, but he had no other choice. His father had refused to meet with him privately.

"You are the prince of this kingdom. Therefore, it is your duty to protect its citizens. You will leave now and attack those elves, or I will throw you in the dungeons for treason." The king spoke forcefully, but managed to contain his anger. He locked eyes with his son, his face serious.

"Orzi, the court prophet, has already predicted your victory," General Luca said. "As long as you leave today, you will be successful."

"How comforting," the prince replied sarcastically. "Father, I do not fear failing in battle. I simply don't understand attacking these elves. Surely you don't mean to extend our borders all the way to Al'marr."

"I most certainly do!" the king shouted, unable to restrain his temper. He pounded a fist against the wooden table. "Do as I command!"

The prince stood and bowed. Without another word, he left the room and headed for the stables. He had no choice but to carry out his father's orders. There was little doubt that his father would indeed have him thrown in the dungeons should he refuse to obey. If that were to happen, he would have no chance at negotiating peace.

Mi'tal was waiting for the prince just outside of the stables. "Your Highness," he said as the prince approached. "I was given word a few hours ago to prepare your troops for battle. All the preparations have been made, and we await your orders."

"How is it you knew of this before me?" the prince asked, obviously annoyed.

"I was told the order came from you," Mi'tal replied, looking somewhat surprised. "A messenger from the palace visited me this morning saying you had commanded it."

"That must have been from my father, then." Aelryk shook his head, attempting to shake away the anger. He did not succeed. "He wants us to attack another clan of elves. This group is near Al'marr and has never been involved in an attack against Na'zorans."

"What do you intend to do, my lord?" Mi'tal would follow any order his prince gave, but he hoped the prince would choose an attempt at negotiation. The prince was young and had so far been brave enough to speak with his father on the subject. Mi'tal hoped that one day the prince would find the courage to disobey the king and bring peace to the land.

"We don't have much choice," the prince replied. "If we don't attack them, my father will probably have us both hanged for treason."

"Would it be possible to attempt to speak with these elves first?" Mi'tal suggested.

"Once we enter their territory we can expect them to throw the first punch. They're not going to allow an army to simply walk into their village. Though they have not yet become a part of it, they must be aware there is a war on their doorstep."

"What of Al'marr, my lord? Might they see this attack as a threat to them as well?"

"The people of Al'marr only care for their spices and gemstones. We won't be crossing their borders or harming their citizens, so I doubt they will take much notice. They don't defend the elves near their lands."

"Very well, my lord," Mi'tal said. "Shall we prepare to leave?"

"Yes," the prince replied. "When we are closer, you will order the men to split their forces. Half of them will remain behind along with the mages. I don't want any more carnage than is necessary."

"My lord, if we ride into their village with only a handful of troops, we are putting ourselves in very serious danger."

"Don't you think I realize that? These elves have so far avoided the war. My guess is they don't want any part of it. They will only fight back if they are forced. We will show our strength and order them to flee. If they refuse, we will signal the rest of our army to attack."

"As you command, my lord." Mi'tal could not decide whether he liked this new plan or not. It would certainly save many innocent lives, but he would much rather make an attempt at peace. He pitied Aelryk that he should have such a father. It was proving a difficult task for the prince to serve the king and appease his own conscience at the same time.

Mi'tal followed only the prince. If Aelryk commanded him to disobey the king, he would do it without a second thought. Such an act would cost him his life, but he would die knowing that he had served his lord. The prince's lord was King Domren, and Mi'tal understood why Aelryk would not fully defy him.

For the first time in his life, Mi'tal found himself wishing death on his own king. The prince was maturing, and he would soon be ready to lead his people. A better world was waiting for Na'zora, if only Domren were gone.

Chapter 27

Ten days of practice had given Yori the confidence to etch runes without his grandfather hovering over his shoulder. Every evening, he would study the scrolls, committing the runes to his memory. He had learned nearly a hundred words in the ancient elven tongue and how to properly etch them into a piece of metal. Some were used for strength or to affect the weight of weapons and armor, while others were used to add power such as fire or lightning to the blow of a sword. Never in his life had he imagined such a thing to be possible, yet here he was performing the magic himself.

All of the Sycamore Clan's warriors now had runed weapons thanks to Yori's newfound skill. Previously, his grandfather had only bothered to rune special weapons for the Overseer and the clan's most skilled warriors. War had not visited their people for a long time, but rune carvers continued to pass along their knowledge throughout the generations.

Darin had not forgotten his promise to Reylana. Yori had etched over a hundred arrow tips which would be used in the war against the Na'zorans. Though he was not a woodworker, he had managed to etch strengthening runes into new bows that would now last indefinitely. Every night Yori went to bed with cramps in his fingers and neck from the tedious work, but he enjoyed every moment. Finally, he had found a purpose in life, and it felt wonderful to be needed and welcome among his own people.

* * * * *

"This has healed nicely," the old woman said. "You should be swinging that sword again in no time."

Reylana flexed the muscles of her left arm which had spent too much time motionless in a sling. They still felt tight, but she was sure they would be back to normal by the time she returned to her brother. "Thank you," she said, stretching her shoulder. She stepped out of the healer's hut and into the bitterly cold wind. She pulled her sword from its sheath and inspected the blade. It looked a bit dull both in color and sharpness. Since she had been unable to fight, she had not tended to the sword's needs. To her, this was almost like ignoring a crying child. She set off toward the smithy to remedy the situation.

Yori could not help but notice the lovely auburn-haired elf coming his way. She was curvy despite the tight leather armor that bound her slender form. She headed straight for Darin, carrying her sword across both hands.

"Good day, Darin," she said. "My blade is in need of some care, I think." She offered the sword to the old elf, who accepted it with a smile.

"I'll soon have it fixed up for you, young lady," he said. "My grandson has been busy with those arrow tips for you. Some will explode on contact, and some will survive to be used over and over again. Would you like us to add runes to your sword?"

"Of course," she replied. "What can you do with it?"

"We can affect the weight, prevent it from becoming dull, strengthen its blow, and many other things."

"Don't do anything with the weight. I'm used to it being heavy, and that's how I like it. If you can prevent it from dulling and make it stronger, I would be in your debt." She looked over at Yori, who she had never noticed before. "Are you new around here?" she asked.

"Sort of," he replied. "I've been here a couple of weeks, but I've rarely left the forge." Yori regretted not spending any time amongst the clansmen. In front of him was someone he wouldn't mind knowing better.

"You're tall," she replied, looking him up and down. "You must be the tallest male elf I've ever met. Would you like to mate?"

Yori's eyebrows shot up in surprise, and the chisel in his hand dropped to the workbench with a loud clang. He glanced over at his grandfather, who was grinning from ear to ear. He flicked his head in the direction of his hut, indicating to Yori to show the girl inside. Reylana stood patiently, awaiting Yori's response. Apparently, her request had been serious.

Without a word, Yori walked to the other side of his workbench and took Reylana's hand. She smiled and followed him to the hut. Once inside, she tugged violently at his pants until they fell to his ankles. She shoved him roughly onto the bed and proceeded to remove only her shoes and pants before climbing on top of him. Taking full control of the encounter, she rode him until her appetite was satiated. Yori felt a sudden surge of pleasure so intense that he clenched his jaw to stop himself from crying out. He had no intention of looking like a fool in front of this woman.

Reylana climbed off of him and retrieved her clothing from the floor. Yori sat up on the bed and stared at her, amazed by the entire event. She leaned over and kissed him on the side of his head.

"After the war is over, we should mate again. I'd love to have a tall son." As she reached for the door, she stopped abruptly and turned to face him. "I'll be back for the sword tomorrow." With those words she exited the hut, leaving Yori behind.

Yori dressed and returned to the forge, a look of bewilderment still apparent on his face. His grandfather laughed at the sight of him and clapped him on the back. "Looks like you're truly a man now," he said proudly. "You're just a piece of meat to the women around here. Romance is a rare thing among our people."

Lem stared at Yori, envying his cousin once again. Yori glanced at him, but looked away without saying a word. His first time with a woman had not gone quite how he had imagined it, but he had no complaints. Retrieving his chisel, he tried to go back to his work. After a few seconds, he looked up and asked, "What was her name?"

"Reylana," Darin replied. The old man laughed and added, "Don't expect her to be true to you. That just isn't our way."

Yori nodded and returned to his work.

Chapter 28

Three white carriages made their way along the road ahead of Reylin's troops. Their scouts had noticed the carriages earlier that morning as they surveyed the path north to the Mountain Clan's village. The carriages were nearing the border, and Reylin's archers readied their bows to prevent their entry into Na'zora. Whoever was inside must be very important, and their deaths would send a loud message to King Domren.

The sword maidens crouched low behind the archers, readying themselves for the charge. The carriages were accompanied by a small unit of guards, but the elves had them vastly outnumbered. Still, the possibility of magefire existed, and they refused to take any chances with elven lives. They would play it safe and have everyone ready to join the fight if necessary.

As the carriages rounded a bend in the road, they finally came within range of the archers. In perfect unison, the elves lifted their bows, releasing their arrows into the chilled winter air. The drivers were struck, blood pouring from their necks. The lead driver had just enough time to halt his carriage before he toppled from his high seat and crashed to the road beneath him. The guards drew their swords and advanced on the woods. Hoping to save as many arrows as possible, the archers moved aside for the sword maidens.

Essa led her troops out of the thicket to engage the enemy. The guards charged at the maidens, attempting to trample them with their horses. The maidens, however, were more agile than the guards had expected. They dodged gracefully to each side until the horses had charged past them and broken their formation among the trees. Now, the maidens charged the mounted guards, slicing at their legs and thrusting their long broadswords into their midsections. Within minutes, the battle was ended with only a handful of elves having to participate. The rest watched silently, lusting for a battle of their own.

Reylin strode toward the rearmost carriage. Drawing his knife, he flung open the door and peered inside. No living thing occupied the carriage. It was filled with luggage and a few small pieces of furniture. Moving to the middle carriage, he flung open the doors as a frightened, dark-haired woman began screaming. He glanced over his shoulder to his archers and smirked.

"Hello, ladies," he said. A second woman sat within, her expression was stern as if with courage. Her breathing, however, was easily noticeable as her chest rose and fell, revealing her fear. The other elves gathered closer to the carriage as Reylin reached in to grab the dark-haired woman by the arm. He pulled her roughly from the carriage, but he caught her as she nearly fell to the ground. She stared at him, her eyes full of fear as he reached in to grab the second woman.

Lisalla recoiled from Reylin's touch, refusing to be dragged from the carriage. "I can remove myself from the carriage," she said defiantly. With all the dignity she could muster, she exited the carriage and stood proudly before her captors. "I am Lisalla, Princess of Ra'jhou. I demand to speak with your leader."

Most of the elves laughed, but Essa remained silent. She approached Lisalla and said, "You are a brave woman. Not many human women would have the courage to make demands. Most of you just cower and bawl like this one here." She pointed to Danna, who was sobbing and shaking with fear.

"Danna is my maidservant. She isn't accustomed to having her life threatened." Lisalla did her best to maintain a calm, regal appearance. In reality, she was terrified of these elves and the fate that might await her. Poor Danna was already terrified out of her wits. Lisalla hoped that by maintaining her own composure, Danna would feel a small amount of comfort.

"I say kill them and send their pretty corpses back to their king," Reylin suggested. "Na'zorans should know better than to travel this area without an army."

"I am not Na'zoran," Lisalla replied. With as much pride as she could muster, she said, "I am the daughter of King Olin of Ra'jhou. I am traveling to Na'zora to marry Prince Aelryk." As soon as she spoke them, Lisalla regretted her words. In her pride, she had given her enemy a good reason to kill her.

"Perfect," Reylin said with a smile.

Essa held up a hand. "You will not kill this one," she declared. "I don't care about the other girl, but you will not kill this princess. She is brave. If her prince wants to save her life, he can stop the attacks on our people."

"So now you're the great negotiator?" Reylin looked at Essa with contempt. Shaking his head, he walked over to the lead carriage and flung open the door. Inside were two well-dressed men huddled together as far from the door as they could get. Reylin motioned to a nearby sword maiden and together they dragged the men from the carriage. Without saying a word, Reylin slit both of their throats. He would hear no negotiation for their lives. His hesitation in killing the women had caused enough trouble already.

"The women are yours, Essa," he said, wiping the bloody knife against his pants. "You can keep them quiet while we continue to the Mountain Clan. Once we've reached their village, they can chose whether these two are allowed to live."

Essa nodded, satisfied with his decision. The Mountain Clan could decide whether humans were allowed to enter as prisoners. If they refused, Essa would kill the women herself. "We will bind their hands and gag their mouths. They will follow us without a fight, or we will kill them."

"We won't be any trouble," Lisalla promised. She knew that as long as she and Danna were alive there was at least a small chance of rescue. All she could do now was obey her captors and hope for a miracle.

Reylin loaded the corpses back into the first carriage and sent the horses running toward Na'zora. "That should let our handsome prince know that his fair princess has been accosted. All we have to do is wait, and he will ride gallantly into battle to save his lady love." Laughter erupted from the elves as Reylin made broad sweeping motions with his arms. Humans had a romantic nature about them that was alien among the Wild Elves. They had use only for practical matters, not fairytale love stories.

The elves freed the carriage horses from their reins, allowing them to graze and roam at their pleasure. They left the two remaining carriages without bothering to rummage through their contents. The trivial belongings of a pampered princess were of no use to the elves.

Essa bound the two women's hands with leather straps and gagged their mouths with cotton strips torn from Lisalla's own skirt. The air was bitterly cold, and Lisalla wished she had the warm blankets from the carriage to comfort her. As it was, she had only a thin yellow dress to shield her from the cold. Danna seemed untouched by the winter air, as she was too distraught over her capture to notice the weather.

The party continued north in search of the Mountain Clan. This would take them to the outskirts of the Kingdom of Ra'jhou, but they had no intention of going any farther. Ra'jhou had never made war against the elves, and they had no idea their princess had been taken captive. If they dared to enter the war to aid Na'zora, Lisalla would be their first casualty.

Chapter 29

Yori stood at the forge with his grandfather studying a scroll laid out on the workbench before them. They exchanged glances as voices began shouting from the center of town. A crowd began to form, and they were both curious to see what was happening. Cautiously, they approached the crowd where the Overseer was attempting to appease the other elves.

"Everyone, please calm down!" he shouted, flailing his arms in an attempt to catch their attention. "We must not act in haste. We do not know the purpose of these soldiers."

"Soldiers?" Yori said quietly to his grandfather.

Darin shook his head and shrugged, unaware of the morning's events.

Reylana shoved her way to the front of the crowd to stand directly in front of the Overseer. "Quiet!" she shouted at the elves. Her auburn hair seemed to flash with anger, and the crowd quieted down to hear what she had to say. "Less than an hour ago, your scouts spotted a large company of Na'zoran soldiers who appeared to be heading this way. They *will* attack you. You have no choice but to defend yourselves."

Once again the crowd roared with many different voices. Clearly, the clansmen did not agree on which course to take.

"Calm down, please," the Overseer said again. "It is true that the scouts have reported a large patrol in our area. However, the Na'zorans would never attack us this close to Al'marr. They would be risking a war on two fronts if they attempted to take land near Al'marr's borders."

"You are a fool and a coward as well." Reylana spat her words at the Overseer. "You must fight!" She drew her sword and raised it before the crowd. Many of the elves cheered in response, while others remained silent.

Yori began to feel anxious at the thought of war. So far, the Sycamore Clan had resided in peace, far from the borders of Na'zora. The king's ambitions must have increased dramatically to reach so far from his original borders.

Darin, being a highly respected elder member of the clan, walked to the front of the crowd. "Overseer," he began, "we cannot expect Al'marr to come to our aid. If the Na'zorans don't cross into their lands, they will not help us. We are nothing to them."

"We cannot be too quick to act," the Overseer replied. "If we arm ourselves and attack them first, we will only escalate the fight. They are probably just patrolling the area and have no desire to fight with us. We have caused them no problems, and we have been no threat to their people."

Many elves sounded their voices in agreement. Darin shook his head and returned to Yori's side.

"I don't think they're just passing by," he said. "I have a bad feeling about this."

"Why would they travel so far from Na'zora?" Yori asked, hoping there could be another explanation.

"The only other reasons would be to attack Al'marr or convince them to join the fight against the elves. Either way, we are not safe."

"Who is willing to fight and who is ready to run?" Reylana asked the crowd. "What harm will it do to ready yourselves for battle if they have no plans to attack? We don't have to attack them first, but we have to be ready to defend ourselves. They destroyed my village as well as many others, and they have murdered our children. I will not sit here and wait to be killed. I will fight with every ounce of strength in my body."

Over half of the crowd cheered at Reylana's words. She spoke forcefully, and her words moved the elves. The Overseer shook his head, clearly disagreeing with the sword maiden.

"It will do no harm for the nursemaids to take the children into the woods for safety. Our warriors can arm themselves, but they must not attack the humans unprovoked. I do not wish to start a war over a peaceful passing of troops."

"Those peaceful troops are the same ones who are murdering your kin just north of here. If you weren't such a coward, you would arm yourself and lead your warriors into battle. We should slaughter these men for their crimes against all elves!" Reylana's face grew red with anger. Clearly the elves were divided, and she was desperate to convince them to fight.

"You would have us run to the slaughter," the Overseer argued. "There is no use in speaking with you." He walked away and returned to his hut.

"Go on and hide then," she called after him. "See if that hut will protect you from their magefire!"

Nat approached Reylana as the crowd began to argue amongst themselves. "Reylana," he said. "There are many of us who would join you in battle. We agree the Overseer is a coward. We should have come to your aid weeks ago when we heard the rumors of war."

Reylana nodded and placed a hand on his shoulder. "Gather whoever is willing to fight. We will do what we can to defend the village."

Nursemaids began leading the children deeper into the woods. They would take to the trees in hopes that the Na'zorans would attack the village and leave the forest untouched. A few of the elderly clansmen joined them, but the majority of the elves would stay in the village. Less than half of them were preparing to fight.

Yori followed Darin back to the forge. "What will we do?" he asked.

"I'm guessing those humans didn't teach you to use a bow," Darin commented. Yori shook his head in response.

"Can you swing a sword?"

"To check the balance," Yori replied. "I've never fought with one."

"Take a hammer, then," his grandfather said. "You may need it." Darin retrieved his bow from his hut. "I haven't used this for many years, but I won't let our village be destroyed without a fight."

Lem came to Yori's side and handed him a hammer. The young elf's eyes were wide with fright, but he was prepared to fight as well. Yori accepted the hammer and squeezed it tightly in his hand. He tried to steady his breathing and stay calm, but his stomach felt as if it were turning cartwheels.

"Let's hope they're just passing through," Darin said. "If not, we're going to be glad we're using runed weapons. Too bad we haven't attached those runed tips to any arrows yet. Those would have been very useful."

Yori turned to his grandfather and said, "Can't we just throw them? The scrap metal exploded when you threw it."

"You're right," Darin said, laughing. "I suppose we could. We won't be hitting any fancy targets, but we'll give them something to remember." The trio dashed behind the workbench to retrieve the sack full of runed arrow tips. Gently emptying it onto the table, Darin said, "Toss these into the center of a group of those bastards and see how they like it."

"Reylana mentioned mages," Yori said. "I've never seen them in action, but I hear they are ruthless in battle. We should try to take them out first if we can."

Darin nodded and said, "If we survive this, you might consider becoming a warrior."

"If we survive this," Yori replied. "I will continue etching runes until the day I die. I want no part of war, now or ever."

"Sometimes we don't get a choice," Darin replied quietly. "We do what we must."

Yori turned his attention to the east, where the forest lay quiet and still. Somewhere within those trees, an army was approaching. He squeezed the hammer in his hand and hoped he would not have to use it.

Chapter 30

Prince Aelryk stopped his horse and held up a hand signaling his troops to halt. Mi'tal joined him at the head of the company to receive his orders. "I've changed my mind about entering their village with a small force," the prince said. "We will send everyone in and fully overwhelm the elves. Perhaps when they see our numbers, they will be more willing to negotiate."

"They may begin the fight before we reach the village, my lord," Mi'tal pointed out. "Wild Elves are extremely stealthy and frequently hide among the trees."

"I'm aware of that, Mi'tal," Aelryk replied. "That's a risk we'll have to take. I won't slaughter an innocent village that has yet to attack us. If we have to kill a few for starting the fight then so be it. No one is to draw their weapons until we are fired upon. I want them to see that we have come peacefully."

Mi'tal gave the prince a nod and proceeded to spread the message to the lieutenants. The company had nearly a thousand mounted troops as well as seven war mages. The mages required constant protection as they had become the main target in every battle with the elves. Mi'tal wondered if the elves would begin the fight simply because the mages were present.

As he returned to Aelryk's side, his hand went instinctively to his war hammer. After all, they were about to charge into enemy territory where his prince would be vulnerable to attack. Though a sword had very little chance of blocking an arrow, Mi'tal still wished the prince would draw his sword for protection. Losing Prince Aelryk would be a disaster for the people of Na'zora.

Nat crouched low upon a branch and watched as the company passed through the trees. Their pace was no faster than a trot, and not a single man had drawn a weapon. He made note of the mages in red cloaks near the rear of the company. After the last man passed by, he hurried back to Reylana and the warriors.

"There looks to be a thousand of them. They're moving at an easy pace and haven't drawn their weapons. They will reach the village within minutes." He had never been in battle, so he trusted Reylana to lead his clansmen.

"That doesn't make any sense," Reylana replied. "They must be trying to trick us."

"Could they really just be passing by?" one of the archers asked.

"I don't know," she said. "Were there any mages with them?"

"Yes, there were seven of them," Nat answered.

"I can't imagine them traveling with mages if they don't intend to fight," she said. "We should follow them and see if they enter the village. The mages always stay near the back of the company, and we can take them out first if we aren't seen."

The warriors followed Reylana as they made their way into the trees surrounding the village. The Na'zorans were indeed heading straight for them. They were vastly outnumbered, but Reylana was determined to take at least a few of them down, even if the village was lost.

As the prince entered the village, he noticed that none of the elves were fleeing in terror as the other clans had done. The elves visible in the village stood their ground, each of them clutching a weapon. He slowed his horse to a walk and lifted both hands in a gesture of peace.

"I have not come with the intention to kill," he declared. "I have come to speak with you."

Hearing these words, the Overseer left his hut to speak with the prince. "I am the Overseer of the Sycamore Clan," he said. "For what reason have you brought an army into our village? We have done you no wrong."

"I have come at the command of my father King Domren, but I will not fulfill his wishes. I would have the continuation of peace between Na'zora and the Sycamore Clan."

"You have a strange way of showing it," the Overseer said, looking up and down the ranks of the prince's army.

"Forgive my intrusion, Overseer," the prince said. "I did not know what awaited me in the Wildlands, and it is not safe to travel without an escort."

"This is much more an army than an escort," he replied. "You are bringing war upon us."

Reylana listened closely from the trees, focusing her eyes on the mages. At the slightest movement from one of them, she would order the archers to attack.

"I have come to issue you an order," the prince continued. "You must vacate this village and move across the Blue River. There you will find safety from my father and his war. If you do not agree, he will send another army to annihilate you. I am giving you the chance to live in freedom and will do everything in my power to stop my father from ever crossing the river."

"Even if we agree, you cannot guarantee our safety?" The Overseer was clearly shaken by the choice before him.

"I do not control my father," Aelryk said, "but I will not allow him to send troops across the river. He plans to extend Na'zora's borders all the way to its eastern bank, and any elves in his path will be killed. Your only hope is to cross the river."

"How do I know we won't be attacked as we leave?"

"My father has sent me to kill you. He will not send more troops until well after I've returned. You have plenty of time to move your people, and I will tell him that I found a deserted village where you once lived. That should satisfy his desire to clear the Wildlands of the elven presence."

"You would lie to your own father on our behalf? What sort of man does that make you?"

241

"I am the sort of man who would do what is right. I have no desire to continue this war. Na'zora has several new farming villages outside of her original borders. We do not need your land. You have my word on that. When I am king, there will be peace."

The elves remained silent, looking to their Overseer to decide their fate. Yori and Darin still stood near the forge, exchanging glances as the prince spoke. They could not believe the prince was defying his own father to spare the elves.

After a moment's consideration, the Overseer replied, "We will leave this land to preserve the lives of my people. I will expect you to keep your word once you are king."

Aelryk signaled his troops to move out. He had no intention of watching the elves to be sure they left the area. His job was complete, and he had avoided any killing.

Mi'tal considered once more the idea of Aelryk as king. If the prince did not believe Na'zora needed any more land, then there was no reason to continue the war. So far, only the Silver Birch Clan had been displaced to build the farming villages, and they might settle for other compensation. The rest of the clans could rebuild their villages where they had once stood. As he thought of the lives needlessly lost, his hand tightened on the handle of his war hammer. A vision of King Domren's funeral filled his mind.

Chapter 31

At the base of the Wrathful Mountains lay the village of the Mountain Clan. As he scouted far ahead of the warriors, Reylin scanned the trees for any sign of elven life. Glimpsing a slight movement on a high branch, he called, "Hello, there. I am Reylin of the Oak Leaf Clan. My kinsmen and I are seeking the Mountain Clan."

The branch swayed again as a young, silver-haired elf climbed down. "Greetings, Reylin. I am Sal of the Mountain Clan. What brings you so far north?"

"There is a war in our homeland," Reylin replied. "Many clans of the Wildlands have been displaced. We come seeking allies."

Sal nodded, understanding Reylin's plight. "I've heard nothing of the war, but we have little to do with any outsiders. News does not travel well here, I'm afraid. Come with me and speak to our Overseer."

"I've brought a large number of warriors with me. Should I tell them to wait here?"

"No, they can come as well. We may not be able to feed everyone, but they are all welcome in our village."

Reylin and Sal moved quickly through the forest to locate the rest of the group. Essa stood at the front, watching as the elves approached.

"This is Essa, leader of the sword maidens," Reylin said.

"Well met, Sister."

Sal openly admired Essa's figure with his eyes. Essa, however, did not return the sentiment. Mountain Clan elves have paler skin than those of the woods, and if Sal represented the other males of the village, they must be even shorter than the males of her own clan. His clear blue eyes were rather fetching, but she had more important matters on her mind.

"Greetings," she replied flatly. She turned to Reylin and asked, "Are we continuing north?"

"The Mountain Clan's village is not far from here. We have all been invited."

"What of the humans?" Essa asked.

"Humans?" Sal echoed.

"We have two human hostages. They are bound and shouldn't cause any trouble." Reylin pointed to the two women.

"I see," Sal replied. "I can't see any problem with them, but the Overseer has the final say. Let's get going." He led the group through the forest to a vast evergreen valley. The mountain breeze brought fresh, cool air to their lungs and renewed their spirits. This was a land untouched by war, where the streams ran with pure, clean water, and the earth was unspoiled.

In the distance, the Wrathful Mountains stood proudly, ever reaching beyond the clouds. Lisalla paused briefly to admire the scene but was soon shoved by an impatient sword maiden. She resumed her march, all the while admiring the mountains and the beauty of the valley before her. She had spent her entire life only a few days away from this place, yet she had never had the pleasure of visiting it. Her heart filled with hope as she admired the magnificent landscape.

As they entered the village, many of the Mountain Clan elves stopped what they were doing to stare at the horde. Never before had there been such a gathering of elves in their land. Sal led Reylin and

Essa straight to the Overseer's hut, where a surprisingly young Overseer waited inside.

"Overseer," Sal began. "These are the warriors of the Oak Leaf Clan. They have come seeking our aid in battle."

"Have they indeed?" he replied, standing. His pale eyes looked from Essa to Reylin as he spoke. "There has been no news of war near our borders, but we mainly keep to ourselves. If it hasn't come directly to our village, we would have no knowledge of it."

"We have with us all of the warriors that remain of the Oak Leaf, Silver Birch, and Mulberry Clans. We have joined forces to fight the Kingdom of Na'zora. They have invaded our lands and slaughtered our people."

"Where is Na'zora?" the Overseer asked.

"It lies south of Ra'jhou and stretches to the east coast."

"Why have they declared war on our people?" The Overseer seemed genuinely concerned. A war against any Woodland Elf clan was a war against his own.

"Their king has decided to extend his borders. We were in the way."

"Have you come seeking refuge or allies?"

"Perhaps both," Reylin responded. "Some of our warriors are past their prime, and others have been injured. Not all of them will be able to continue fighting. It is my hope to join all of the elven clans together into a single force."

"That would seem to be the most effective way to fight," the Overseer replied. I will call a meeting of my people to discuss the matter. We have not been involved in a war for many generations, but I feel certain my people will wish to join your cause."

"Thank you," Reylin said. He turned to leave the hut, followed by Essa.

"That was easier than I expected," Essa remarked.

"I've never met any member of the Mountain Clan before today, but I was always told that they were honorable elves. I think they just proved that rumor to be true."

The elves began to mingle with their mountain kin, and the mood became less somber. For a short time at least, they were welcomed into a thriving village that reminded them of the homes they had lost. Untouched by the hand of war, the elves flourished among the mountains.

At the base of a small evergreen, Lisalla and Danna had been secured with ropes while the elves enjoyed the hospitality of their kin. No one saw the women as a threat, and they were left completely unguarded. Reylin approached the women as they sat motionless in the sunlight.

"These bonds are too tight," Lisalla said as he approached. "I would be more comfortable if you could loosen them just a bit."

"So you can kick my teeth in while I'm bent over?" Reylin laughed as he spoke and made no move to loosen the leather straps on her wrists.

"You may bind my feet first if you like," Lisalla suggested. "I only ask for a small comfort, not to be set free."

"You have resigned yourself to remain my prisoner then?"

"Not in the slightest," she replied. "Eventually you will either free me or kill me. I am of no use except as a bargaining chip in this war. Once I've served my purpose, you will be rid of me in one way or the other."

"You're smarter than you look," Reylin replied, kneeling next to her. He removed the leather strap that bound her hands and tossed it to the ground. He remained in close proximity, which made Lisalla feel uneasy. She did not know his intentions, and she wished he would move farther away from her.

His eyes moved over her form, drinking in the curves of her body. "You really should wear more clothes," he said. "Your nipples are showing."

Without considering the consequences, she slapped him across the face.

Reylin replied with laughter. "I'm only mentioning it because it seems unbecoming of a princess to expose her breasts."

"For your information, I was sleeping when you attacked me. These are my nightclothes, and you did not have the decency to allow me to change before you dragged me away."

"Maybe you should have asked while you were issuing orders to speak to our leader. I might have allowed it. Then again, I might like to have the both of you travel along naked."

Lisalla tried to stand, but her waist was still roped to the tree. Danna wept into her hands, fearing what might become of her mistress.

"If you dare lay a hand on me, I will kill you." Lisalla stared straight into Reylin's eyes as she made the threat.

"With what?" Reylin laughed again. "Don't worry, dear lady. I have no intention of raping you or your bawling maid. No elf would dare touch a human woman. The very thought is repulsive." He moved over to Danna and untied her hands as well. "We're not as evil as you've heard. Any elf sick enough to rape a member of his clan would be castrated and impaled at the head of the village for all to see. We don't tolerate savagery among our own."

Lisalla had not considered the idea of laws among the Wild Elves. In fact, she had never given them much thought at all until she was taken prisoner by them. So far, they seemed brutal and uncaring. "Your women are bigger than your men. I doubt they would be easy to subdue."

"They are taller, for sure," Reylin explained. "But they aren't stronger. Meaner, maybe." He laughed and shook his head. "Anyway, such a crime has not been committed in my lifetime. I've only heard stories from ages past."

Lisalla remained silent, wondering why Reylin did not join the rest of his clan in eating and drinking. Everyone else seemed to be enjoying themselves while Reylin kept watch over two women who had no hope of escape. Even if they managed to free themselves from the rope, they would soon perish in the Wildlands. Neither of them knew anything about the woods, and both of them were underdressed for the winter conditions.

"I could use something warm to wear, as could my maid," Lisalla said.

"I'm sure you could," Reylin replied. "What would you have me bring you?"

"A blanket? A coat? Surely there are some spare pieces of clothing around this village."

"Maybe, but do you really want to dress as an elf? It might get you killed in the next attack."

"I don't fear death," Lisalla declared. "I would rather die warm and standing on my own two feet rather than cowering against the frozen earth."

"Well spoken, my lady," Reylin said with a grin. "I'll find you something." After a few moments, he returned with two fur blankets along with two long-sleeved leather shirts and two pairs of pants. "Enough for both of you," he said, tossing them the garments. With a quick stroke of his knife, he released them from the rope that held them to the tree.

"Thank you," Lisalla said. "Now turn away so we can change."

"So you can run?"

"So we can change," she repeated. "We've nowhere to run. I doubt I could make it far before an arrow found its way into my flesh."

"No kidding," Reylin said, removing his bow from his back. "I'll compromise and turn my head to the side."

Lisalla sighed, but did not argue. She handed Danna a shirt and pants and pulled her new clothes on, letting her dress drop to the ground. Instantly, she felt much warmer.

"I am grateful to you, Reylin," she said. "You have shown yourself to be a decent man."

"High praise indeed," he said mockingly. "You can join me in getting something to eat."

The women followed him to the fire pit at the center of the village. The mountain elves eyed the women curiously but said nothing. They were quick to accept anyone their kinsmen accepted.

"Tell me, Reylin," Lisalla began as she ate. "Why are you fighting this war?"

"Because King Domren is murdering my people for their land. He wants to own everything west of Na'zora. Maybe once we're all dead he will invade Ra'jhou."

"He could try," she replied, "but if I'm married to his son, I doubt he would make such a move. I have never heard anything good about King Domren. I hear he oppresses his own people, and justice is a thing of the past."

"I don't care how he treats his own," Reylin stated. "They have the power to be rid of him. Maybe one of them will do us all a favor and kill him."

"It's possible but unlikely," she pointed out. "People usually love their king, even if he doesn't deserve it."

"He murdered my parents," Reylin said. "They were part of a small group of elves asked to negotiate a land treaty with Na'zora. He offered to draw up a map and settle the borders permanently. Instead, he slaughtered the elves to show his strength and started a war with the Silver Birch Clan. They had been the most receptive to the humans and were the first to be scattered by their hands."

"That's terrible," Lisalla commented. "It is a despicable thing to disrespect a banner of truce. If he called them in to negotiate and then killed them, he is the most wicked sort of man imaginable."

"That's exactly what he is, and if I get the chance, I will kill him myself."

Chapter 32

Reylana descended the trees in a fury. In a flash, she stood before the Overseer. "You're just going to let them push you across the river? What happens when they keep pushing until you land in the sea?"

"They will not be able to cross the river," the Overseer said smugly. "The God of the River will protect us from harm."

"He doesn't even exist!" She shouted. "If you think some make-believe, magical god is going to protect you, then you're an even bigger fool than I thought."

"How dare you insult-" the Overseer began, but he was quickly cut off by Reylana.

"Shut up!" she shouted. "I have no time for cowards." She turned to the gathered elves and asked, "Who will fight with me?"

Scores of hands went up followed by cheers from the warriors willing to fight. Yori looked down at his feet and remained silent.

"What about you?" Reylana asked as she approached him.

"I have no desire to go to war," he replied.

"We need you. Our weapons are insufficient, and you can sway the odds in our favor."

"Prince Aelryk seems like an honorable man to me," Yori replied. "He spared all of our lives and promises a future of peace. I don't want to be responsible for countless deaths."

"So you're a coward too," Reylana declared, turning away from him. "I'm leaving to rejoin my brother's army. Anyone who wants to come is welcome. Bring your weapons."

Nearly four hundred warriors prepared to set out for war. They gathered their weapons, including the arrow tips that Yori had made. All of them carried at least one runed weapon. Though he feared his kinsmen would still be outnumbered once the clans were united, Yori felt that he had already done enough to help their cause. He did not think it was right that Na'zora's king was forcing the elves from their homes, but he did not agree with the elves slaughtering humans in retaliation. Somehow, there had to be a chance for peace. If only the prince turned out to be a man of his word, the war might come to an end.

The elves who remained in the village began packing their winter provisions for the journey across the river. Yori and Lem began packing up the tools from the forge. The forge itself would have to be rebuilt once they reached their destination.

"Why didn't you go with them?" Lem asked. "You should have gone."

"That was the same prince who freed me from prison when his father was going to have me killed. You could have gone if you're so in favor of the war."

"I'm no use with a bow, and I can't etch the runes. I would have just been in the way."

"Then don't judge me," Yori replied.

* * * * *

Three days later the Sycamore Clan was ready to cross the river. Several rafts had been constructed from fallen timber, and the shaman had been fasting in preparation for his ceremony to praise the River God. The clan could not hope to cross the Blue River in safety without the god's blessing.

Yori watched spellbound as the shaman approached the riverbank at dawn. Dressed all in blue feathers, which had been specially dyed for the occasion, he danced proudly along the bank. His ankles and wrists were adorned with shell bracelets that rattled as he moved. As he danced, he chanted words that Yori did not understand, but he could certainly feel their power. It was clear to him that earth or water magic was involved, but he did not fully understand it. Instead, he listened closely to the chanting and admired the graceful, bird-like movements of the shaman.

As soon as the shaman finished the dance, he approached the Overseer and declared, "The River God will allow us to cross in safety."

Darin took note of Yori's interest in the ceremony. "We used to have lots of ceremonies like that when I was young. We praised all the forest gods in those days."

"Why did you stop?" Yori asked.

"Different generations have different priorities it seems."

"It's a shame to lose something so magical," Yori remarked.

"Yes, but the world is changing," his grandfather replied. "We aren't as connected to the earth as we once were. Perhaps in time we will be again."

They boarded a raft to cross the Blue River. Yori looked down into its depths as they floated gently across the current. As they neared the halfway point, the blue of the river's depths became more intense. Staring deeply into the water, Yori caught a glimpse of a face. For a split second, its features appeared silver amid the blue depths. An expression of pure serenity spread across the face before it disappeared back into the blue. Yori remained silent and did not mention what he had seen. Perhaps the River God had truly smiled on their crossing.

When the raft reached the far bank, Yori hopped off first to offer a hand to the rest of the elves as they disembarked. Carrying the majority of his grandfather's belongings, he chose a flat patch of earth where they could build the new forge. "Will this spot work?" he asked his grandfather.

"Looks just fine to me," he replied. "I'm guessing they plan to rebuild the village close to the bank. There is a fire elemental living in a tower just a few days' walk from here. No one wants to live too close to him."

"What does a fire elemental look like?" Yori asked.

"Beats me," Darin replied. "He probably has red hair, though." He smiled lightheartedly at his grandson.

For a moment, Yori was tempted to go and see for himself but thought better of it. He felt out of place now that the village was being relocated. Reylana's words echoed in his ears, and he wondered if he was indeed a coward. The thought of war gave him nothing but bad feelings. His heart ached to see the elves treated fairly and for an end to the violence. No one should have to die for a piece of land.

"Grandfather," he said. "I've been thinking about the Sunswept Isles. I've heard they enchant weapons and armor using gems."

"I believe I've heard that as well," Darin replied. "They're all sorcerers, so they use their spells on the gems and set them into the metal. I'm told they can create very powerful enchantments."

"What if you used those gems and runes together?" Yori was curious whether such a thing had ever been attempted.

"I imagine you'd have a very powerful weapon," Darin replied. "I don't think the Enlightened Elves bother with runes, though. I'm sure those snotty, self-righteous bastards consider them beneath their intelligence." He thought for a moment and then asked, "Who would you give such a weapon to if you could create it?"

Yori was surprised by the question. He had not paused to consider what could be done with something so powerful. "Well," he began, "I don't suppose I would want it in the hands of the attacker. Maybe I would give it to whoever was trying to defend their home."

"What if the people defending their home are committing atrocities of their own?" his grandfather replied. "In war, it isn't always easy to determine who is good or bad."

"You're right about that," he said with a sigh. He had refused to travel with Reylana and provide more weapons for the elves, even though his refusal might be their downfall. However, he did not see the need to continue killing Na'zorans when the prince honestly desired peace. He could see no reason why the two sides could not end the violence and come to an agreement. "I'm not sure I belong here any longer." His tongue felt heavy as he spoke the words.

"It can't be easy for you being a child of two worlds." Darin placed his hands on his grandson's shoulders. "I have taught you everything I know, and you have proven yourself highly skilled. You could use more practice, but you don't have to stay around here to get it."

Yori hugged his grandfather tightly. He tried to swallow the lump he felt in his throat as tears began to form in his eyes. "I love you, Grandfather. Thank you for everything."

"I love you too," the old elf replied. "Your father had the traveling spirit in him as well. Where will you go?"

"I think I'll try the Sunswept Isles. I'd like to learn how their magic affects steel."

"You might have trouble finding someone to teach you. They aren't exactly a friendly bunch." Darin laughed as he spoke.

"They'll think I'm too tall for a Wild Elf. Maybe I can fool them into thinking I'm one of them."

"Maybe so," Darin replied, clapping Yori on the back. "At least stay for dinner. You can be on your way in the morning."

"Don't you need my help with the new forge?" Yori asked.

"Lem is more than capable of helping me rebuild the forge," he replied. "We'll be here waiting for you when you get back."

Yori did not know why he felt the urge to travel and learn about other magical weapons. He knew very well that anything he created would likely be used in war, since weapons are not typically used for peaceful purposes. Still, he wanted to learn all that he could. Someday he might return to the prince and serve him in times of peace. Even without the threat of war, it was best to have a way of defending one's self. Evil could take on any guise, and his skills may be needed one day.

Chapter 33

Mi'tal strode beside the prince as he marched heavily down the stone corridor of the palace. He had not bothered to change out of his battle clothing, and his chainmail rattled as he walked.

"My lord, is it wise to barge into your father's council chambers like this?" Mi'tal asked. Aelryk's dark eyes shot an annoyed glance his direction.

The pair continued at a brisk pace until they reached the arched wooden doors of the council chambers. Not waiting for the guards to open them for him, the prince swung the doors wide with the strength of both arms. The councilors inside sat stunned, staring at the prince.

"A marvelous entrance as always," King Domren spat. "What do you want?"

"I want a word with you, Father," the prince demanded. "These fools can stay or go. It matters not."

"We are in the middle of a discussion. You can wait outside," the king replied with a dismissing wave of his hand.

"This will not wait!" Aelryk shouted. "You will hear me now!"

The councilors glanced at one another, wondering if they should leave the room. The temptation to listen in, however, proved too strong. The king had not ordered them to leave, and they silently agreed to stay and witness the spectacle.

"How dare you barge your way in here and give me orders! I should have you thrown in the stocks!" The king rose to his feet and stared red-faced at his son.

"You can throw me where you like, but first you will listen. You are a tyrant and a fool. I will not continue to slaughter peaceful elves. You cannot possibly hope to defend all of the Wildlands, and you're risking war with Al'marr and Ra'jhou!"

"Al'marr barely has an army and Ra'jhou will fight alongside us. That was the price of your bride. We will eradicate the elven presence, and our people will inhabit all the land east of the river. In time, we will have the west side as well."

"You're completely mad," the prince replied. "You can't think to take over the west bank."

"Why not?" the king asked. "No one could possibly stop me."

"There is a sorcerer there more powerful than all of your mages combined. You would be sending your army to certain death."

"That is a fairy tale, my gullible son."

"The elves of the Sunswept Isles speak of battles with this sorcerer. They all failed to subdue him. Human mages have nothing on Enlightened Elves, and they will be slaughtered."

"Then I'll find more," the king replied with a shrug.

"What will you do with all of the land you're planning to take? It is nothing but forests and meadows."

"Those things can be easily removed," King Domren said, taking his seat once again. "We will build new towns and farming villages and our population will grow. Every family will be required to enlist a son into my army until we have enough men to conquer all of Nōl'Deron."

Aelryk could not believe his ears. If his father truly intended to destroy the forests, he was determined to stop him. "I will not allow that to happen," he said calmly.

"Are you threatening your king?" The king rose to his feet again, staring angrily at his son. "You will leave my presence this instant."

Aelryk stared at his father for a moment before turning to leave. He glanced quickly at his father's councilors, who appeared nervous and uneasy. If they valued their lives and fortunes, they had no choice but to agree with the king. Plainly, however, many of them disagreed with the king's plan.

Mi'tal had waited outside the door and rejoined Aelryk as he stormed from the council chambers. "Where are you going, my lord?" he asked.

"I need to borrow your hammer," he replied.

"May I ask for what purpose?"

"I feel like breaking something!" The prince clenched his fists as he continued down the corridor. Exiting the palace, Mi'tal drew the hammer and offered it to the prince.

"Put it away," the prince said, seeming calmer now that he was outside in the fresh air.

Mi'tal slipped the hammer back into its holster and said, "It is ever at your command, my lord."

A young boy in peasant clothing approached the prince. Clearly out of breath, the boy had been running at top speed to deliver a message. "Your Majesty," he said, panting. "Your Highness, I mean. I have a message from General Luca, sir, Majesty." He leaned his hands on his knees and doubled over to catch his breath.

"What is it?" the prince asked, losing patience.

"A carriage, my lord, was found. The princess's carriage. She is gone, my lord."

"What do you mean? She was taken prisoner?"

"Yes, Your Majesty, sir. She was taken by elves. The other carriages were found north of Duana. Some of the drivers and guards were killed with elf arrows, sir." The boy stood up straight again having recovered his breath. He spoke with his head bowed out of respect for the prince.

"Did General Luca send anyone to find her?"

"I, umm..." the boy began. "I don't know, Majesty. He said to inform you right away. I've been running for two days with only an hour or two of sleep. I'm sorry, sir. I didn't think to ask questions."

"It's not your fault, young man," the prince said reassuringly. He gave the boy a few coins and turned to Mi'tal.

"We must find her," he said. "I can only hope they've decided not to kill her since she was not found among the dead."

"Perhaps they mean to use her as leverage," Mi'tal suggested, smoothing his black hair with a gloved hand.

"We can only hope as much," the prince replied. "I need you to find out where they've taken her. Do whatever you can to negotiate her release and secure peace with the elves. I will remain here to keep an eye on my father. I will do whatever it takes to prevent another massacre."

"Of course, my lord. I will do what I can." Mi'tal knew that this would be an incredibly dangerous mission. Assuming he managed to make it behind enemy lines without a dozen arrows in his heart, he had no idea if they would listen to reason. There were several clans scattered throughout the Wildlands, none of which had a village that was marked on any map. Every village the Na'zorans had known about had been destroyed. Unsure of where to begin looking, he proceeded to the stables to fetch his horse.

Instead of taking men along for the journey, Mi'tal decided it was best to travel alone. He would appear less of a threat if he was unaccompanied and bore a white banner of peace. Perhaps the elves would take pity on a man alone and hold their fire long enough for him to speak. His only regret was being too far from King Domren to assist the prince in ascending the throne. For now, his other plans would have to wait.

Chapter 34

Lisalla walked unbound at the head of the company next to Reylin. The elven army now numbered over twelve hundred strong. Luckily, the Mountain Clan warriors already possessed runed weapons, thanks to the skill of their clan's rune carver. Every evening when the company stopped to rest, he worked diligently etching runes into the blades of the sword maidens or the tips of the archers' arrows. In time, all of their weapons would carry the magical symbols that would sway the odds in their favor.

The forest remained frozen, locked in winter's grasp. A few inches of crunchy snow blanketed the earth, preventing Lisalla's feet from warming. She still wore the soft slippers she had brought from her homeland, and they provided little in the way of warmth. Hugging the fur blanket around her shoulders, she tried to focus on walking and forget her winter surroundings.

When they stopped for the night, Essa took out her broadsword and began polishing the blade. Sal, who had been admiring her at a distance, finally found the courage to approach her.

"That's a fine blade," he commented. Essa ignored him and continued to rub a cloth along the sword. Sal waited a moment and spoke again. "Are you going to have our rune carver etch it for you?"

"Maybe," she replied, still looking at the blade.

Sal took a deep breath and let it out. He took a seat next to Essa and said, "We could die in battle tomorrow, you know. Would you like to mate tonight?"

"You could die today," she replied, glaring at him and tightening her grip on her sword.

"I don't mean to offend," he said, raising his hand to touch her dark hair. She grabbed his wrist and squeezed it.

"Don't touch me," she said through clenched teeth. "Get away from me," she added, shoving his arm away.

"I'll mate with you," one of the Mountain Clan women said. "Come on, Sal."

Sal smiled at the woman and turned back to Essa. "Looks like you're going to miss out," he said before taking the other woman's hand. They ascended into the trees together, while Essa remained focused on her blade.

Reylin, who had not overheard any of the conversation, took a seat next to Essa.

"Why are men always so preoccupied with mating?" she asked, obviously annoyed.

"All I did was sit down!" Reylin replied in a surprised tone.

Essa shook her head.

"Anyway," Reylin began, "I wanted to ask your opinion on what to do next. I think we should give the rune carver time to work on everyone's weapons. After that we can resume the fight."

"That's a good idea," Essa replied. "It was a nice surprise that the Mountain Clan had a rune carver. Still, he is only one man. The work could take a long time, and I hate to sit idle."

"We could watch the road for travelers in the meantime. Maybe Reylana will return soon with the Sycamore Clan's rune carver."

"They could all be dead, for all we know." Essa put her blade back in its leather scabbard. "But I hope not. It's a long journey. I think we should move to a more central location where all of the clans can meet if they decide to join us."

"I agree," Reylin said. "We should make sure there are patrols near the border at all times, though. We don't want to be taken by surprise, even if we all join together. The next strike should be ours."

Essa nodded in agreement. "What are you planning for the princess?"

"I'm not sure," he admitted. "They probably know by now that we have her, but I don't know if they care. She's just one girl after all."

"Yes, but she is a very rich girl," Essa replied. "I think they will come looking for her. Ra'jhou might even send an entire army to find her. Are you prepared to fight both kingdoms?"

"I suppose if we have to," he said. "Maybe we could bargain her freedom for their help against Na'zora."

"They would certainly be a welcome addition to our army," she replied. "I think she likes you. Maybe you should see what she knows about her kingdom's politics."

"I'm not so sure she wants to be my friend," he began, "but I can try." He stood and approached the campfire where Lisalla and Danna were sitting quietly.

Lisalla nodded as he approached. Danna's eyes grew wide, and she stared at the ground. "Why does this one recoil when I approach?" he asked, gesturing to Danna.

"She's frightened," Lisalla replied.

"Has she no voice of her own?"

Danna began to sob, burying her face in her hands. Reylin shook his head in disbelief. "She is a coward and a disgrace," he said.

"She isn't accustomed to being a hostage or going along on forced marches!" Lisalla protested. "You could have a little compassion."

"It would be compassion to put her out of her misery. Would you like that?"

Lisalla's mouth clamped shut, and she gave no reply.

"I've come to ask you about your father, the king. If we release you to him, will he fight on our side against Na'zora?"

"My father does as he pleases. I cannot say what he would give for my safe return." After a moment, she added, "You could send Danna with the message. It can't hurt to try."

Danna paused in her sobbing to look at Lisalla. She glanced at Reylin and then back to the princess. "Please let Lisalla go home," she begged.

"Go back to your bawling," Reylin commanded.

"My father has agreed to help Na'zora. That was the price of my dowry."

"I see," Reylin says. "Was he gathering an army to march against us?"

"No," she replied. "I don't think he truly intended to fight. He just wanted me married and gone."

Reylin laughed. "The joys of being a princess, I suppose."

"He might pay you for my return, but I do not know if he will go to war. There has not been a war in Ra'jhou during my lifetime. My father is no war leader."

"So what you're saying is it's hopeless to ask."

"I'm trying to answer you truthfully. I do not know how my father will react." The princess looked in Reylin's eyes as she spoke. She never glanced away, hoping to convince him of her honesty. Earning his respect may very well be the key to saving her life, and she intended to have it.

"If I send this girl with a message, will she return with an army?"

"She will do exactly as I tell her," Lisalla replied. "She is my loyal servant."

"Yes, but if your father commands differently, she will have no choice but to obey. Perhaps it's better to bargain you to your prince."

"I am told he is an honorable man, but we have never met. Again, I do not know what he would give for my life."

"Maybe I should kill you both and be done with it," Reylin said casually. "I'll decide in the morning." Without another word, he walked away leaving Lisalla and Danna to ponder their fate.

Lisalla's heart sank, knowing that she had failed in her attempt to free Danna. She doubted Reylin would choose to send the girl as a messenger when there was a chance she could send back an army to attack them. He would not want their exact location known, and in order to negotiate, someone would have to be able to find them. She regretted being born a princess who was not allowed to learn about war and politics. She was only expected to know how to dress in the latest fashions and how to please her husband. It was truly a waste to teach a daughter such things. She vowed to herself she would teach

281

her own daughters better, should she survive to bear children. Elven women were fighters, and human woman could learn to fight as well.

Chapter 35

As dawn arrived over the new Sycamore village, Yori packed up his few belongings. His worn-out knapsack had been replaced by a sturdy, oiled-leather bag crafted by the hands of his elven kin. He rolled up his animal skin clothes and placed them inside the bag. Today, he would wear the green shirt the prince had given him in an effort to blend in with the humans of Al'marr. They were more accepting of elves than the Na'zorans, but he was going to seek passage on one of their ships. He did not know how readily an elf would be taken on board, so he planned to keep his ears covered once he reached Marrel.

"Stay safe," his grandfather said as he prepared to leave the hut. "You're always welcome here." He grabbed Yori and hugged him tightly.

Taking a deep breath, Yori turned and slipped out the door. Once again, he hoped to avoid a long goodbye. It was already hard enough to leave, and he was still unsure he had made the right decision not to join the other elves in battle. Later in life he may come to regret it, but his plan was to focus on today. Perhaps he would learn something in the Sunswept Isles that he could share to better the lives of the Wild Elves.

Several rafts sat idly on the west bank. Yori chose the smallest one to carry him back across the river. Though he intended not to look into the water's depths again, he thought he heard a voice coming from the blue. Peering over the edge of the raft, he looked down into the deep blue river. A silver mist danced and twinkled amidst the blue, but it took on no discernable shape. The voice faded, leaving only the sound of the rushing water to fill his ears.

He knelt on the raft and shoved the oar deeply into the rocks below to stop its motion. Leaning in close to the water's surface, he quietly asked, "Is there someone there?" He waited and heard no response. Rising back to his feet, he began paddling once again toward the east bank. Without warning, a fountain of water shot up next to him, sprinkling him with water. He thought it surprisingly warm, considering the season. A blue light encompassed his raft, and he gasped in surprise. Though he had stopped paddling, the raft continued steadily toward the east bank and stopped gently when it reached land. The blue light faded away.

Yori climbed onto the shore and looked back at the river. He saw a silver light dance upon its surface for a moment before descending back into the depths. Had the River God blessed his journey? Perhaps the god had wanted him to make it safely to the other side, but for what purpose he did not know. Perhaps it approved of the choice he had made, or perhaps it thought him a coward and wanted him to leave. Yori couldn't be sure.

"Thank you," he said to the river. "I hope you will watch over my people while I'm away. They may need your help." A second fountain of water shot up from the center of the river, sprinkling water droplets in every direction. Yori smiled and felt a sense of peace. Surely this god was watching out for the Sycamore Clan.

The forest was still dark, its thick branches allowing very little light to seep through from the overcast sky. A few unseen critters scampered beneath the rotting leaves as he made his way through the trees. Before reaching the edge of the woods, he turned and stared back in the direction of the river. He wanted to freeze the image of the forest in his mind to keep with him on his journey.

As he arrived at Marrel, he noticed several changes to the town. Colorful banners and ribbons adorned every building and merchant stall, and a large stage had been erected at the center of town. It appeared there was some sort of winter festival taking place, but he did not intend to stay long enough to join in the fun.

Yori stopped in the fletcher's stall to inquire about the town of Marron. Inside, Hydon sat busily tending to his arrows. He looked up as Yori approached and said, "Good morning, Brother. What brings you here today?"

"I'm traveling to the Sunswept Isles," he replied. "I was hoping you could give me directions to Marron."

"I can't imagine why you'd want to go there," Hydon said with a laugh. "But Marron is at least a full day's walk south. You might see if some of the mining wagons could give you a ride. They travel back and forth every day delivering gems. They'll take you right to the docks where you can purchase passage to the isles. Do you have any money?"

"I have a little," he replied, undervaluing the coins the prince had given him.

"Don't let them cheat you. I hear those sea captains try to take advantage of travelers. It shouldn't cost any more than one silver coin."

Yori nodded. "Thank you, Hydon."

"Safe journeys," he replied before returning to his work.

Yori hurried past the marketplace to the warehouses where he had helped Atti unload his goods when he first arrived in Al'marr. It wasn't long before he spotted the gem wagons. Stout men were loading heavy wooden chests with iron locks onto wagons. No other goods would have need of such hefty locks, so Yori assumed they must be filled with precious gems. Approaching one of the men, Yori asked, "Are you heading to Marron?"

"Sure am," the bearded man replied, loading a chest into a wagon.

"Do you think you'll have room for a passenger?"

The man turned and looked Yori up and down. Apparently, Yori didn't look much like a thief. "I suppose so," the man replied. "You've got to help load the wagons first, though. There's five of them, and these chests are heavy."

"I'm stronger than I look," Yori replied with a smile. He was shorter and thinner than the bearded man, but years of hammering iron and steel had provided him with a decent amount of muscle. He slid a chest to the side of the loading dock and lifted it onto his shoulder. The bearded man raised his eyebrows and nodded in approval.

"We'll be at this until lunchtime," he said. "The miners will let us eat with them before we head out."

"Sounds great," Yori replied, lifting another chest. The chests were indeed very heavy, but Yori did not mind the work. Offering the man coin would probably have spared him the physical labor, but he preferred to help out rather than sit back and watch.

Lunch consisted of boiled potatoes, a small strip of dried meat, and a large chunk of bread. As soon as he saw the food, he missed the fresh cuisine of the forest. The elves collected berries that they could make into jams that kept all through the winter. The hunters supplied fresh meat nearly every day, and they drank teas from the dried leaves of dozens of different plants. He allowed his mind to wander and tried to imagine what he would be eating once he reached the Sunswept Isles. Everything he had heard of the Enlightened Elves had been negative, so he could not imagine their food being very good.

"All set to leave?" the bearded man asked.

Yori nodded, returned his empty plate to the cook, and tossed his leather bag over his shoulder.

"Can you drive a wagon?" the man asked. "One of our drivers has been throwing up since last night. I thought he was drunk and needed to sleep it off, but I guess he's really sick."

"I can do it," Yori replied. He had driven a wagon for his uncle many times and was not bad at managing stubborn mules.

Along the road to Marron, Yori took notice of the landscape. The area near the city was drab and brown, but as they moved farther away, the land came alive. Fields of gold stretched on for miles, and the trees grew tall and proud. Tiny farmhouses dotted the landscape, and chickens roamed freely beside the road. Children were playing despite the cool weather, and they waved cheerfully as the wagons rolled by.

As they neared the coast, the smell of the sea filled Yori's nostrils. The air seemed denser and warmer in Marron, and the sound of the waves filled the air. Catching his first glimpse of the ocean, Yori sat in awe. Never before had he seen so much blue. The waves crashed fiercely against the shore, leaving a white foam behind on the sand. Fleets of cargo ships littered the coastline, each being loaded or unloaded by hundreds of workers.

Gulls screeched noisily overhead as Yori's caravan came to a halt near one of the ships. Hopping down from his seat, Yori walked around to the back of his wagon to help unload. The bearded man waved a hand, telling him not to bother.

"You don't have to unload," he said. "They pay these men to do the work from here. They don't want us mucking up their precious boats."

With a nod, Yori said, "Thanks for bringing me along." He looked up and down the long row of ships, wondering which one to try first. The ship he was closest to seemed as good as any, so he followed the men who were unloading the chests full of gems as they made their way up the ramp to the deck.

The ship's captain was closely supervising the cargo being brought on board. When Yori appeared on his deck, he became visibly angry. His face reddened, and the veins in his forehead bulged as he shouted, "You don't belong here! Go back where you came from!"

"I'm sorry for the intrusion, sir," Yori began. He did not have a chance to finish his thought before he was interrupted.

"I said get off my ship!" The captain approached Yori and towered over him. The glare in his gray eyes nearly burned a hole through Yori's head. "I've got to get these gems to Master Yarion, and I don't have time for sightseers."

An idea burst into Yori's mind, and he quickly removed his cap to reveal his ears. Standing as straight as he could and sticking his nose in the air, he said, "Master Yarion is my father. That bastard owes me an explanation!"

His pretense at arrogance must have been convincing enough for the captain. "I'll be damned," he said in disbelief. "In a million years I'd never guess one of those haughty elves would make it with a human woman."

"Obviously he did," Yori replied, still feigning arrogance. "My mother has finally told me the truth, and I will have his explanation."

The captain laughed and said, "Fine by me. I'd love to give that old sorcerer a shock. It's one gold coin for your fare."

"Gold?" Yori said stunned. "I'll give you a silver, and I won't let my father blow your ship to bits as you sail away."

The captain eyed Yori suspiciously but bought the act. "Fine," he said. "Just stay out of the way."

Yori handed him a silver coin and proceeded onto the deck of the ship. He smiled to himself, pleased with his own performance. He doubted it would be so easy to convince the Enlightened Elves that he was one of their own kind. They could probably smell the Wild Elf in his blood. At any rate, he was aboard the ship that would bear him to the isles.

The sun finally broke free of the clouds, and its rays sparkled on the water's surface. After what felt like hours, the ship was finally loaded and ready to set sail. Yori stayed out of the way of the sailors as they went about their duties. Wondering what kingdoms might lie far off in the blue, he leaned on the starboard rail and stared off into the vast ocean.

As the ship began to move, the ocean breeze swept over him. His sandy hair danced on the wind, and he closed his eyes to stop them from watering. The wind was more intense than he imagined, and he found it difficult to take in a full breath. The ship began to sway, followed shortly by Yori's stomach. Observing the magic of the sea would have to wait until he was acclimated to the motion of the ship. Despite his queasiness, his spirits remained high. Adventure awaited him just beyond the horizon.

Chapter 36

Snow fell in large, chunky flakes as Reylana led the Sycamore warriors to rejoin her brother's army. The heavy snow was nearly blinding, and she was having a hard time recognizing her surroundings. Tracking the movements of his company was impossible with the fresh snowfall. It was still early in the afternoon, but the blizzard showed no signs of relenting. "Let's make camp here for the night," she declared. "We'll have better luck finding them after this storm has ended."

The elves climbed into the trees to wait out the storm. Nat took a seat on a wide branch next to Reylana. "We should have tried harder to convince Darin to come with us," he said.

"He was too old for this journey," she replied. "But we should have dragged his fool grandson with us whether he wished it or not."

Nodding, Nat said, "That could have worked too."

"We can only hope my clansmen have done better at convincing the other clans. Perhaps one of them has a rune carver. We still stand a better chance with greater numbers, even if most of our weapons are not etched with runes."

"All of us here have runes, and we have a few to share with our kinsmen. We could use a mage or two on our side in place of a rune carver."

"I don't think that's going to happen," Reylana said. "I've never heard of any of our kind with that type of power. Shamans always focus on repairing the earth, not destroying it."

"I've never encountered a mage," Nat said with a shrug. He grinned and added, "I'm looking forward to using them for target practice, though."

Reylana stretched out on the branch and closed her eyes. There was no need to keep watch. Even humans couldn't be stupid enough to travel in this weather. Relaxing, she let her mind wander until she soon fell asleep. In her dreams, she saw the forests burning. Her kinsmen were dying all around her as

294

magefire blasted through the air. As she made her way toward the mages, the ground in front of her erupted, sending dirt and dried leaves in every direction. Only gaping pits remained where once earth and trees had existed. With no other option before her, she retreated to find safety in the woods. Many elves joined her, running from all directions. Their efforts had been defeated by the mages, and the Wildlands were now destroyed. No forest would remain once the mages had finished. The elves had nowhere left to run.

She awoke in a cold sweat, the visions from her dream refusing to leave her mind. Darkness loomed all around her, but the snowfall had become lighter. Though she had never prayed before in her life, she felt the urge now. *If there is truly a Goddess of the Forest, please help my people. We cannot do this alone.* Immediately after thinking the words, she felt foolish. She knew that there were no magical creatures out there that were willing to help. If the elves were to survive, they needed true leadership and a damn good battle plan.

She sat up and looked over at Nat, who was fast asleep. He seemed courageous enough, having spoken out against his clan's Overseer. Also, he had managed to convince nearly half the clan to join in the fight. She hoped he would prove wise enough to lead a group into battle, though she knew he lacked experience. She herself had not experienced battle until Na'zora declared war on her people. She had proven herself a quick learner, and so could Nat.

As dawn finally broke, the clouds separated to allow the sun to peek through the sky. The snow had ended, leaving at least ten inches behind on the ground. Today's march would be slow as they grew ever nearer to joining the others. Reylin's group was on the move, but she was sure she would be able to find them.

With a firm shake, she roused Nat from his sleep.

Yawning, he said, "Good morning."

"Send some scouts out ahead. We need to figure out where Reylin's group has gone. I'm betting he'll be somewhere near Na'zora's border and not too much farther north. He'll want to stay central, I'm sure."

Nat descended the branches to find his clansmen and dispatch the scouts. Reylana descended from the tree as well. Her mind went first to the thought of food, but all she had brought was dried meat and nuts. Not exactly a feast, but it would have to suffice for now.

One of the scouts came back within minutes of heading north. "There are elves ahead of us," he said.

"I saw tracks not a few hours old. I'd say it was a scout who turned back before he reached us."

Reylana sighed in relief, knowing she would rejoin her brother that day. The deep snow made their journey difficult, and Reylana cursed every time she tripped over a hidden obstacle. Her legs were beginning to ache already, and she wished for some magefire to thaw her path.

Up ahead, a familiar voice called out. "Where's my fiery-haired sister?"

"Reylin?" she called, craning her neck to see ahead.

Reylin strode her direction accompanied by a Sycamore scout. "It's good to have you back, Sis," he said, wrapping an arm around her shoulders.

"It's good to be back. The snow was so thick last night I couldn't tell where we were. I'm still not completely sure," she admitted.

"You're not far from our old village," he replied. "Everything looks different in the snow." Shaking his head, he said, "Women make terrible guides. They never know where they are."

She punched him in the shoulder and said, "If we spent as much time goofing around in the forest pretending to hunt, we'd probably know better."

"Oh just stick to what you know and swing your pretty sword," he said jokingly.

Reylana smiled briefly, but her thoughts took a more serious turn. "Have we lost many of our clansmen since I left?"

"Not too many," he replied. "Though, we have seen some battle. You've missed out."

"I wouldn't have been much use with a busted shoulder, but it's healed now."

"We've gained a few friends," he said with a grin.

As the army of elves came into view, Reylana's mouth dropped open.

"I've got about twelve hundred friends here," Reylin said. "How many did you bring again?" He chuckled and looked back over his shoulder at the Sycamore warriors. "Only about four or five hundred, I'm guessing. Looks like I win."

"I didn't know it was a contest," she replied, still staring at the army. Never before had she seen such a gathering of elves. The elves of the Wildlands usually kept to their own clans and had no need for each other. It amazed her to see so many come together.

"I'm still hoping some clans across the river will join us. We haven't heard anything from them yet."

"I couldn't convince the rune carver," Reylana said, the disappointment clear in her voice.

"No worries," he replied with a smile. "I've found one of those myself. The Mountain Clan has a rune carver, and he's been very busy." He held his head high with pride but couldn't stop himself from laughing.

Shaking her head, Reylana said, "It's good to see you again, Reylin." She wrapped both arms around him and squeezed him tightly.

Chapter 37

In the thick forest, Mi'tal felt much colder than he had riding through Na'zora. He was grateful for the generous helping of ground pepper he had picked up in Duana's marketplace. After sprinkling it inside his boots, he found his feet were much warmer.

The white banner with blue trim mounted to the back of his saddle floated lazily on the cold breeze. He could only hope the elves would recognize it as a symbol of peace when he encountered them in the Wildlands. Without knowing where the elves might be hiding, he took little comfort in the banner's presence. Having the chance to speak before he was shot would be more helpful than the banner, but their archers were difficult to spot, even in the bare trees of winter.

High above in the trees, Sal watched intently as a single horse and rider approached. The man was still a good distance away, but he was clearly heading in Sal's direction. A white banner streamed behind the rider, and he recognized it as a banner of peace. A single rider alone posed little threat, but he could be a distraction from the army that might be following him.

Sal climbed hurriedly down the tree and raced back to camp. He spotted Reylana first and asked, "Where is Reylin?"

"He's scouting the southern edge of camp. Why?"

"There's a rider approaching," he replied.

"We better tell Essa," she said, searching the camp with her eyes. Spotting Essa with a group of sword maidens, she sprinted to her side followed closely by Sal.

"This had better be important," Essa said, glaring at Sal.

"It is, he replied. There's a rider approaching the camp."

"Is he a scout?" she asked.

"I don't know," Sal answered, smoothing down his silver hair. "He's alone and carries a white banner. Perhaps he has come to speak with us."

"Or he's a spy," Reylana offered. "He may be attempting to locate our camp so he can return with an army. I don't think we should trust him."

Essa weighed Reylana's opinion heavily. She was a trusted ally and quite skilled in battle. Her brother Reylin, however, was quick to distrust all humans, and he had probably influenced Reylana to the same way of thinking.

"If this man is alone, I will listen to what he has to say. If there is any hint he is spying for an army, I will kill him."

Reylana started to argue, but a stern glance from Essa's dark eyes stopped her.

"Should I escort him into the camp?" Sal asked.

"Yes, but don't talk to him except to tell him you will bring him here. I don't want him getting away with any information."

With a nod, Sal turned and ran back to his post. The rider was much closer now, and Sal began to approach cautiously. He was close enough to see that the man was armed, so he readied his bow just in case. Knocking an arrow to the string, he called out to the rider. "Halt! Who are you, and what do you want?"

Mi'tal immediately stopped his horse and raised both hands in the air. Looking around, he failed to see the person who was speaking, but he was grateful to have been spoken to rather than shot. "I am Mi'tal of Na'zora, servant to Prince Aelryk. I come with a message of peace."

Sal emerged from his hiding place in the thick forest, his bow still at the ready. "I will lead you to my camp."

Mi'tal slowly dismounted his horse and took the reins in his hand. Never before had he seen a Wild Elf quite like Sal. He wanted to ask where he was from but thought better of it. With an arrow still pointed at his heart, he didn't want to risk upsetting the elf.

Sal lowered his bow and drew a dagger. He kept both eyes on Mi'tal and only glanced at the path ahead to be sure he was going the right direction. This man knew the camp was near, and if he decided to run, Sal would have to kill him. He would not fail Essa.

As they entered the camp, Essa strode over to meet Mi'tal. Being among the tallest of Wild Elf women, she stood equal to him in height. "Take his weapon," she commanded. "Bind his hands as well. He doesn't need them for speaking."

Reylana grabbed the hammer and laid it next to a tree. Sal sheathed his dagger and bound Mi'tal's hands with a thin strap of leather. Both of them remained close at hand in case Essa required their assistance.

"Why have you come here?" Essa asked.

"I have come on a mission from Prince Aelryk," Mi'tal replied. "He has sent me to negotiate peace with your clan."

"There are many clans here, not just my own," Essa stated proudly.

Reylana stepped forward, her hazel eyes fierce. "The prince led the raid on the Sycamore Clan. He forced them across the river and threatened them if they did not comply." She looked at Mi'tal and spat on the ground. "He doesn't want peace. He wants obedience."

"King Domren commanded that raid," Mi'tal replied. "The prince had no choice in the matter. He spared your lives and moved your people to safety."

"What if they had refused?" Reylana shouted back. "Would he have killed them?"

"He would have spared whoever he could," Mi'tal responded.

"Silence!" Essa shouted. "I have heard what happened with the Sycamore Clan, and I have not decided about this prince of yours. He may be honest, and he may be laying a trap. Is there an army with you?"

"No, my lady," Mi'tal replied, not knowing how to address the elf. "The king and his armies have no idea I've come. The prince himself has sent me."

"You are brave to come here alone," Essa said. "You were very lucky not to be shot on sight." She looked over at Sal with a curious expression. "Some of our kinsmen are not as hostile as others, it seems." Essa was a dedicated warrior, and she understood why Sal had stayed his hand. He had returned to his commanders for their decision before acting. She had no doubt that he would have killed Mi'tal had she ordered it.

"There will be trouble when Reylin returns," Reylana said coolly. Her brother was not going to like having a Na'zoran in his camp.

"Reylin is not our leader," Essa said. "There are other clans among us now, and they should have a say in any peace talks. Reylin will never talk peace. He sees only war."

"Reylin has done everything he can for our clan, and he is the only leader we've had for months." Reylana could feel the redness rising in her ears as she defended her brother. He and Essa did not get along well and had been competing for leadership since the Overseer was killed. Essa led the sword maidens, who were staunchly loyal to her, but many of the archers preferred Reylin to make the decisions. The two so far had managed to get along, but a rift could easily form should they find themselves unable to compromise.

"I don't doubt his loyalty or his skill in battle," Essa said in an unusually soft tone. "Reylana, you must realize that your brother's behavior is unpredictable. He is not the right person to negotiate peace. I doubt he will ever stop fighting, even if a treaty were signed."

Reylana stared at Essa and did not respond. She knew Essa was right. Reylin's temper was uncontrollable, and his heart only lusted for revenge. If there was a chance for peace, Essa would be better suited to the task. She was a fair and honest warrior, and she loved her clansmen deeply.

"Tell me what this prince has to say," Essa said, turning back to Mi'tal.

"The prince wants an end to the fighting. His father is determined to take all of the land east of the river, and someday he will also try to take the land to the west as well. Your people will be annihilated if King Domren has his way. You can help avoid this by ceasing to raid villages full of innocent citizens

307

and helping us to find Princess Lisalla, who has disappeared en route to Na'zora."

"Your princess is here with us," Essa said. "She has not been harmed."

Mi'tal's face reflected his surprise. "She is Prince Aelryk's betrothed, and he will give anything to have her returned safely."

"How will he convince his father to stop fighting?" Essa asked.

"If you stop the raids and return the princess, it will be a show of good faith. The prince can prove to his father that you're ready to negotiate, and the talks can begin."

"That doesn't answer my question," she replied. "King Domren is in charge of the armies, not the prince. You said yourself the king forced the prince to attack the Sycamores."

"The prince did not harm a single member of the Sycamore Clan. He convinced them to move where it is safe. His father would be livid if he knew." Mi'tal was grasping for words. In truth, he had no idea how the prince planned to stop his father from fighting.

"I think this peace will have to wait until Domren is dead," Essa commented.

Knowing there was no Na'zoran around to hear his treasonous words, Mi'tal declared, "I would kill this king if I had a chance. I swear it. Prince Aelryk is the rightful king of Na'zora." His words hung heavily in the air.

Essa stared into his dark eyes for a moment. "I believe you," she said.

Reylana shook her head. "Essa," she said.

Essa held up a hand to silence her. "Even to an enemy, Reylana, would you declare that you despise your Overseer and would kill him?"

"If I had a problem with my Overseer, I would take it up with him personally. I wouldn't sneak away to talk about it with others."

"Half of the Sycamore Clan believed this prince to be honorable. That is why they followed his command. You told me so yourself," Essa pointed out.

"The prince is an honorable man," Mi'tal declared. "He is the opposite of his father. Once he assumes the throne, you will have peace. He has sworn this to me, and I have risked my life to bring you the message."

Essa thought for a moment and said, "Go back to your prince and tell him that once Domren is dead, we will negotiate peace. I give him my word on it."

"Yes, my lady," Mi'tal replied.

"You can't just let him walk out of here!" Reylana shouted.

"I can, Reylana, and I will." She turned to Sal. "Release his hands."

Sal obeyed without hesitation.

"We will move our camp, so if you are planning to return with an army you will be disappointed," Essa said. She retrieved his hammer and held it out for him to take. "You may go."

"Thank you, my lady." Taking the hammer, Mi'tal mounted his horse and rode from the campsite. With every breath he tensed, expecting an arrow to find its way into his flesh.

"You've doomed us all, Essa," Reylana said.

"No," Essa replied. "I have ensured there will be peace in our future. I am a warrior, but I do not wish to fight forever. Our old village is gone, and we must make a new one. I would not have it destroyed before it's built."

Reylana shook her head. She was sick of this prince and his promises of peace. It would have sent a better message to return the prince's servant in pieces. They still had the princess, however, and surely his betrothed was worth more than his servant.

Chapter 38

At midday another scout arrived at Reylin's post to relieve him from his duties. He climbed out of the tree and returned to the camp. As he entered, several elves looked away from him, deliberately avoiding his gaze. The camp seemed strangely silent, and Reylin grew suspicious. Seeing Reylana, he called out to her. "What news, Sis?"

Reylana rushed over to her brother's side. "There was a Na'zoran here this morning," she said. "He wanted to talk peace and locate the princess we're holding."

"Where is he now?" he asked. "Dead?"

Reylana took in a deep breath and released it quickly. "Essa let him go."

"What?" he shouted. "Why?"

"She wanted him to carry back a message that we will discuss peace."

Without a word, Reylin shoved passed Reylana, determined to speak with Essa. "What have you done?" he demanded as he reached her.

"A man came with a message from the prince. I sent him away with my own message." Essa shrugged as if the incident were no big deal.

"You should have sent for me," he said angrily. "I could have killed him since you were too weak."

"How dare you!" she shouted at him. "I made my choice for the good of the clan. Would you have me make an enemy of this prince as well as the king? He may be our only chance for peace once Domren is dead."

"He may also reveal our location and send an army to crush us!" Reylin shouted back. "He probably got a good look at the size of our army as well."

"It doesn't matter," she replied. "We can move the camp, and he doesn't know we have runed weapons. We will be victorious the next time they attack."

"You should have killed that man," Reylin continued. "Now he knows we are led by a weak woman."

Without hesitation, Essa slapped Reylin hard across his face. "I am not weak. You have no sense when it comes to leadership. All you see is killing."

"You're exactly right," he replied. "All Na'zorans deserve death." He marched over to the captive women and grabbed Danna by her hair. As Lisalla screamed in horror, he dragged the dark-haired woman to the center of camp and slit her throat as she cried out. Her limp body fell to the earth, her blood staining the snow beneath her.

Lisalla ran to her maid's body and wept. "How could you be so evil?" she shot at Reylin. "She was no threat to you."

He grabbed Lisalla, his hand clutching her throat. Before he could make another move, Essa grabbed him from behind and yelled "Stop!" Once he was safely away from Lisalla, she released him. Hundreds of elves gathered around to witness the spectacle. "If you kill this one, the prince will never forget it. There will never be peace."

"We won't need their peace once they're all dead," Reylin spat.

Reylana approached her brother and softly placed a hand on his arm. "Come and talk with me, Brother," she said. The two moved deeper into the forest, leaving the others to tend to the captives.

"She had no right to release that man," Reylin began. "Where were you?" He stopped walking and stared at his sister.

"I was next to her," she replied. "I did not agree, but she is my commander. She gives the orders."

"If you know better than her, then you don't have to listen. You should have killed him yourself."

"Listen to what you're saying," she said. "Our clan works together, and we respect those who are in charge. Essa leads the sword maidens of the combined clans. The women trust her judgment, as do many of the men."

"She's wrong," he replied.

"She may be wrong, but I respect her decision. If she is right, her actions will bring about peace in the future."

"We can bring peace by ridding ourselves of the Na'zorans." Reylin's anger was finally beginning to subside a bit.

"That wouldn't bother me one bit, but I think it may be more than we can handle. They still outnumber us, and they still have those damned mages."

"We need to plan another raid now that we have better weapons," he suggested. "We don't want them to see us as weak."

"I agree," Reylana replied. "There are other clans among us now, though. We have to make sure everyone is in agreement."

Together they returned to the camp, their feet crunching the frozen snow beneath them. Essa still stood near Lisalla, watching Reylin closely as he approached.

"We want to plan a raid now that we have better weapons," Reylana informed her.

"That's a good idea," Essa replied.

"What, you don't want to wait for peace?" Reylin said mockingly.

"I said I would negotiate peace once Domren is dead. While he lives, I will continue the fight. I won't hide in the woods until he comes for me." She glared at Reylin as she spoke.

In an effort to calm the situation, Reylana said, "We're all in agreement then. Let's talk with some of the other clans as well."

Essa nodded. At the western edge of camp another disturbance was taking place. Hearing the commotion, the three raced to the scene. An Oak Leaf scout was returning to camp, followed by a large group of elven warriors. The clans across the river had come to join the fight.

The fair-haired scout led the group to Essa and Reylin with a smile on his face. "These are warriors from the River Clan and the Willow Clan. They've come to help us fight."

Reylana's face broke into a smile as she grabbed the scout and hugged him. Releasing him, she stared out into the crowd of elves. Hundreds had come to join the fight. The elven army now numbered over two thousand strong.

"Fetch the rune carver," Reylin told the scout. "He's got a lot of work to do."

Chapter 39

The stars shone bright silver against the black sky as Yori stared up at the heavens. The ship would arrive at the Sunswept Isles by morning, and he was enjoying the fine weather as he sailed. The closer they came to the isles, the warmer the weather became. Winter, it seemed, held no sway over islands full of sorcerers.

He finally returned to his cabin, hoping to catch some rest. The following day was sure to be a busy one, and he didn't want to appear tired and dull before his future teachers. As he drifted to sleep, he dreamed of a strange red land where no other life existed. Alone he traveled, searching for another living soul. A red wasteland stretched endlessly before him, and the sky reflected the red of the earth.

Streaks of hot red lightning filled the sky above him, and he felt the heat on his skin as they struck the ground beside him.

He awoke with a start and shook his head. It was nearly dawn, so he went back out onto the deck to observe their approach to the isles. In the distance, he could see land. There were two separate islands that he could make out, and behind one there was a huge cloud of smoke. He wondered briefly if there was a third island which was currently on fire. Shaking the thought from his head, he continued to watch as the islands grew closer. The ship's crew was preparing to dock, and Yori's anticipation rose.

No one spoke to him as he departed the ship. Heading down the ramp to dry land, he hoped to spot someone who could point him in the direction of a teacher. Master Yarion did not sound like the friendly sort, but perhaps he had a servant or two who was more willing to chat.

Yori took a moment to observe his surroundings. Tall stone spires rose high into the sky everywhere he looked. There were no trees to be seen, and the earth was covered in flat stone, preventing any grass from pushing its way to the surface. Though he had grown up in a town filled with people, he was used to seeing the forest. In Enald, trees grew in various places within the town, and grass was no rarity. Here, it seemed, the Enlightened Elves had no use for nature. Gulls mobbed the shore, but no birds could be seen as he moved farther away from the sea.

He spotted a tall elf giving orders to some of the dock workers and decided to try his luck at a conversation.

"You stink of Wild Elf," the tall elf said. "Don't come too close."

Yori stopped in his tracks in disbelief. His previous assumption had been right. There would be no fooling these elves into thinking he was one of them. "I'm looking for training in weapons enchantment," he said.

The tall elf began to laugh and shook his head. "That's very amusing. Now off with you!" He stopped laughing and waved Yori away.

"I wasn't joking," Yori called out. "Do you know where I can find a smith?"

The tall elf laughed again. "You're a funny little thing."

Yori stared back at the elf. Everything he had been told of the Enlightened Elves was true. This was the first one of their kind he had ever met, and he could already tell the elf thought Yori was beneath him. "Look, can you tell me where to find a smith or are you not smart enough?" Yori thought he'd try giving the arrogant jerk a taste of his own medicine.

The smile came off of the elf's face as he said, "Try the city square." He pointed over his shoulder, stuck his nose in the air, and walked away in a huff.

Insulting their intelligence seems to work, Yori thought. *I'll have to remember that.* As he located the city square, he found the most immaculate marketplace he could ever have envisioned. Everywhere was white stone, and there was no hint of trash or dirt on the streets. The merchant stalls were small versions of the tall towers that filled the skyline. Bronze-skinned elves dressed in long, colorful robes strolled lazily about the market, casually inspecting goods as they passed by each stall. No one seemed to be in any kind of a hurry, and no one was yelling over the crowd to advertise their wares.

There was little noise, and Yori thought he would easily hear the sound of a hammer should he come near a smith. To his disappointment, however, he heard nothing of the kind, and no smoke could be seen coming from a furnace. He was beginning to wonder if these elves had some magical method of crafting weapons that did not require a forge.

With a sigh, he began to browse the long line of stalls for any sign of a blacksmith. The elves eyed him suspiciously and moved away from him as he passed. He was failing to blend in among such tall elves. Everyone here was at least a head taller than him, despite the fact that he was average height for a human. He supposed it was easier to look down on other races if you literally had to look down at them.

His clothing probably did not help matters. He was dirty from his travels, and it had been a while since he had a bath. Seeing what appeared to be an inn, he wondered if they had a "no Wild Elf" policy. Finding a place to stay might prove difficult. He decided he might fare better if he had a bath and some decent Enlightened Elf style clothing to wear. Luckily, he saw a shop selling robes nearby, and a pretty young elf maiden stood within. *She looks friendly enough*, he thought.

As he approached the stall, the girl's mouth dropped open, and she stared at Yori without saying a word.

"Hello," he said. "Do you accept coins from the Kingdom of Na'zora? I have silver."

"Um, yes," she replied, glancing to each side. "Aren't gold and silver coins accepted everywhere?"

Yori had no idea they would accept the same currency. "I need to purchase something to wear," he said.

"What color do you take?" she asked.

"It doesn't matter," he replied. "Whatever fits will do."

Again the girl's mouth dropped open. "It certainly does matter!" she protested. "You must have a specialty."

"Specialty?" Yori asked, wrinkling his brow.

"Yes," she replied. Seeing that Yori still didn't understand, she added, "Your magical specialty. These robes enhance your abilities."

"I see," Yori said, trying not to sound like an oaf. "Is earth magic an option?"

The girl giggled slightly with her mouth closed, and she lowered her head. Once she had composed herself, she said, "Of course it is. Green or brown?"

Good grief, he thought. "Green, I think," he replied. Green would match his eyes, at least.

"I might have a green one in the right length," the girl replied as she searched through a pile of clothing.

As the girl continued to search, an older man appeared from behind the booth. "Are you looking at my daughter?" he asked, eyeing Yori suspiciously.

"No, sir," he replied, shaking his head.

"You should be!" the elf shouted. "She's rather beautiful. Just don't touch her, or I'll melt you." The man's eyes flashed red, suggesting the truth behind his threat.

Yori nodded quickly, not knowing what to say.

The girl offered Yori a plain green robe and smiled. "My father is only teasing," she said. "See if this is the right size."

Slipping the robe over his clothes, Yori could tell it was a perfect fit. "It's perfect," he said. "How much do I owe you?"

"Five silver," she replied. "I thought you'd want the cheapest one."

"Thank you," he said as he handed her the coins. She was correct in her assumption. He did not want to spend much on clothing, but this robe had cost him five times the price of his journey by ship. There was little choice, however, if he intended to blend in among the locals.

He made his way to the inn to inquire about a room and a bath. It was nestled within one of the tall towers, and he was anxious to see what the inside looked like.

Within the tower was a polished marble floor and several tables made of white stone. A long twisting staircase led high into the tower. Behind the stone bar, an elf was busy wiping down crystal clear, long-stem glasses. "May I help you?" the elf asked.

"I need a room," Yori replied, approaching the bar.

"Goodness, how did you get to be so short?" the man asked, looking him up and down.

"Spell went wrong," Yori lied.

The elf nodded sympathetically. Apparently, not all Enlightened Elves could smell his mixed blood. "You can have a room on the third floor for three silver," the elf said.

"Thank you," he replied, handing the elf the coins. "Where can I find a bath?"

The man seemed puzzled by the question. "Each room has its own, of course. I trust you can heat the water yourself." He went back to wiping the glasses.

Yori walked slowly up the stairs, preparing himself for a cold bath. As he entered the room, he could not believe its size. For only three silver, the room was nearly as large as his uncle's entire cottage and had indoor access to water. This place was beyond belief.

Removing his clothes, he slipped into the tub and turned on the water. It was freezing cold and his entire body tightened as it splashed on his skin. An idea came to him, and he climbed back out of the tub. In his leather bag were three chisels gifted to him by his grandfather. Choosing the medium-sized chisel, he climbed back into the tub and began to etch fire runes into its stone surface. His eyes flashed green as he focused on the runes. Suddenly, the water began to heat as it reached the level of the runes. Smiling, he sat the chisel down outside the tub and sank deep into the warm water.

After twenty minutes of scrubbing, he declared himself clean enough for anyone and tossed his dirty clothing in the tub to soak. If only he could etch runes into cotton, his clothes would always be clean.

Wearing his new green robe, he exited the inn and strolled through the marketplace once again. He walked for nearly a mile before he came across a stall selling weapons. Beautiful, gem-inlaid daggers were spread neatly on a marble countertop. Inside the stall were a variety of jeweled swords, some of them with colored blades. They were marvelous to behold, but he did not dare to touch them. They might hold strange enchantments that he was not prepared to handle.

An older, white-haired elf greeted him. He was tall and thin and wore a dark red robe. "You aren't from around here, are you?" he asked with a smile.

Yori detected no arrogance or disgust from this elf. "No," he replied. "I'm from Na'zora."

"I thought as much," the elf replied. "I visited there once, a few hundred years ago."

325

Yori had no idea these elves lived so long. "Did you enjoy it?" he asked, trying to make casual conversation.

"Not one bit," the white-haired elf responded. "Are you looking to purchase a weapon?"

"Actually," Yori said, "I'm hoping to learn about enchanting them."

Yori expected the elf to laugh, but instead he replied, "Interesting." Silence followed.

"Do you know where I might learn?" Yori asked.

"Let me guess," the elf began. "You forge weapons with a large furnace and a heavy hammer."

Yori nodded.

"That isn't how we do things around here. Here, we use magic in all aspects of the craft. I'm afraid you lack the necessary skill."

"What skill would that be?" Yori asked curiously.

"For starters, you don't have the correct blood. It takes an inborn magic that your kind do not possess." The man hesitated a moment before continuing. "That isn't meant as an insult. I am merely stating a fact."

"Then it's impossible for me to learn?" Yori was beginning to wonder if the entire journey was wasted.

"I didn't say that, exactly," the elf replied, considering the question. "You couldn't possibly forge the weapons using our method, and you could not enchant the gems." He scratched his chin as he thought. "You might be able to use our gems to complete the process, though. I'd be interested to see if it works."

Yori stood silent, confused by the man's words.

"I'm not sure an unenchanted sword could support the gem, though," he said, thinking out loud. "It would probably destroy it."

"I can craft a runed sword," Yori stated proudly.

The elf's eyebrows shot up. "Indeed!" he exclaimed. "That might work. I'd be interested to see the results."

"I'd be interested in working with you," Yori replied with a smile.

"Excellent," the elf replied. "You will find that most of my people prize learning and study, though not all will be so keen to have you as an apprentice. For now, you will be an amusing little experiment." The old elf chuckled. "You may call me Master Eldon."

Yori wasn't sure he liked the sound of being an experiment, but the man seemed decent enough. He had not treated Yori as an inferior being, and he seemed genuinely curious about combining the two magics. He was glad to have found someone willing to work with him, at least for a while.

Chapter 40

Dashing into town at top speed, Mi'tal finally arrived back at the palace. Without a moment's rest, he stabled his horse and ran into the palace to the prince's chambers. Inside, there was only a young page, tending to the prince's bed sheets. The boy paused and looked up as Mi'tal burst through the doors without knocking.

"Where is the prince?" he shouted to the boy.

"He's at the barracks, sir, practicing drills with his troops," the boy replied.

Mi'tal raced off down the corridor and back outside the palace. The barracks were nearby, but he was already beginning to tire from his sprint through the palace. Mustering all of his strength, he raced down the path to the barracks. He could hear the sound of swords clanging in the rear of the building and made his way to the source of the noise.

The prince was sparring with a soldier as Mi'tal arrived. "Your Highness," he called. "I bring urgent news."

Aelryk immediately lowered his sword and rushed to Mi'tal. His opponent bowed as he walked away.

Moving forward to meet the prince, Mi'tal said, "The elves have indeed taken Princess Lisalla. They say there will be no peace until the king is dead." He made no mention of his declaration to the elves.

"Was she hurt? Did you speak to her?" The prince asked hurriedly.

"No, my lord," he replied. "I was bound myself and was not given the chance."

"We must rescue her," Aelryk replied. "My father isn't going to do anything to help. He will only attack the elves and make her situation worse. If they want my attention, they've got it."

"What do you propose for a rescue?" Mi'tal asked.

"I'm not sure," he began. "Do you think you can locate their camp again?"

"Yes, my lord, as long as there isn't a heavy snowfall. However, I wouldn't expect them to stay in the same place. They know I'm aware of their location."

"Then we'll have to act fast before they can move far." The prince's dark eyes narrowed as he asked, "How many soldiers do they have?"

"I couldn't say for sure. They made mention of other clans that had joined them, so there could be many more than there were. If all of the clans have joined forces, our own numbers could be outmatched. I have no idea how many might dwell west of the river."

A guard from the palace marched purposefully toward the prince and bowed. "Your Highness, the king has requested your presence in his council chambers."

With a nod, Aelryk said, "I'm on my way." He gestured for Mi'tal to follow him as he walked back to the palace. He walked slowly, not caring if he kept the king waiting. As they reached the council chambers, Aelryk said, "Wait here. It shouldn't be long."

Inside the council chambers, the king sat casually in his high-back chair. The councilors stared at Aelryk as he entered.

"Now that you're here, we can begin," the king said. "I have received a message from King Olin of Ra'jhou. He has heard that his daughter was captured by outlaws and is threatening war with Na'zora if she is harmed. He says we are responsible for her safety, and if we do not secure her release, he will declare war."

The councilors murmured to one another but did not raise their voices loud enough for the king to hear.

"What are you going to do about it, Father?" the prince asked.

"Nothing," he replied.

The stunned councilors looked at the king in shock. Glancing at each other, they wondered which of them would speak first. Failing to find their courage, the men remained silent.

Staring at the councilors with contempt, Aelryk said, "I will tell you what these fools will not. You cannot risk open war with Ra'jhou while you are still fighting with the elves. What if the elves return Lisalla to Olin in exchange for his alliance?"

"Then I will just have to crush Ra'jhou as well as those elves," the king said dismissively. The threat from Ra'jhou clearly meant nothing to him.

"How do you expect to win such a fight?" the prince asked.

"I have reinforcements on the way. They will tip the scale in our favor once and for all."

Aelryk had no idea who the king might be speaking of. "Are you going to elaborate?"

"No," he replied. "You're dismissed."

"Father-" the prince began.

Domren cut him off, shouting, "Dismissed!"

Knocking his chair over as he stood, the prince replied, "I will find Lisalla, and I will secure her release. If you continue your reckless fighting, it will be the death of this kingdom." He stormed out of the room, leaving the cowardly councilors behind.

Mi'tal followed the prince away from the council chambers.

"Could you hear that?" the prince asked.

"Yes, my lord," he replied.

"My father is a fool," Aelryk began. "Ra'jhou has a massive army, and they have defeated us in battle in ages past. Risking war with them is irresponsible. If they ally with the elves, there may be nothing left of Na'zora or her people."

Mi'tal nodded sympathetically. "I agree that is a risk we should not take."

"We must find Lisalla and get her to safety before the elves can bargain her to King Olin. There is no other way."

"Of course, my lord," Mi'tal replied.

"You look like you've ridden through a nightmare, my friend." The prince managed a weak smile. "I will have one of my father's lieutenants prepare my troops and round up as many mages as he can find. You should go and rest. We'll head out in the morning."

"Do you plan to attack the elves?" he asked. "They may harm the princess if they see you coming."

"They allowed you to live long enough to speak with them. I'll have to hope they do the same for me. I will insist on her release and only attack them if she has been harmed."

"My lord, I fear you are risking your future hopes for peace by riding into their forests. Wouldn't it be better if you stayed behind?"

"Only Lisalla matters now. Peace can wait."

Chapter 41

Master Eldon led Yori to the back of the shop where jewels were laid out on white marble tables. Blades, hilts, and pommels lay strewn about the table in various stages of completion. "I think you should focus on the simplest gems. Red, blue, green, and clear is a good start."

Yori stared up at the elf, a blank look on his face. He had no idea what Master Eldon meant by the colors.

"Shall we take a step back then?" the elf said, noticing Yori's puzzled expression. "You come to me wearing a green robe, meaning you know a thing or two of earth magic. Your gem of choice would be an emerald. Red represents fire which would require a ruby. Blue is water and uses a sapphire. Clear is the air, and it requires a diamond. That being said, there are all sorts of variants in gem colors, and each has its own purpose. You should stick to the basics."

"For now," Yori replied.

The old elf eyed him curiously. "Indeed." He seemed to be considering whether Yori would ever be capable of learning more. "One thing you should know right away is that any color in between will not work in the hands of a human or Wild Elf. Those enchantments would be far too strong for anyone other than an Enlightened Elf to control. Any shade of violet is going to have the most kick to it. Human mages have died trying to wield the power locked within those stones." He shook his head and chuckled to himself.

"So orange, yellow, white, and all the other colors are off limits?" Yori asked.

"Yes," Eldon replied. "You will not be able to enchant your own gems. That is a task for those of us who have spent long years studying the arcane sciences. Any gem you require will have to be enchanted here and shipped to you from the isles."

"You're assuming I won't be staying here," Yori pointed out.

Laughing, the elf replied, "I know it to be a fact." He lifted a ruby from the table and passed it to Yori. "What do you think of that?"

"It's hot," he replied, feeling the heat emitting from the stone. Holding it up to the light, he inspected its facets. "It's beautiful," he commented.

"Of course it is," the elf said. "I enchanted it myself. You can watch as I set it in the hilt I've prepared for this sword." Taking the gem back, he sat it on the table, his hand hovering slightly above it. The gem began to glow red, and sparks shot from its center. Untouched, the gem moved along the table to the hilt of a sword. Extending his other hand slightly higher than the first, he directed the gem to place itself inside the hilt of the sword. The metal glowed red for a moment before cooling back to a silver sheen.

Yori looked at the elf in amazement. "I've never seen anything like that. How did you craft the metal?"

"In nearly the same manner," Eldon replied. "We don't need hammers or forges. We use our own knowledge of the arcane to heat the metal and shape it to our whim. Few of us are truly masters of this craft." He held his head proudly in the air, looking down at Yori.

"How long does it take to learn all of that?" he asked curiously.

"It can take up to a thousand years to learn the process correctly," he replied. "You won't live that long, I'm afraid."

"I didn't know anyone lived that long," Yori remarked.

"I am two thousand and four years old. That is considered elderly among my people. Many are killed by their own experiments or in disputes with other sorcerers well before they reach my age."

"Sounds like a dangerous place," Yori commented. No sooner had the words escaped his mouth than the ground began to shake beneath his feet. He looked up at Eldon, his eyes wide with shock. "Did you do that?"

The old elf laughed again and shook his head. "No, that was our dear friend Yelaurad. He is mightiest among our gods and lives in the volcano on the Red Isle."

"The Red Isle?" Yori asked.

"Yes, it is a barren wasteland of red, scorched earth. The only thing that lives there is Yelaurad in his volcano. He likes to send us messages from time to time just to remind us he's still around. He belches smoke and rattles the ground. A rather obnoxious sort of god, that one." Eldon shrugged and turned his attention back to his work.

"How will I set these gems into the metal without your magic?" Yori asked.

"That is where the experiment comes in," the elf said, a twinkle in his bright blue eyes. "I assume you can read Ancient Elvish."

Yori nodded, eager to prove his abilities.

"I have some scrolls in my tower that you should look over. They're rather elementary in their writing, of course, but I don't think that will bother one such as yourself. We use them to teach children, but perhaps you will find them useful."

Yori chose not to be insulted by Master Eldon's words. He was, after all, a child when it came to learning this new type of magic. He wasn't sure he would be able to learn it, but maybe with help from the runes he could figure out a way.

"You may stay with me during your studies," Eldon said. "I have apprentice quarters to spare." Shooing Yori from the shop, the old elf turned and cast a spell over it, sealing the entrance with stone.

"I take it you have no use for mechanical locks around here," Yori commented.

"No, those would be far too easy to break. It would take all of a sorcerer's power to break into my shop, and even then he would find the weapons inside useless. They will only respond to their master until I tell them to do otherwise."

This bit of information intrigued Yori. Enlightened Elf magic must be entirely different from any magic he would find in the forests. "With all the power you have, why do you need a conventional weapon?" he asked.

"We do not have an unlimited supply of power, though some of us have more than others," Eldon replied. "A weapon can carry hefty enchantments that are too draining for a sorcerer to conjure at a moment's notice. Also, you wouldn't want to cast a spell that could drain your entire magical store. Carrying a sidearm is the best way to go if you fear you may be attacked."

"Do attacks happen often?" Yori wondered out loud.

Master Eldon laughed. "All day long, young man."

He continued to laugh as they made their way down the street towards one of the stone towers. Each tower looked basically the same to Yori, and he wondered how people could tell their homes apart. He decided they must use magic for that as well and entered the tower behind Eldon.

The interior of the tower was breathtaking. The expanse of the room was surreal. What had seemed like a cold stone spire was warm and inviting. All around him, he saw ornately carved wooden furniture, white marble sculptures, and brass lamps shining brightly on every wall.

"There are quarters for you on the seventh floor," Eldon said, pointing at the spiral staircase. "Third door on your left. I trust you can find it yourself. I'll have one of my apprentices bring you those scrolls."

"Thank you," Yori said as he ascended the stairs. Arriving at his room, he was once again impressed. It was easily twice the size of the room at the inn, and it had multiple rooms for his use. There was a sitting area with tall bookcases lined with hundreds of different books, a laboratory room with vials, flasks, and all sorts of other equipment, and a large metal table with a glowing orb at its center. The bedroom held an enormous bed topped with deep red velvet cushions. Never in his life had he slept anywhere so fancy. These quarters were finer than any in the king's palace in Na'zora.

Setting down his leather bag, he headed to the window to take in his surroundings. From this height, he could see far into the distance. The sea lay before him, gleaming in the sunlight. Despite being

341

only midday, few people could be seen moving about the streets. Perhaps most of them had returned home already as Master Eldon had done.

A knock sounded from his door, and an elf in a red robe stepped inside. Under one arm, he clutched several scrolls. "These are for you," he said, placing them on the large wooden desk. "Master Eldon says to tell you a meal will be prepared in the next ten minutes. You're invited to join us." With a huff, the elf turned and exited the room.

"Thanks," Yori called after him. Clearly not everyone was thrilled about his presence here, but being snubbed didn't bother Yori in the slightest. He had come here to learn, not make friends.

Chapter 42

"Why are we waiting for dawn?" Sal asked. "Why not attack now, while the villagers are still sleeping?"

"Essa insisted," Reylin replied. "Since our weapons are much better, she insisted we at least wait until the people were awake."

"Ah," Sal said. "She's a true warrior, then. She wants them to put up a fight."

"It still won't be much of one," Reylin commented. "But two attacks happening at once will certainly send a message to their king. Essa and Nat will attack Duana with the rest of our army this morning, and we will burn Enald to the ground. Domren is going to think it's an invasion."

A thousand elven troops hid in the trees just outside the village of Enald. They waited for sunrise, when the villagers would begin to emerge from their homes. Children would not be attacked directly, but every adult was a fair target. The houses and shops were to be destroyed, forcing the humans out of their homes as the elves had been.

"I'm surprised this village has no lookouts," Sal remarked. "Do they not realize there is a war taking place in the woods?"

"They're going to realize it today," Reylin replied.

The snow had held off for the night, providing clear paths for the elves to make their way to Enald. By now, Essa's troops would be in position, allowing the elves to attack both cities at once. King Domren would be forced to retaliate and bring the war back into elven territory. Once there, they planned to have an even greater advantage.

As the sun finally began to peek over the horizon, the elves began descending from the trees. The shadowy figures of Enald's citizens began to move about the streets, preparing for their daily chores. The sword maidens readied the charge as the archers spread out to cover three sides of the town.

Reylana had agreed to lead the sword maidens while Essa went north. She waited a few moments to ensure the archers had reached their posts before giving the order to charge. Just as the streets began to fill, she lifted her sword, signaling the maidens to attack. They charged toward the city just as arrows began to fly through the air.

Screams erupted from the citizens followed by panic and chaos. The runed arrow tips hit their marks, causing homes and shops to burst into flames. Terrified citizens ran from the burning buildings, not realizing they were under attack. They ran straight into the charging sword maidens and were quickly cut down.

Reylana turned away as a woman dashed from her home cradling a small child in her arms. She could see no way of killing the mother without harming the child, so she did not pursue. The maidens broke formation, chasing fleeing citizens in every direction. The archers focused their fire on the town, destroying as much as possible.

As she pursued a man through the streets, Reylana caught sight of a stable full of horses that had caught fire. Seeing no reason to harm the animals, she ran inside and quickly opened their stalls, allowing them to run freely. Pausing for only a moment, she hoped the beasts would someday run free in the forests, should the forests manage to survive the war.

A large man with an iron bar approached her from behind. He grunted as he lifted the weapon, catching her attention just in time to step out of the way. Swinging the heavy bar again, he aimed for her head. Rolling to one side, she narrowly avoided the weapon, which struck the ground with a heavy thud.

The man was no fighter and was beginning to tire already. With difficulty, he tried to raise the bar once more over his head, but Reylana was too fast. From her lowered position, she swung her blade forcefully, striking the man in his thigh. Blood gushed from the wound, and he fell to one knee, clutching at his injured leg. From the amount of blood spraying from the wound, Reylana could tell it was fatal. Instead of wasting her time watching him die, she turned and ran back out into the streets.

The archers began to close in as the city burned. Catching sight of Sal and a few other silver-haired archers, Reylana ran to his position. "Where has everyone gone?" She had not seen a single citizen since coming back out of the stables.

"Most of them are running east," Sal replied. "It's been chaos since the moment we attacked. If we'd attacked them in their beds, I think we would have killed more of them."

"You're probably right about that, but destroying the town was more important than casualties." She left Sal and pursued the townspeople who had fled. Several sword maidens ran ahead of her in the distance. Unsure how far it was to the next town, Reylana hoped the women would not pursue too far. They were already dispersed and vulnerable should there be an army ready to retaliate.

Corpses lay strewn in her path as she continued to run. Apparently the elves were faster than Enald's average citizen and had managed to catch quite a few of them. The sun rose high in the sky, and Reylana decided it was best to regroup. She raised her sword, reflecting the sun's rays in her runed blade. A white light projected hundreds of feet ahead of her, and the sword maidens stopped running as they caught sight of it.

"Regroup!" Reylana shouted as loudly as she could. She hoped the maidens who were farthest away had gotten her message. She continued to shout until she could see the women returning to her position. "We need to get everyone back together," she said as the women approached. "We've spread out too far, and we should get back to the archers."

One by one, the women returned to Reylana. Once they had all gathered, they ran back to Enald to rejoin Reylin's troops. Reylin strode through the center of the town, a large smile on his face. The entire city was smoking, and there were no signs of any of its citizens.

"How's that for forcing people from their homes?" Reylin asked as he approached his sister.

"I just wish we had more of those arrow tips," Reylana replied. "We should gather any metal we find for our smiths."

"Good idea," Reylin said. "I saw a smithy just at the edge of town." Reylin pointed to his left.

Nodding, Reylana took two of her sword maidens and headed for the smithy. The rest of the elven army regrouped at the center of the town. They cheered their victory and dared the king to send an army for them to fight. Their blood was running hot, and they were eager to continue the battle.

Chapter 43

Smoke filled the sky over the city of Duana as Essa rallied her troops to the edge of town near the forest. Their dawn attack had taken the city completely by surprise, sending its panicked citizens running in all directions. Their marketplace was completely destroyed, and the elves had grabbed anything they deemed of value. They had found a few new weapons as well as a small store of arrows.

Nat and his archers had discovered a merchant stall full of lamps and oil which had provided the fuel to burn the city. Not only had they saved runed arrows from waste, but they had also been able to toss the burning lamps at the mobs of citizens who tried to flee. No elven lives had been lost, and the town was destroyed with very little fighting.

Essa raised her sword in victory as her troops gathered at the tree line. They were still eager to fight, and they cheered loudly as they raised their weapons high in the air. The celebrations came to an end as the high pitched whinny of a horse broke through the air. An army had come to pursue the elves.

"Reform the charge!" Essa commanded, turning to face the sound of hooves. Through the smoke, she could just make out the silhouette of horses coming their way.

The archers quickly ascended the trees and waited for a clear shot. As the horses broke free of the smoke, the elves loosed their arrows. Fire rained down upon the Na'zorans as the runed arrows exploded. Frightened horses threw their riders and fled. Many of those riders were quickly trampled by the horses still coming from behind.

The archers continued to shoot, sending more riders to the ground as their horses were struck with fire. The maidens stood ready behind the trees, hoping for their chance to join the fight. Once the remaining horses reached the tree line, they wouldn't be able to stay in formation. Their riders would be at the mercy of the elven blades.

Prince Aelryk and Mi'tal had managed to stay on their mounts despite the fire from the elves. Their mages were somewhere toward the back of the line, probably stumbling over fallen soldiers as they tried to rejoin the group. Aelryk had not expected to find Duana under attack, and he didn't realize the elves had acquired such weapons.

The elves continued to fire relentlessly from the trees. Aelryk turned his horse and signaled his troops to follow. The mages needed to blast the elves out of the trees if his troops were to have a chance at fighting them. While they remained aloft, he could not hope to advance.

Near the rear of the line, he found the mages. All of them still remained on their mounts, awaiting the prince's orders.

"I need you to concentrate fire on those trees. We have to take care of those archers."

The mages began conjuring their fire, and after a few moments they began to fire white streaks of lightning at the trees. The arrows stopped flying, but there was no sign the elves had been injured. As the mages ceased their fire, a strange silence filled the air.

Nat climbed ever higher among the branches until he felt he was in the proper position. Licking a finger and holding it skyward, he tested the direction of the wind. Knocking a runed arrow to his bow, he aimed high in the air. His arrow flew, arcing high out of sight. Silently, he counted down from ten. As he reached one, he heard the sound of his arrow hitting its mark. Smiling to himself, he began descending the branches.

The arrow landed in the midst of the mages, exploding as it hit the ground. All six of them were thrown from their mounts as the terrified beasts were burned with fire. Two of the mages were trampled to death as the horses fled. Aelryk's horse was visibly frightened, and it took nearly all of his strength to keep it under control.

Mi'tal rushed to the prince's side. "We've lost too many to pursue the elves into the woods, my lord."

Nodding in agreement, the prince replied, "That was only their archers. I'm betting their swordswomen have improved their weapons as well. We have to retreat."

"What of Lisalla?" Mi'tal asked.

"We'll have to find another way," he replied, looking off into the woods. "We must return to the palace and gather the rest of our army."

Mi'tal sounded the retreat. From the forest, cries of victory could be heard as the Na'zorans sped away. The archers descended from the trees to celebrate with the sword maidens on the ground.

Essa made her way over to Nat. "Well done," she said, clapping him hard on his back.

He nodded and smiled proudly at her.

"We mustn't give them a chance to return," Essa said. "We'll head for the troll forest immediately."

The elves began to make their way to the section of evergreen forest known as the troll forest. Legend states that thousands of years ago, before the Wild Elves came into existence, this section of forest was home to horrible, vicious trolls. Now, it would serve as cover for the elves if the Na'zorans managed to locate them.

"Does Reylin know to meet us here?" Nat asked as he walked.

"Yes," Essa replied. "We discussed everything before our group traveled north."

"I hope they've had as much success in the south as we had here."

The elves continued to cheer and sing songs of victory as they marched. The winter air could not chill their spirits as they celebrated. They had destroyed the homes of many humans and sent their army fleeing in fear. The tide of the war had finally turned in their favor, and the victory tasted ever so sweet.

Chapter 44

Yori pushed his chair away from the desk and rubbed the back of his neck. After hours of staring at the scrolls, he was no closer to learning how to set the gemstones without using magic. The bits and pieces he could make out suggested various spells, but he had no idea how to go about casting them. Clearly, these scrolls were not designed for his type of magic.

A knock came from his door, and one of Eldon's apprentices called to him. "Master Eldon would like a word with you. He's on the first floor. Don't keep him waiting."

Relieved to have an excuse to stop studying, Yori began the long walk down the spiral staircase. As he neared the bottom, the ground began to shake violently. He clutched at the handrail to stop himself from falling on his face. No other elf in the room seemed to notice the trembling, and they casually went about their business. Once the shaking subsided, Yori proceeded down the stairs to find Master Eldon.

"Ah, there you are," Eldon said as Yori approached. "Have you had any luck with those scrolls?"

"Not really," Yori admitted. "They all suggest spells, but I don't think I could cast them."

"I'll just have to do a bit of research on my own, then," Eldon replied, shaking his head. "Let's head over to the shop, and I'll show you how I forge a dagger." Standing, he clapped his hands loudly, calling two of his apprentices to his side. Both of them wore red robes and hateful expressions. "Come along," he said.

Yori followed a few steps behind the sorcerers. So far, the apprentices had not been kind, and he preferred to stay out of their way. Angering someone who could set you on fire just by looking at you didn't seem like a good idea.

Master Eldon waved his hands in front of the shop, and the solid wall of stone dissolved once again. Strolling inside, he mumbled some instructions to the two apprentices and sent them away. "This way, Yori," he said, as he approached his workbench.

Eldon placed a flat sheet of steel on the workbench and hovered both hands a few inches above it. Closing his eyes, he focused his energy into the metal, which took on an orange glow. As the color flickered, Yori could tell the steel was the right temperature for shaping. Master Eldon began to wiggle his fingers slightly, keeping his wrists and arms perfectly still. Yori stared in disbelief as the form of a blade took shape in the center of the glowing metal sheet.

"Unbelievable," Yori whispered.

Having finished his work, Eldon dropped one hand to his side and began to move the other hand in a circular motion. A bluish tint came over the dagger to cool it, and tiny sparks flew from the edge as he sharpened it without the need of a grinding stone. Once he was satisfied, he lifted the blade and handed it to Yori.

"Try etching some runes into that," Eldon said. "I'll make a hilt for you."

Yori accepted the blade and took out his chisels. He wasn't sure which runes he should etch, so he chose a simple set of runes that would prevent the blade from becoming dull. By the time he had finished, Eldon had already crafted a simple hilt for the dagger.

Looking at the runes on the blade, Eldon smirked. "You couldn't think of anything better than that?"

Yori shrugged apologetically. "I've never added fire to a blade before. I've added fire to arrow tips, but with blades I've only added runes to improve its function."

"Don't you think adding fire to it would improve its function?"

"I wouldn't want it to explode in someone's hand," Yori commented.

"That's not how it works." Eldon thought for a moment and added, "Unless of course you etch something that will cause it to explode. You need to learn another word for fire." He strode over to a shelf and took out a large blue volume on weapon crafting. Yori could not make out the full title, but the words "blade" and "enchantment" were clearly visible.

Thumbing through the dusty volume, Eldon found a suitable page and laid the book on the table. Pointing at a graphic of a partially crafted hilt, he said, "Examine this closely."

Yori looked at the picture and tried to make out the words in the description. Clearly, a red gem was being added to the hilt of the sword. The pieces Yori could read stated: *Fire strengthens steel, giving the wielder an advantage. The heat will radiate at various levels, burning one's opponent, shooting sparks in an attacker's eyes, melting the enemy's weapon, and sometimes melting the opponent himself.*

Realizing what he had just read, he stared up at Master Eldon, his jaw dropping open.

Upon seeing Yori's expression, Master Eldon nearly burst with laughter. "It's quite amazing what you can do with gemstones, is it not?"

Nodding his head, Yori replied, "It certainly is."

"Now," Eldon began. "Try etching something more along those lines. I can bring you a dictionary if you need me to." The old elf chuckled quietly.

"That won't be necessary," Yori replied. He knew just what to etch next. Turning the blade to the other side, he began etching again. This time, he chose a derivative of fire that also insinuated strength and passion in the ancient elven tongue.

Master Eldon watched and nodded approvingly as Yori completed his work. "Excellent choice," he declared. "Now let's see if you can set a gemstone into this hilt." With a magical burst, Eldon opened a drawer that contained various gems laid out on a soft cushion. Choosing a small red stone, he said, "This one should do nicely."

Using the same method his uncle had taught him, he delicately set the precious stone into the metal. The dagger glowed red, but after a few seconds the color faded away. Even the etched runes lost their small amount of color as the pair stared in disbelief.

"What would cause that?" Eldon asked, scratching his chin.

Yori shook his head. "I guess that gemstone didn't like what I did to it." He had no idea why the runes would lose their effectiveness, but it had to relate to the gem or the magic contained inside it.

"I'm going to have to fix this," Eldon declared, turning the blade in his hand. "This is going to require more research on my part. I might have to visit the university."

The sound of footsteps told Yori the apprentices had returned. They walked in stride with one another as they approached the workbench where he sat. As Yori looked over his shoulder at them, they glanced at each other and shook their heads. He turned away, hoping they would keep their comments to themselves.

"Here, hold this," Eldon said, passing the dagger to one apprentice.

"Achh!" the elf shouted as he dropped the dagger and staggered backwards.

Eldon chuckled. "At least that part still works."

The apprentice retrieved the dagger from the floor and glared at Yori as he handed it back to his master.

"You two should take this young elf to see the duel. I'm going to head over to the university for a bit." Eldon turned to Yori and said, "We'll continue this lesson in a day or so. I'm sure I can find something by then."

Eldon hurried off, leaving Yori behind with the two apprentices. He stood and managed a weak smile. The apprentices looked at each other and rolled their eyes.

"So what are you, anyway?"one of them asked.

"An elf from the Wildlands," Yori replied, not bothering to mention his human blood. He knew that would only make him more disgusting to their eyes.

The elf shrugged at his answer. "Let's go," he said.

After magically sealing the shop, they continued down the street through the massive marketplace. Yori would have enjoyed stopping to browse the wares, but he barely had time to glance at the shops as he matched the hurried pace of the apprentices.

At last they arrived at a large coliseum. The entire structure was made of polished white stone that sparkled in the sunlight. Inside, hundreds of spectators had gathered to witness the daily duel.

"What are they dueling about?" Yori asked.

"Does it matter?" one apprentice replied. "They have some dispute, and they've come here to settle it."

"How do you determine the winner?" Yori asked, fearing the answer.

Both apprentices laughed at the question and continued inside the coliseum. They found seats near the upper row just before the duel began. Two sorcerers, one in a blue robe and one in brown, stood at the center of the stage. Neither carried any visible weapons as they paced, sizing each other up.

Without warning, the blue sorcerer shot sparks at his opponent, who barely had time to put up a shield. As the sparks faded, the brown sorcerer was already wrapping his opponent in what appeared to be some sort of webbing. Yori glanced over at the apprentices, who sat on the edge of their seats. A blue light flashed, and the blue sorcerer was somehow freed of his bonds. The crowd roared with excitement. Yori remained silent, unsure how to respond. He assumed the spell must have been rather difficult if it could impress this crowd.

The brown sorcerer wasted no time in attacking again. This time, he emitted a green light from his fingertips, enveloping the blue mage in some type of sphere. The sphere began to fill with water until it burst, freeing the blue sorcerer from his prison. He quickly shot a stream of blue light at the brown sorcerer, hitting him in the face and knocking him off balance.

The brown sorcerer hit the ground hard, and the blue sorcerer stood over him triumphantly. A purple glow encircled his hands as he prepared for his final attack. The brown sorcerer, however, was not yet finished. With a swipe of his foot, he knocked the blue sorcerer to the ground and pummeled him with an unseen energy attack. The force of his blows drove the blue sorcerer into the earth itself, leaving a shallow pit in the center of the arena. Shaking his hands as if to dry them, he commanded the dirt to fill over the top of the blue sorcerer.

The elves jumped to their feet, cheering the victory of the brown mage. Yori was the only person in the coliseum to remain seated. Never before had he witnessed such a scene. One elf had clearly killed the other in front of hundreds of witnesses, yet no crime had been committed. Disputes in the Sunswept Isles were apparently settled in this fashion, and the crowds enjoyed it immensely. Yori wondered what two people might fight over that would require such drastic measures. Surely they could have settled their dispute more peacefully.

The crowd began to disperse, and Yori followed the apprentices back to Eldon's tower. The old sorcerer had not yet returned home, so Yori proceeded to his room to await dinner. He sat down in front of the desk and once again looked over the scrolls. Reading, he hoped, would take his mind off of the spectacle he had just witnessed. He chose a scroll about purple gems and studied it closely, hoping to forget about reality for the time being.

Chapter 45

King Domren sat tall and proud on his throne as Aelryk stormed into the throne room. "There you are," the king said. "I've been awaiting your return."

Bowing before his father, the prince said, "My men and I were forced to retreat. The elves have acquired some very powerful weapons. They killed nearly a quarter of my men, and wounded hundreds. The city of Duana has been decimated."

"Yes," the king said. "Enald has been destroyed as well. It's very clever of them to take out two market districts."

Aelryk glanced back at Mi'tal, who was standing at the back of the room. Mi'tal's face wore an expression of surprise. The news that elves had managed to attack and destroy two of Na'zora's largest cities was shocking. "What is your plan, Father?"

"The college has sent over a little gift." The king's face broke into a wide smile. "Months ago I ordered them to cease all training that did not involve battle skills. I now have fifty mages at my command who are ready for war."

The disbelief was clear on Aelryk's face. He had been kept completely in the dark about his father's plan. "So you've been planning this all along, yet you did not bother to share it with me."

"That's right," the king replied. "Why should I? You've been against this war from the start." He leaned forward, taking a closer look at his son. "You are a magnificent leader, and your men would follow you into the sea if you rode there." He frowned, adding, "Unfortunately, you are weak. You don't have the stomach to do what must be done. You'd have tried to talk me out of it had you known my intentions. I didn't want to listen to your whining."

Aelryk could feel the heat rising to his face. "Whining? All I've ever tried to do was offer you sound advice. It's more than I can say for those pitiful dolts you call councilors."

"My son, if you're going to be king you must learn a thing or two." He sat back in his chair and shook his head. "Councilors who disagree with you can be replaced. The rule of Na'zora belongs to one man alone. Someday that man will be you, and I expect you to uphold your father's legacy."

Aelryk stared at his father, maintaining his silence. No one in the room dared to speak. The councilors who were present didn't even dare to glance at one another, for fear of making a sound.

"Prepare your troops," the king said, cutting through the silence. "We will be riding out again tomorrow."

"We don't know where the elven army is," the prince pointed out.

"Yes, we do," the king stated proudly. "Orzi has given me their precise location." So far, the prophet had not been wrong in his advice to the king. His words were golden to the king's ears.

With a bow, Aelryk turned on his heels and strode to the door. Mi'tal followed closely behind as he exited. Once they were outside in the sunlight, the prince paused to speak.

"Did you have any knowledge of these mages?" the prince asked.

"Not in the slightest, my lord," Mi'tal replied. "I would assume only General Luca was aware of it. He would never divulge the king's secrets. Not to me, at least."

"Nor to me, it would seem." The prince stared at the ground, lost in thought.

"Shall I prepare the troops, my lord?" Mi'tal asked.

With a sigh, the prince replied, "Yes. If my father is riding into battle, we must go as well. Once those mages are unleashed, Lisalla may be in grave danger. Without us, there will be no chance of stopping my father. He won't care if the princess is among the casualties as long as she's accompanied in death by many elves."

* * * * *

Three days of riding brought the king's army within range of the elven encampment. Their arrival, however, had not gone unnoticed. Scouts had seen them approaching, and the elven army was given a day to prepare for the coming battle. Reylin's troops were low on arrows and had busied themselves crafting more. Unfortunately, they did not have enough time to craft new metal tips and were having to make do with sharpening the wooden shafts. Essa's troops still had a small amount of runed tips, and they planned to use them wisely. They would only be shot into the largest groups of enemy soldiers, in hopes of taking down as many men as possible with a single arrow.

The sun was already high in the sky when the scouts sent word that the enemy had arrived. The archers began ascending the trees, taking cover in the thick evergreen boughs.

"All sword maidens split into small groups," Essa told the women. "Find a place low in the branches where you can take cover, but be ready to strike at a moment's notice. We want to avoid the possibility of a mounted charge, but once the forest has forced them to disperse, we must be ready to fight."

The women began choosing their groups and setting off into the woods. The elves would not meet the Na'zorans at the edge of the woods. Instead, they would force the humans to come deep into the forest if they wanted to fight. The archers would be ready to fire as soon as they came within range.

King Domren commanded the troops to wait as the mages rode to the front of the line. The battle mages had been confident they could fire far enough from the tree line to avoid the elves' arrows. They stopped well away from the forest's edge to prepare their attack. Ten of the mages formed a circle around the rest and spread their arms wide. Focusing their eyes skyward, the mages began to chant. White magic encompassed the entire party, forming a protective barrier. The battle mages were now free to begin their work.

With great effort, the mages conjured their blasts in groups of four. They touched their palms together, forming a link that concentrated their efforts into a single spell. Half of them chose to create massive fireballs, while others focused on energy blasts. Once their spells were prepared, the shielding mages dropped their protective layer to allow the battle mages to fire. As they sent blast after blast into the forest, the earth began to shake. Limbs were flying through the air as trees were struck, and dirt and debris spewed in every direction.

The elves, who were expecting magefire, clung tightly to the trees. The force of the blasts were much stronger than they had been before, and the archers were unable to return fire. All of their energy was focused on grasping the limbs to stop themselves from falling. Smoke began to rise as parts of the forest caught fire. Energy blasts continued to pound the forest, tearing pits into the earth and toppling trees.

Smoke and dust filled the air as Reylin descended from the trees. Most of the other archers had already climbed down, unable to maintain their grip through the constant waves of magefire. "We should just fire in their direction," Reylin suggested. "Maybe we'll hit some of them."

"No," Nat replied. "We're going to need our arrows if they enter the forest. We can't waste them firing blindly into the smoke."

"He's right," Sal said. "The mages didn't come within range. I would have seen it from my position."

"What do we do then, run?" Reylin asked angrily.

"We should press deeper into the forest," Nat suggested. "They can't continue this onslaught. Their mages will tire soon enough, and then we can fight the rest of them on our own turf."

"Agreed," Sal replied.

Reylin remained silent but nodded his approval. His personal choice would be to unleash as many arrows as possible on the mages, but many elves may be lost in the process.

"Let's spread out and inform the sword maidens," Nat said, turning to leave.

Essa was already heading their direction to discuss the situation. "We need to fall back," she said as she reached Nat.

"That's what we decided as well," he said.

With a nod, she went to inform the women. Once the group was together, they marched deeper into the forest, hoping the army would pursue. If their mages ran out of power, the elves would have a fighting chance.

The mages continued pounding the forest relentlessly. Fires were burning throughout the forest, and giant limbs were snapped from the trees. In a show of force, the mages concentrated their fire to uproot a massive conifer which shook the earth as it fell. As the giant roots were ripped from the ground, dirt and rocks flew all around the Na'zoran army. The soldiers raised their arms to shield their eyes from the dust.

Domren signaled the army to move ahead. The mages were beginning to tire and had already been consuming potions to replenish their magical stores. Soon, they would all be useless. Magefire was a powerful weapon, but it had its limits.

Aelryk's troops moved ahead first. If he could find the elves before his father's men, perhaps he could negotiate Lisalla's release. As they moved into the woods, Aelryk could barely make out the figure of Mi'tal riding next to him through the haze of smoke filling the air. The men began to choke and cough on the thick, polluted air. The massive amount of debris on the ground was making passage difficult for the horses. They moved slowly, attempting to take careful steps, but many of them were still tripping and unbalancing their riders.

"We can't continue like this, my lord," Mi'tal called to the prince.

Aelryk held up a hand, signaling his men to halt. He knew Mi'tal was right, but his heart ached to continue forward. Somewhere in this forest was Lisalla, assuming she was still alive. "Perhaps I could go on alone and speak with the elves," he said.

"I wouldn't recommend it," Mi'tal said, coming closer to the prince. "I don't think they're going to be in a talking mood after that attack."

Sighing, Aelryk said, "You're probably right." He looked forward into the forest, hoping that Lisalla was safe and well somewhere among the trees. "Let's get back to the king." Turning their horses, the men moved out of the woods.

Domren rode forth as the prince emerged from the trees. "What's the problem?" he asked impatiently.

"You can't see an inch in front of your face in there," he said. "We'll be slaughtered if we try to follow those elves."

"If they made it through the smoke, so can you," the king protested.

"They can smell every branch in those woods. They know it by heart, and they don't need their eyes to navigate it. Maybe you should learn a thing or two about your enemy."

Domren glared at the prince. Turning his horse, he rode back to his troops. "General Luca," he called. "We've given them enough to think about for today. Let's get back to the palace."

The army began to move out, leaving the elves to their ruined forest. Aelryk took one last look over his shoulder, taking in the destruction. Where once had stood a tall, proud evergreen forest was now a burning pile of rubble. Hoping the destruction had not spread too far into the woods, he led his troops homeward. Once again, he had failed to find Lisalla and bring her to safety. He vowed never to fail her again.

Chapter 46

Fires raged all around as the elves fled deeper into the forest. The smoke was too thick to navigate by sight, but the elven scouts of the Mulberry Clan knew this forest by heart. Only a few hours away, their village lay in ruins. The elven army made its way through the evergreens to a dense deciduous forest. If the Na'zorans were in pursuit, they would have difficulty traversing the thick underbrush of these woods. Only the light-footed elves dared to enter this forest.

At the edge of the woods, they rejoined the small group of elves that had stayed behind. Lisalla was among them, her head bowed and her heart heavy. She had refused to speak or eat since Danna's death, and she had sworn to escape at the first opportunity.

No longer caring whether she survived, she decided that dying alone in the wild would be preferable to a senseless death at the hands of an angry elf. At the very least, she would die knowing she had tried to save herself. She did not intend to die weeping.

"This looks like a good place to stop," Essa said as they reached a dense grove of trees. "If they're behind us, we will have the most cover here."

For the next several hours, scouts came and went as they patrolled each direction in search of the Na'zoran army. There was no indication that they had been followed, and the sun was fading fast. As darkness began to overtake the forest, the elves settled in for the night.

"They must not have been able to make it through the mess they created," Reylana commented.

"They should be ashamed of themselves for damaging such a beautiful section of forest," Sal said. "Do these humans have any care for nature?"

"They only care about taking it away from us," Reylin replied. "They'll be back soon, and we need more weapons."

"How do you suggest we get them?" Essa asked.

"We raid more villages and take them away from the Na'zorans."

"I don't like that idea," Nat said. "They had about fifty mages with them. They could be posted anywhere along the border, and I'd rather not risk losing any more of our kinsmen."

Those who had been slain in the last battle had been left where they fell. In their hurry to flee the magefire, the elves had not had the chance to carry their bodies into the trees. Many of the fallen lay beneath massive trees that were uprooted by the energy blasts. Nothing could be done for them. The earth itself would have to accept the remains.

"I agree," Essa said to Nat. "We need weapons, but getting them from Na'zora is too dangerous. We don't know what they're planning."

"We know exactly what they're planning!" Reylin shouted. "They're planning to kill all of us and take every inch of the Wildlands for themselves!"

Reylana came to her brother's side and placed a hand on his shoulder. "There's no need to get angry." Her voice was calm and kind, but did little to soothe his temper.

"Your friends here are ready to give up. They want to hide in the woods and wait until the king dies so they can kiss the prince's ass."

"That prince is ten times the man you'll ever be!" A voice shouted from the darkness. Lisalla had once again been tethered to a tree. She could no longer contain her hatred for Reylin.

"Speak again and I will shove a rock in your mouth!" Reylana shouted. "You have no idea what my brother has suffered at the hands of these men. Our parents were murdered by your prince's father, so don't presume to know what kind of man the prince is. A dog does as its master commands!"

Lisalla did not reply. Aelryk was a far cry from his father, that much was certain. Though she did not know him, she had heard the words of his servant promising to make peace with the elves. In her heart, she knew the prince to be wise and fair.

"We aren't giving up," Essa said, "but I refuse to lead this army into a massacre. They probably expect us to run over and attack them. They'll be ready for it."

"We should wait and send more scouts to patrol the area," Nat suggested. "In the meantime, we can focus on crafting new arrows and making repairs to our weapons."

"That's a good idea," Sal replied.

"Agreed," Essa said. "We need to prepare ourselves for the next attack. We will need hundreds of arrows crafted. The next time we're attacked, we may have to use all of them on those mages."

"We would have done better in this battle if that damned half-breed rune carver had joined us," Reylana spat.

"So that's it then?" Reylin interrupted. "We just sit here and wait?"

"You don't have to sit," Nat answered. "We need you to help scout the area." He didn't understand Reylin's frustration.

"Shut up!" Reylin shouted. "No one was asking you. You're just some little fool we picked up. Your opinion is worth less than shit!"

"Reylin, please," Reylana said, attempting to soothe her brother. "Come and walk with me," she said. Taking Reylin's arm, she led him away from the others. Glancing back over her shoulder, she sighed as she looked at Nat. He had been a wise leader and a brave warrior, and she didn't want her brother to continue insulting him. She hoped he would calm down after he had a little time to clear his head.

"After everything I've done for them, they just replace me," Reylin said.

"They haven't replaced you," Reylana replied. "The army has grown, and other clans have to have their say. That's all it is, Reylin."

"They don't listen to me at all anymore. I'm nothing to them." He took a seat on a fallen log.

"They're going to let the Na'zorans run them out of the Wildlands. We'll have to hide across the river like the Sycamore Clan."

"That won't happen," she promised. "Not while I'm alive, at least." She sat next to her brother on the log and placed a hand on his back. "You are a valuable member of our army," she began. "Who knows where we'd be if it wasn't for your leadership in the beginning."

"The others don't see it that way," he said. "From now on, I'm going to do things my way whether anyone likes it or not. No one has to follow me."

"Get some rest," Reylana suggested. "I think we're all exhausted." She rose, leaving her brother alone with his thoughts. Heading for one of the campfires, she happened to pass Lisalla. She paused and looked at the woman as she sat motionless on the cold ground. "I'm getting something to eat. Do you want anything?"

Lisalla looked away from her and did not speak.

"You haven't eaten since your maid was killed," Reylana said. "Are you trying to follow her in death?"

Lisalla looked up at Reylana, her eyes cold. "What does it matter now?"

"I'll bring you some food, and you will eat it. If you don't, I'll shove it down your throat. We need you alive."

"Why?" Lisalla asked. "If the prince is like his father, he won't care whether I'm released."

"No, but the king of Ra'jhou might care." Reylana shrugged and continued to the campfire.

Lisalla remained silent and stared into the darkness. The moon glowed brightly overhead, and the chill of the night made her shiver. Fighting back tears, she thought of Danna and the days they had spent discussing frivolous matters such as weddings and shoes. Danna had deserved more out of life, and Lisalla had many regrets. If only she had found Danna a husband in Ra'jhou, she would still be alive. Lisalla could have easily traveled without her.

She cursed her father for sending her through a war zone. He must have known what was happening, but he did nothing to protect his daughter. What was he doing now? Would he make any attempt to save her? The uncertainty weighed heavily on her mind.

Closing her eyes, she wondered if anyone would care if she died. Perhaps Reylin or one of the others would murder her and leave her body lying in the woods until beasts scattered her to pieces and time claimed the rest. It didn't seem a fitting end for a princess, but that was her reality. Aelryk would find a new bride, and she would be forgotten. Her life had no purpose, and no one would mourn her passing. Unable to contain her grief, she wept softly, her warm tears splashing against her cold flesh. Winter's wind swept over her, and she welcomed its cold embrace.

Chapter 47

Lying on the soft bed in Master Eldon's tower,

Yori awoke just before dawn. His habit of waking early had not left him, despite being far from home. With no reason to get out of bed at this hour, he lay still, staring up at the ceiling. It was covered in wooden tiles, each one delicately carved into a different shape. Some resembled leaves or vines while others appeared to be a random geometric shape. Yori assumed they must be magical symbols of some sort, but he was unfamiliar with their meaning.

Out of nowhere, Master Eldon suddenly burst into the dark room. "I've got it!" he exclaimed.

Startled, Yori rolled over too quickly, not realizing he was so near the edge of the bed. He crashed onto the floor in an undignified position.

"Don't just lay there," Eldon scolded. "We've got work to do!" He spun around and disappeared into the hallway.

Picking himself up from the floor, Yori groped for his clothes in the darkness. He rubbed the sleep from his eyes and followed the white-haired elf down the stairs. Yori could have sworn he heard cheerful humming. Never before had he seen Eldon so excited. As they descended the stairs, the old elf continued to glance at Yori over his shoulder, grinning like a mischievous child.

As they reached the ground floor, Eldon rushed to his desk. Grabbing a scroll in his hand, he said, "Silver is the answer. I've found it right here." He pointed to a passage on the scroll, which Yori struggled to read. Obviously he was taking too long, and Eldon grew impatient. Tossing the scroll back down on the desk, he said, "Silver can hold the power you need."

Ripping open the front door, he marched down the street to his shop. Yori trailed behind him, still unsure of what he was talking about. He knew better than to question the sorcerer. He had already learned that they were easily offended and had no desire to anger his teacher.

As Yori arrived in the shop, Eldon was already digging through a wooden chest. "Here," he called to Yori. "Try this on for size." He tossed Yori a shining silver ring.

Yori slipped the cold metal band around his finger and immediately felt a surge of discomfort. A spark erupted on the surface of his hand, causing him to jump back. Frantically, he pulled the ring from his finger and dropped it onto the ground.

Eldon laughed hysterically, his hand holding his stomach. "I couldn't resist," he said through his laughter.

Yori stared at the elf, wondering if he'd lost his mind.

"Give it to me," Eldon said. "I'll remove my imprint so you can wear it."

With great care, Yori retrieved the ring from the ground. He handed it back to Master Eldon, who squeezed it tightly between both hands. In the blink of an eye, the enchantment was removed, and the ring was safe for Yori to use.

"Now you can see if this will work," Eldon said, handing the ring back to Yori.

"What do I do with it?" he asked.

"Stones of the purple variety add extra power to items which can greatly benefit a sorcerer. You, unfortunately, are not a sorcerer. Your tiny mind can't possibly hope to wield such power, so we must settle for the bare minimum."

Yori stared blankly at him for a moment. "I'm afraid I don't follow," he said.

"Of course you don't," Eldon replied with pity. "Silver can hold a power enhancing spell that should be safe for you to use. We can't add a purple stone, of course, because it would probably kill you. However, I believe you can etch runes that will enhance your power. Give it a try." The old elf smiled triumphantly. All of his studying on Yori's behalf was finally about to pay off. This was his solution, and now it was up to Yori to succeed or fail.

Taking a seat at the workbench, Yori's mind raced with the different possibilities of runes to carve into the ring. Whichever word he chose would determine the strength of the enchantment as well as its overall effect.

Settling upon a word, he took out his chisels and began etching. The runes formed a word he had learned while reading Master Eldon's scrolls. Not only did the word mean power, but it literally translated to "magical strength".

Peering over Yori's shoulder, Eldon nodded as the word took shape. "Excellent choice," he said.

Yori's eyes blazed with green fire as he completed the etching. The runes immediately responded with a purple glow. He placed the ring onto his forefinger and held it up to admire it. "This is an expensive gift," he said.

"Consider it an offering to one who is less fortunate," Eldon said. "Let's see if that's solved our problem."

He brought out the same dagger that Yori had worked on before. Eldon handed him a new red stone that felt warm to the touch. Taking a deep breath, Yori set the stone into the hilt and attached it to the blade. The entire dagger took on a faint reddish glow.

"Well done!" Eldon exclaimed. "I knew it would work. The answer was so simple I had forgotten it."

Yori beamed with pride. The ring had indeed done its job, providing him with the extra power he needed to set the enchanted stone without damaging it. He admired the dagger and glanced back at the ring on his finger. It felt warm as well, its runes shining brightly.

"It seems we're all finished here," Eldon said. "There isn't anything else I can teach you."

"Thank you for everything, Master Eldon," Yori said sincerely.

Waving his hand, Eldon dismissed the comment. "Don't forget to retrieve your things before you leave." He sat down at his workbench and did not look up again. It would seem their master and student relationship had come to an end. Yori took the hint and left.

The sun was just coming up as Yori walked back to Eldon's tower. Once again, he made the long journey to the seventh floor to retrieve the rest of his belongings. He packed his clothing into his leather bag and started back down the stairs. Chaos had erupted on the first floor as two apprentices were having an argument. They had resorted to tossing magical blasts at each other.

"I'll roast you alive!" one of them yelled.

"I'd like to see that, you lizard sucking coward!" the other replied.

Energy blasts flew through the room, toppling books and displacing the furniture. Master Eldon was going to be beyond angry when he returned home. Yori didn't understand how two such educated elves didn't have enough sense to take their fight outside, but he was not about to interrupt them. *I'm getting out of her just in time*, he thought.

As he made his way to the docks, Yori paused near the stall where he had purchased his robe. Hoping for one last glimpse of the pretty elf inside, he leaned his head into the shop. No one was around except for her father. Instead of risking his anger, Yori decided to keep moving.

The docks were already buzzing with activity at the early hour. Yori strolled over to the nearest ship and approached one of the sailors. "Are you heading to Al'marr?"

"We make a stop there before heading on," the man replied, looking slightly uncomfortable.

"Do you have room for a passenger?" he asked. "I can pay with silver."

The man glanced nervously from side to side. "No payment is necessary, sir. We'd be pleased to have you aboard."

Surprised by the generosity, Yori replied, "That's very kind of you." As he ascended the ramp to the ship's deck, he realized he was still wearing the green robe, and the sailor must have thought he was a sorcerer. He smiled to himself, pleased to have pulled off such an illusion. Perhaps his new ring had given him a more magical appearance as well.

After an hour or two, the ship was finally loaded and ready to set sail. Once again, Yori looked upon the vast blue of the ocean and felt its salty breeze on his face. This time, the sea was taking him home, but to which home still remained to be seen. With all the studying he had done on the isles, he had not spared a thought for where he would live. He stared out into the blue hoping that both of his families were safe from the war.

Chapter 48

Prince Aelryk rode to the front of the army to be at his father's side. "Father," he said. "I don't think you should lead this attack."

The king looked at him with disdain. "I don't care what that old wise-ass prophet has to say. I'm the most capable war leader who ever lived. Without my presence, these idiots will surely fail."

"But Father, Orzi has never been wrong. He has foreseen your death, and you should heed his words."

"Away with you!" the king shouted. "Go and lead your own troops. They're too stupid to do this without you."

Clenching his teeth, the prince turned and trotted back to his company. Stopping next to Mi'tal, he said, "My father is a fool."

Mi'tal remained silent, not wishing to openly criticize the king. He was well aware of Orzi's prophecy. A few days back, he had predicted that the king would fall in battle. Orzi, however, had not been specific about which battle and had simply stated that it would be in a battle against elves. King Domren had dismissed the warning, believing it impossible for him to be slain by elves. The prophet, however, had not mentioned whether it was an elf or human who killed the king.

"You must help me and keep a close watch over him, Mi'tal. He believes himself invincible, and that is a dangerous way of thinking."

"I will do my best to watch him, my lord," Mi'tal replied.

Up ahead, the king gave the signal to move out. Mages moved to the front of the line, preparing a shield wall to protect the king and those who would fight next to him. The elves were hidden deep in the forest, and there was the possibility of an ambush. The remaining mages were distributed within the ranks to avoid having the entire group wiped out in one shot. If the elves still had a store of exploding arrows, this would not be an easy battle to win.

They entered the forest at a snail's pace, each man holding his weapon at the ready. The elves could be hiding anywhere, waiting for the right moment to pounce. Silence filled the forest, broken only by the soft footfalls of the Na'zoran horses. King Domren rode proudly at the front, protected by his mages and personal guards.

As the army moved deeper into the woods, the elves had indeed been alerted to their presence. With great stealth, they eased their way through the trees, surrounding the human army. This time, they would not be defeated by the mages. Their first priority was to eliminate the conjurers before turning fire on the rest of the army. The sword maidens crouched in the thick brush, waiting for their opportunity.

A bone-chilling shriek pierced the air, disrupting the silence of the forest. Startled, the Na'zoran army came to a halt, searching for the source of the cry. In response, two more shrieks went up. The elven archers were announcing their presence and letting each other know that the army was now surrounded.

Arrows fired from all directions, striking the red-robed mages. Despite being surrounded by soldiers, they were easy targets to hit. The mages surrounding

Domren continued to hold their shield, hoping to protect the king and themselves. Soldiers moved in to protect the mages, but they too were pierced with arrows. Nearly half of the mages had fallen before anyone discovered the treetop locations of the elves.

Noticing the source of the arrows, the mages began to return fire. They blasted energy at the treetops, and the archers struggled to maintain their balance. The arrows kept coming but at a much slower rate. Some of the mages scrambled to protect one another with magical shields, while the rest continued to fire.

With most of the mages subdued, the sword maidens sounded the charge. Essa dove into the melee first, her broadsword coming down hard on the thigh of a mounted soldier. From behind the soldiers, Reylana's group charged into the action. Their battle cries startled the horses, sending many riders to the ground.

Chaos descended upon the ranks, sending men in all directions as the maidens charged into the fray. The archers continued to fire relentlessly, focusing mostly on the mages. As the mages continued to use power to shield one another, they were quickly becoming too drained to return fire. Their magical strength weakening, they were unable to shield each other on every angle, and the archers wasted no time exploiting the weakness.

Reylin could see that the battle was in his favor, so he decided it was time to use his last few runed arrows. Knocking one to his bowstring, he aimed for the center of the army where no maidens had yet invaded. Loosing the arrow, he watched with pride as it struck the ground, sending flames and sparks into the enemy ranks. Men scattered and horses reared in fright, throwing their riders. Nat and Sal followed suit, releasing the last of their runed arrows as well.

Aelryk managed to avoid the flames and keep his balance on his horse. Mi'tal sat on his mount, ever-faithful at his prince's side.

"Can you see the king?" Aelryk cried.

Mi'tal craned his neck to see over the fighting. As he did so, a sword maiden charged him, swinging her sword wildly. Without a moment to spare, he maneuvered his horse out of the way, sending the maiden crashing into another soldier. He caught a glimpse of a shield wall that still protected the king. "He's up ahead, my lord," he called to the prince. "He is still protected."

The prince's horse was struck with an arrow, sending the poor creature into a panic. It threw Aelryk violently to the ground as it attempted to outrun the pain. Mi'tal immediately dismounted to help the prince to his feet. Grabbing Aelryk's hand, he pulled him upright. The men barely had time to draw their weapons before two sword maidens rushed in on their position.

Mi'tal swung his hammer with great force, coming down hard on the maiden's arm. The bone cracked audibly, and she dropped her sword to the ground. Her fighting spirit was not quelled, however, and she grabbed a dagger from her leather bodice. Once again she advanced on Mi'tal. With another swing of his hammer, he landed a fatal blow to her skull.

Mi'tal searched the crowd to find that the prince had managed to fight off his attacker as well. The mages' shield was no longer glowing in the distance, and Aelryk was pushing his way through the crowd in an effort to reach his father. Mi'tal saw an opening to the side and took it. If he could reach the king before Aelryk, he might have a chance to end the war. He had no intention of fighting the prince, should he choose to defend his father.

The few mages who were left continued to bombard the trees with energy blasts. None of them had the strength left to produce fire, but they could still dislodge a few elves from the trees. Three of them concentrated their blasts at what they believed to be the most aggressive archers. They were firing more rapidly than the others, and the mages were determined to take them out. With their powers combined, they fired an enormous bolt of lightning at the tree. As it fell, its massive roots were ripped from the earth, and elves came tumbling from the limbs. Reylin was among them, his right leg shattering as he hit the ground.

With every ounce of his strength, Reylin pulled himself back to his feet. The fallen tree would provide some cover, allowing him to continue to fight. His broken leg was bleeding heavily, and he could barely breathe through the pain. As he moved a hand over his chest, he could feel that several ribs had been broken when he came crashing out of the tree. Steadying himself as best he could, he knocked an arrow and searched the crowd for any sign of Domren.

Chapter 49

Managing to avoid the raging battle, Mi'tal moved quickly toward the king. He had been dismounted and was swinging away at a sword maiden. His guards were focusing on the elves as well and would never suspect Mi'tal's true intent. Tightening his grip on his hammer, he made his way behind the king. His heart raced as he lifted the hammer high into the air, intending to kill with a single blow. *For Na'zora,* he thought. He was certain the king's guards would immediately strike him down, but his life was a small price to pay to free his kingdom from tyranny. He hoped that Aelryk would forgive his treason one day and remember him as the friend he had always been.

Out of nowhere, an arrow struck the king through the neck just as Mi'tal's hammer was about to come crashing down. The king toppled to the ground with the arrow still sticking out of him. Blood gushed from the wound, staining his bright armor a crimson red.

"Save the king!" a guard shouted as soldiers rushed in to lend aid.

Aelryk, who had not managed to make it to the king's side, looked to the tree line where the arrow had originated. A lone red-haired archer stood, leaning to one side. It was obvious he was wounded, but the prince felt no pity. He plowed through the fighting, knocking soldiers and sword maidens alike out of his path. Reylin looked up as the prince approached, but made no effort to defend himself. He was far too weak from blood loss, and his broken ribs prevented him from taking in a full breath. With a single stroke of his sword, Aelryk slashed Reylin's chest. Blood poured from his mouth as he fell to his knees, collapsing onto the soft earth.

Hurrying to his father's side, Aelryk once again blasted through the crowd. The king lay motionless on the ground, his eyes staring blindly at the sky. Aelryk felt a chill on his spine as winter sent a cold blast of air against the perspiration on his skin. His father was dead.

"You are our king now," Mi'tal said, coming to his side.

Aelryk stared blankly at his father's body, not hearing Mi'tal's words.

"Your Majesty," Mi'tal said, attempting to catch Aelryk's attention. He laid a hand on the prince's shoulder. "You are our king. You can put an end to this war."

Aelryk looked up at him, the shock of his father's death being put aside. Remembering his promise of peace to the elven people, he nodded to Mi'tal and patted him on the shoulder. Now the king of Na'zora, he had sworn to put an end to the fighting.

"The king is dead!" he shouted to the soldiers. The ground fighting continued, but at the sound of the prince's voice, the few remaining mages ceased their fire. "Stop this fighting at once!" he commanded, trying his best to shout above the noise. He feared the elves would not heed his words, but he intended to do as he had promised.

"Fall back!" he shouted. His words echoed throughout his army as the men did their best to break away from the fighting.

Hearing the prince's words, Essa commanded the maidens to stop as well. "Maidens to me!" she cried.

Reylana lowered her sword and backed away slowly from her opponent, who took the opportunity to retreat. As she turned, she caught sight of Reylin lying lifelessly on the ground. She ran to his side as tears clouded her vision. "Oh, Reylin," she sobbed as she fell to her knees beside his body. At the death of her parents, she had not wept openly. Her grief for her twin was far greater, and she could not hold back the tears.

Finally managing to take in a breath, Reylana ran deep into the forest. The war had claimed her brother just as it was coming to an end. *It's just as well*, she thought. *He never would have accepted peace.* Continuing to run deeper into the forest, she pushed the thoughts of her brother from her mind. The time would come to grieve more for Reylin, but for now, she had a mission to accomplish.

Aelryk moved to the front of his army to face Essa. He laid his sword flat across his hands and thrust it into the ground at her feet. Retrieving her sheathed blade from her scabbard, she thrust it into the ground beside his.

"From this day forth, let us have peace," Aelryk said.

"No elf will attack a citizen of Na'zora without provocation," she replied. "King Domren is dead, and you are now the king. You must ensure your people no longer attack us."

"I swear to you, I will see it done. I will draft a peace treaty along with the leaders of the elven clans. Together we will come to terms and end this fighting."

Essa nodded, her eyes fixed on Aelryk. She believed him to be a man of his word, and she intended to be a part of his peace treaty. "The elven leaders will negotiate with you," she said. "We desire peace for our forests, just as you do for your citizens."

Aelryk extended his hand to Essa, who grabbed his forearm and gripped it tightly. Grasping hers as well, he looked into her stern, dark eyes. He felt a sense of relief that he had not encountered her during the battle. She was probably the fiercest warrior he had ever encountered, if she could be judged by her eyes alone.

From the trees behind Essa, a blonde-haired woman emerged followed by an auburn-haired elf. Reylana had brought Lisalla to her prince as an offering of peace. Lisalla hesitated and looked back at Reylana.

"Go on," Reylana said.

Lisalla drew in a deep breath and slowly made her way to her betrothed. Aelryk stood in awe of her beauty as she came ever closer. Her blonde ringlets danced on the wind, and her stunning blue eyes reflected the cold, piercing the frosty air as a needle through cloth.

Aelryk stepped forward and took Lisalla in his arms. They embraced for the first time, and Lisalla's eyes filled with tears.

"The king is dead?" she asked. Her voice was soft and quiet.

"He is," Aelryk replied.

"Perhaps it is for the best," she said quietly. "If he was half the tyrant I heard he was, Na'zora will be better for it."

"He was my father, Lisalla," Aelryk said. "He was also my king, and his loss pains me."

"Yes, but now you are the king," she replied with a smile. "Now you can have peace."

Aelryk turned his attention back to Essa. "Your delegates can return to the palace with us. I can guarantee their safe passage."

Essa, Reylana, Nat, and Sal all agreed to accompany the king to the palace. Some of the remaining clan Overseers would be sent, and at least five members of each clan would be present for negotiations. All of their futures depended upon this treaty, and none of the clans would be left out.

Chapter 50

After catching a ride on one of Al'marr's gem wagons, Yori found himself back in the village of Marrel. He had changed out of his green robe and donned the more comfortable clothing of the Wild Elves. Eager to see how his grandfather was faring, he hurried into the woods. The paths from the Sycamore village to Marrel were still worn, reassuring Yori that his clan had not been wiped out while he was away. He hoped they were safely settled on the far side of the river.

The snow had melted away, leaving a sogginess to the forest floor. A cold breeze stung his skin as it joined the moisture of the woodlands to create its icy blast. Though the Sunswept Isles were always warm and sunny, Yori happily accepted the winter of his homeland. His nose was reddened and his eyes watered thanks to the frozen air, but he did not complain.

Near the outskirts of the original Sycamore village, a scout called out to Yori from the trees. "Yori?" he called. "Is that you?"

"It is," he replied, scanning the branches above. He finally spotted the elf, who was waving happily as he sat among the treetops.

"Glad to see you've come back."

"Thanks," he replied. "Has the river frozen solid, or will I need to use a raft?"

"The Blue River never freezes," the elf replied. "You won't need to cross it, though. The war is over, and we've returned to our old village. The new king has promised peace."

Yori's heart leapt at the news. "That's good to hear!" he called. "Does that mean King Domren is dead?"

"Cold and stiff," the elf replied happily. "The new king is drafting a treaty with all of the clans."

"Then the prince kept his word," he commented. It was indeed good to hear that the prince had kept his promise. Peace had finally returned to the land, and the elves would no longer be driven from their homes.

"I'm just as surprised as you are," the elf replied.

Waving goodbye, he quickened his pace until he reached the village. Stopping at its edge, he gazed on his father's people. Elves moved here and there, going about their daily lives. Fresh elk meat was roasting, sending a pleasant aroma to his nostrils. His stomach growled in anticipation of the fine elven cuisine.

At the far edge of town, he saw his grandfather's furnace fire glowing a deep orange. The sound of the hammer let him know that Lem was hard at work, probably being yelled at by Darin. He hurried across the village to reunite with his family.

"Yori?" Lem was obviously surprised to see him.

A wide smile spread across Yori's face. "Yep," he replied. "I'm back. Where is Grandfather?"

"I'm sorry, Yori," Lem said, looking down at the anvil. "He's gone."

"Gone?" he replied, his heart sinking at the thought that the old elf had died.

"He's across the river helping them dismantle the forge. The stubborn old elf keeps insisting we should leave no trace that we were ever there. He says it's bad for the forest."

Yori sighed in relief. Seeing that his grandfather's workbench had been left messy, he set down his bag and began tidying the area. Various tools were strewn about, most likely left there by Lem. Without supervision, he was rather forgetful and a bit careless. The tools needed to be cleaned and properly stored to avoid unnecessary wear and tear. As Yori busied himself cleaning, he heard a familiar voice coming from the edge of the village.

"That's it. Set it right there and don't drop it. They can't be reused if they're all busted up." Darin was directing two elves carrying heavy loads of brick. One elf bent to place the bricks on the ground, but Darin shouted, "Not there! Over there!" He pointed off to his right. Shaking his head, the elf did as he was commanded.

Happy to see his grandfather hadn't changed in the short time he was away, Yori strolled to his side. "Are these guys giving you trouble?" he asked jokingly.

Darin turned around, wrinkling his brow. Seeing Yori, his face broke into a warm smile. "You've made it back," he said. Clapping Yori on his back, he added, "I'm glad those snooty islanders didn't roast you on a spit."

"I learned a lot from one of them," Yori replied. "Master Eldon taught me how to set their enchanted gems among weapons."

"Really?" Darin asked curiously. "Does it combine with the runes?"

"It does."

"You'll have to tell me all about it." He paused a moment and added, "That is, if you're planning to stick around."

"I'll stay a while if you'll have me," Yori said with a smile.

"You're always welcome here. Always." Darin put an arm around Yori's shoulders and said, "Come on. There's one more load across the river, and you can help us carry it."

Yori gladly accompanied the elves to the river. As the raft pushed away from the shore, Yori knelt and looked into the blue water. A silver mist swirled just below the surface, and he could not resist the urge to touch it. As he placed his hand lightly in the water, the runes of his silver ring flashed. The runes that had once been purple took on a faint blue tint. Removing his hand from the water, he inspected the ring. The band itself had taken on a bluish tint as well.

None of the others on the raft seemed to notice what had happened. Yori remained silent, not fully understanding what had occurred. Pressing the ring to his heart, he suddenly remembered a promise he had made. Perhaps the River God was reminding him to show him the path he should follow.

Once they reached the shore, Yori helped the elves load up the last of the bricks from the forge. As they crossed the river for the last time, Yori saw no sign of the being that lived in the water. Being blessed by the river's magic, he no longer felt uncertain about his future. He knew what he should do and where he should make his home.

"You seem a million miles away," Darin commented as they reached the shore.

"Just thinking," he replied. "I'm going to keep my promise to the prince," he declared. "He has kept his promise to us, and I should do the same."

Nodding, Darin replied, "I understand, but stay here with us for a few days. I like having you around." His green eyes sparkled as he looked upon his grandson.

"I will," he replied. "I hope I'm able to visit here once in a while. The forest is in my blood, and I don't want to stay away from it too long."

Chapter 51

Reylana paced anxiously outside the palace.

Na'zora's palace district was a far cry from her forest home. There were few trees and only tiny gardens spread here and there. The palace itself included a larger garden, but the winter's chill had claimed every plant.

"Stop pacing," Essa said. "You're making me nervous."

Halting in her tracks, Reylana took a seat next to Essa on the stone steps of the palace. "I bet the other clans are giving too much away," she said, shaking her head.

"They have to negotiate for themselves. If they stay strong, they will do as well as we have done."

"We're moving farther north than I had hoped," Reylana admitted. "I will miss the forests where I was born."

"That forest is no more," Essa said flatly. "There is a healthy forest waiting for us, and our people will thrive there."

"Everything's going to be different," Reylana replied, looking at her feet. "I have no one, and I don't even have my homeland anymore."

Essa looked at Reylana, her eyes sincere. "You have your clan. We are your family, and you are needed. Together, we will make a new life."

Reylana nodded, trusting in Essa's words. "Let's get back in there," she said, standing.

The two elves returned to the king's throne room where scores of elves and humans had gathered. A large wooden table had been brought in for the occasion, and the king sat among the elves rather than on his throne. Choosing not to perch himself on his throne and look down upon them was a wise choice. Reylana respected the decision, hoping it was a reflection of the new king's true nature. Though she doubted he truly considered the elves his equal, at least he was making them feel as if they were.

The newly appointed Overseer for the Silver Birch Clan was speaking forcefully, trying to convince his clansmen that his idea was best. "That land is destroyed," he said. "We cannot return to our former home, so we must make do with what we're given. The Forests of Viera are unspoiled."

"Your former village will never be the same," Aelryk said. "There's no point in trying to rebuild. The mages have ensured it would be uninhabitable by my father's command."

"What will become of it?" a Sycamore clansman asked.

"Na'zora will clear the land, and part of it will become farms. We will not be expanding our borders very far. We only wish to make use of the land that is now useless to you."

Though the new king's words sounded logical, the elves murmured among themselves. Making a new life in a new forest could prove difficult, but some of them were eager to take on the challenge.

"Where will Na'zora's borders end?" Reylana asked, lifting her voice above the noise.

"We will rebuild all of the farming villages that were destroyed in the fighting," Aelryk began. "That land was already ours. We will take only the nearest sections of forest that are no longer sufficient for your people. Those areas will be converted to farms which will feed our growing population."

"So basically Na'zora gives nothing, the elves have to move, and Na'zora gains farmland." With sarcasm, she added, "That seems fair."

Rising to his feet, the Sycamore Overseer spoke again. "The Forests of Viera will make a fine home for my clan. We will accept that land on the condition that it never be touched by Na'zora. You may not spread your borders or build farms in its vicinity. Nor may you create settlements between Viera and Enald." He looked around the room proudly, hoping the elves would no longer object.

"Agreed," the king replied.

Sounds of approval came from the seated elves. The Overseer nodded and sat back in his chair.

"Viera is a small forested area," Essa said. "You may find it inadequate someday."

"I'm not opposed to future negotiations," the king declared.

"You will be too busy running your kingdom to care about us elves," Reylana said. "I, for one, would be happy if you just forgot about us as long as you leave us in peace."

"Let's discuss the Sycamore Clan," Aelryk suggested. "You have stated that you've already returned from your new village across the river and intend to occupy your original area. That is acceptable."

"It had better be," Nat replied. "I expect my clan to be left alone in future. Na'zora will never need to extend its borders to Al'marr. Unless, of course, you want to start a war with them. We would gladly fight on their side."

A hush came over the crowd upon hearing Nat's threat. His expression was serious, and he intended to keep his promise. He stared at the king, expecting an angry response.

"I assure you that I have no plans to take your land." The king's voice was calm, his expression revealing no dishonesty. "Until we can learn to trust each other, we must abide by the terms spelled out in this treaty."

"Then make sure you add a line about staying away from us," Nat remarked. "I don't want it to slip your mind."

Aelryk made no effort to reply and turned his attention to the parchment in front of him. After a few moments of silence, he said, "I believe we've covered all of the clans and their territories. All that remains is to draft a final copy and have all of you sign it."

"Assuming the final copy is correct," Reylana replied. "I'd hate to see you trying to trick us with your fancy words."

"I assure you, my lady, that the treaty will read exactly as promised. Everything that has been declared during these negotiations will be upheld by Na'zora."

The elves began to mingle as the Na'zoran scribes busied themselves drafting the final copies of the treaty. Nat joined Essa and Reylana, the three of them moving as far from the king as possible.

"I think we're all losers here," Reylana commented. "Well, maybe not you, Nat." She gave him a weak smile.

"We've lost our sense of security," he replied. "We still have our homes, but this war has changed us."

"Most of the clans are moving farther from Na'zora," Essa pointed out. "The Silver Birch Clan is moving closer."

"That will lead to their demise," Nat replied.

"I hope this king keeps his promise to them, but I'll stand with them in battle if he doesn't." Reylana's voice was determined. She did not trust Aelryk, and she was willing to continue the fight if she had to.

"With so many of us moving, I'm sure Na'zora will feel free to expand," Essa said. "They won't get too close to us for now, but in time I think they'll overstep their boundaries. We must prepare our children to fight and keep close ties with the other clans."

"Agreed," Nat said.

Once the documents were prepared, each clan took its turn looking over the words for discrepancies. Finding no tricks, they placed their signatures on the treaty. They were now free to return to the Wildlands and make new lives for themselves. Peace had been promised, friendship had not.

Chapter 52

Once the treaty had been completed, the people of Na'zora began preparations to crown their new king. On that same day, he would wed Princess Lisalla, the woman who would be their queen. Despite the massive rebuilding that lay ahead of them, the citizens were determined to celebrate.

Aelryk intended to have his coronation and wedding in the palace courtyard overlooking the ocean. Hundreds of citizens could gather on the beach and still have a decent view of the ceremony. All Na'zorans were welcome, regardless of their rank or class. This was to be a day of celebration. The dark cloud of his father's reign had ended, and a new era of peace and prosperity lay ahead.

Lisalla's maids buzzed around her, preparing her for her wedding. The lavender gown which she had brought from Ra'jhou had been retrieved from her carriage, and today she would finally wear it. She brushed a hand lightly over the tiny pearls that accentuated the bodice and admired herself in a full-length mirror.

The gown was stunning, but a sadness found its way into Lisalla's heart. She could not help thinking of Danna and how much she had looked forward to this day. It pained Lisalla that her friend was gone, and she missed her deeply. Her mind wandered back to the day Danna had been killed, the image forever embedded in her memory.

As the maids began to decorate her hair with ribbons and flowers, Lisalla did her best to brush off the sad thoughts and put a smile on her face. Today was a day to celebrate, not mourn. Her new life was about to begin.

Out in the courtyard, a huge crowd had assembled to witness the day's events. It was nearly midday, and the coronation was soon to begin. The winter air was chilly, but that did not deter Na'zora's citizens from gathering to greet their new king. The ocean sent a warm breeze to comfort them and bring joy to their hearts.

As Lisalla appeared in the courtyard, a silence fell over the crowd. She walked softly to her seat, her satin shoes making no sound against the stone pathway. Taking her seat, she looked upon the crowd and the faces of her people. Both young and old, whether peasant or noble, returned her gaze, and she smiled warmly at each of them. Her heart swelled with love for her citizens. Na'zora was her true home from this day forth, and she knew her life here would be happy.

Aelryk finally emerged from the palace to take his seat in the courtyard. In near-perfect unison, the assembled guests dropped to one knee. As the king took his seat, the crowd rose to observe his coronation.

General Luca, who had served as First Advisor under King Domren, lifted a golden crown from a soft velvet cushion. His flowing blue robe danced on the wind as he held the crown high in the air and proclaimed, "Na'zorans, I present to you Aelryk, son of Domren, your true and undoubted king!" With great dignity, he strode to the king and placed the crown upon his head before kneeling in reverence. The crowd erupted in cheers and applause.

King Aelryk stood and reached for Lisalla's hand. Placing her hand in his, she smiled gently at her betrothed and curtsied respectfully. He kissed her soft, pale hand and looked deeply into her blue eyes. From this moment he would love her, and no other woman would ever come between them. He vowed in his heart to be a faithful and loving husband.

The pair made their way to the marriage altar, which had been placed only a few steps from the throne. A golden chalice full of deep purple wine awaited them. Lifting the chalice before his new bride, Aelryk said, "I vow to love you and honor you in all things. I take you as my wife and pledge my fidelity." After taking a long sip from the chalice, he passed it to Lisalla.

Trying to fight her nerves, Lisalla lifted the glass before her husband. "I vow to love and honor you in all things. I take you as my husband and pledge my fidelity." Pausing for a moment to take a quick breath, she smiled playfully and drank from the goblet.

After she returned the goblet to the altar, Aelryk took her in his arms and kissed her passionately. The warmth of his touch soothed Lisalla, and her nerves soon melted away. Lovingly, she placed a hand on the back of his head and gently stroked his dark hair. As they separated, she looked into his eyes and saw kindness.

The couple once again joined hands, turning to face the crowd. The citizens cheered for their new king and queen, raising their voices in celebration. Together, Aelryk and Lisalla returned to the palace along with scores of followers. A feast had been prepared to celebrate the momentous day, and hundreds of citizens had been invited. Tonight they would celebrate with music and dance along with fireworks presented by the court mages.

As the couple walked slowly through the long marble corridor of the palace, Lisalla placed her arm in her husband's. "May I offer you some advice, my king?" she asked, her voice soft and kind.

"Always," he replied.

"Above all else, love your people," she said. "Do what is best for them, and you will be a good king."

"I shall endeavor to do so," Aelryk replied. "You must also do something for me."

"What is that, my lord?" she asked.

"You must never fear to speak your mind and offer your advice to me," he said. "I would have a wife who is also involved in governing this kingdom."

"I promise," she replied.

Chapter 53

After spending several days with his grandfather, Yori had finally made his way back to the city of Enald. The town still showed signs of extensive damage from its recent attack by the elves. People walked hurriedly through the streets, going about various tasks. Some busied themselves repairing the damage and removing debris.

Yori continued through the streets to his uncle's smithy. It still stood and appeared mostly unharmed. There were new wooden shingles to the roof, and some of the posts had been replaced, suggesting that the shop had been damaged but was already repaired.

Inside the shop, he caught sight of his uncle at the anvil. He was hammering away, completely unaware of Yori's presence. Seated at the far corner of the shop was Meladee. Her dark hair covered most of her face as she played with a cloth doll.

Glimpsing movement at the corner of her eye, she looked up at Yori with a start. "Yori!" she yelled, rushing past her father to reach him.

Ren looked up and spun around in time to see Yori kneel and grab the little girl. He lifted her high in the air before hugging her tightly to his chest. She kissed his cheeks and giggled, throwing her arms around his neck.

"You've been gone forever," she said, scolding him as he returned her to her feet.

"I'm sorry, Meladee," he replied. "I had a lot to learn. Will you forgive me?"

"Ok," she replied, grinning.

"It's good to see you again," Ren said. "I didn't know if you'd be coming back."

"I wasn't really sure myself," Yori responded truthfully. "I've traveled quite a bit this winter, but it feels good to come home."

"You've probably heard that the war is over," Ren said. "We took some damage here, but the entire town pitched in to repair the smithy. With all the work I have lined up to repair the town, I've had to hire two new apprentices. You're still welcome to work for me if you like."

"Thanks, Uncle," Yori replied. "But I should have a job waiting for me in the palace district." He grinned, trying to imagine what it would be like working for the king.

"That's true," Ren said. "I bet that job pays much better. With all that you've probably learned while you were away, I think you might be ready to run your own smithy. I'd like to hear about these runes if you're going to stay a while."

"I think I could be persuaded to stay a day or two."

"Trella has been missing you too. No doubt she'll want to cook all of your favorite dishes while you're here."

"That's it," Yori replied with a smile. "You've convinced me."

"Yay!" Meladee shouted. "We're building a new house. It's a big one. There's even going to be a room for you." She looked cheerfully up at Yori and took his hand.

"Whenever you want to visit, our door will always be open," Ren said.

Yori looked down at Meladee and winked. She giggled and tugged at his arm, leading him to the site of her new home.

A few days later, Yori arrived once again at the palace district. Trella had sewn him a new red headband, and he checked to make sure it was covering his ears. The war had ended, but the negative sentiment toward elves remained unchanged.

Despite the layer of snow on the ground, the marketplace was bustling with its usual activities. As Yori walked along the streets, his spirits were high, reflecting the general atmosphere of the city. Everyone seemed to be smiling.

Moving unnoticed among the crowd, he stopped at the palace gates to request an audience with the king. Two guards in shining chainmail stood proudly, watching as the people went about their duties.

"Excuse me," Yori said to them. "I was sent on a mission by the prince, and now I have returned. I need to report back to him."

The guards looked him up and down. One of them replied, "The prince is now the king."

Yori smiled knowingly. "Yes, I've heard the news. May I see him?"

"You can wait inside, but the king is very busy. One of his councilors might come and speak to you." Opening the gate, the guard waved him through.

Within the stone walls of the palace, Yori felt trapped. Having spent time in the forests, he no longer felt as comfortable indoors as he once did. Despite his uneasiness, he stood with his back straight, trying to appear dignified. He felt a bit silly, but he didn't want to be mistaken for a servant or dismissed without the chance to see the king.

After nearly an hour, a gray-haired councilor in a yellow robe strutted down the hallway. "You have a report for the king, I'm told," he said. Staring at Yori with disdain, he awaited a response.

"Yes," Yori said. "A few months ago he sent me to learn a special craft. I have returned to offer him my service."

"The king himself sent you?" the councilor asked suspiciously.

"He was the prince at the time, and yes, he sent me himself." Yori returned the stare, showing the old man that he was not intimidated by his tone.

"What was this craft?" the councilor asked, narrowing his eyes.

"That is between the king and myself," Yori replied. Growing impatient, he added, "He's not going to be pleased when he learns you've kept me from my duties."

The old man snorted. "What name shall I give to the king?"

"My name is Yori," he replied. "I am the blacksmith he pardoned and sent on a mission."

"Wait here," the man said. He turned and strode back down the hallway, disappearing through a tall wooden door.

Yori sighed and continued to wait. Several minutes later, the councilor once again appeared at the end of the hallway. He beckoned for Yori to follow him.

The doorway led into the king's throne room, where a large number of people had gathered. Apparently Yori was not the only one who had business with the king. The councilor motioned for him to take a seat among the crowd, but a voice commanded him differently.

"Yori," Aelryk said. "I didn't actually expect you to return."

Yori stood dumbfounded, unsure how to address a king. Their previous meeting had been so informal that he had not stopped to consider how he should behave in the king's presence.

Waving frantically, the old councilor summoned Yori up to the front. With a tilt of his head, he signaled Yori to stand in front of the king. Yori obeyed, standing awkwardly before the throne. Silence ensued, and he glanced back at the councilor who was lowering his head, apparently trying to tell Yori to bow.

Yori bowed awkwardly before the king, trying to fight his own embarrassment. The king suppressed his laughter, understanding how out of place the young half-elf must feel.

"Have you completed the task I gave you?"

"I have, Your Majesty."

"Good," the king replied. "Have you mastered the craft of rune carving?

"I have."

"And have you come here to fulfill your promise to work for me?"

"Yes, Your Majesty, but I have a condition."

Aelryk raised an eyebrow. "Oh? What might that be?"

Yori took a deep breath and let it out. He knew he was in no position to make demands of a king, but his conscience would not allow him to remain silent. "I will work for you on the condition that the weapons I craft will not be used to harm the elves of the Wildlands."

433

The king nodded, a faint smile on his lips. "I have every intention of upholding the peace treaty. I understand your request, and I give you my word."

Yori gave a single nod. "Then I am at your service, Your Majesty."

"Good," Aelryk replied. "I will have quarters arranged for you here in the palace."

"If you don't mind," Yori began, "I would prefer to live on the north side of town near the large grove of trees. I prefer to remain close to nature."

"I will have a home constructed for you," the king said. "The palace armory is now yours. I trust you to oversee its daily operations and produce quality weapons and armor for my troops."

Yori felt a surge of pride. Being placed in charge of a king's armory at his young age was no small accomplishment. "Thank you, Your Majesty," he said.

"You may encounter some prejudice while the war is still fresh in everyone's minds. In time, I hope we can move beyond that. You are dismissed."

He bowed again before taking his leave. Exiting the palace, he followed the dirt path around to the armory, where a dozen smiths were hard at work. These men were now under his supervision. As he entered the army, he noticed a small purple flower had lifted its head and pushed its way through the snow.

About the Author

Lana Axe lives in the Missouri countryside surrounded by dogs, cats, birds, and reptiles. She spends most of her free time daydreaming about elves, magic, and far-away lands.

For more information, please visit:
http://lana-axe.com/